The Left-Handed Sword

Will Kalif

The Left-Handed Sword

Table of Contents

1. Darkness Arrives

"We dance around the circle and suppose while the secret sits in the center and knows" – Robert Frost

The car wound its way gracefully along the single lane highway. He shifted it gently into second gear and the warm Newport air caressed the hood as it made its way toward the old city. It was a toreador red blur that darted its way easily along the curves.

There is a certain magic surrounding Newport. It's very old New England and two hundred years after the rest of the country declared its independence from Europe, Newport still remembers its European roots and flavor. It is something that is embedded right into the cobblestones.

It is the French Riviera of America. The beaches are long and narrow and for miles they come right up to the road. The homes are large and beautiful, replete with hand-woven rugs and imported Italian marble. The whole city reeks of money and of something else.

When people inhabit a place on the earth for many generations the place tends to remember things, and the spirit of the people stays behind long after the people themselves have left. This is a phenomenon that is everywhere in the world; we just don't notice it.

A human being absorbs everything that he sees, hears, and experiences, and then it becomes a part of him. And the same is true for everything in this world. If you place a sturdy rock in a stream the stream slowly changes it. Over time, the flow of water, no matter how gentle, senses the insulting edges of the rock and softens them. We think of this as how the water affects the rock and this is true. But it also how the rock remembers the water.

The same is true with living things. If you plant a grapevine near a pumpkin patch the wine will have a hint of pumpkin. If you grow thousands of people over one patch of land the land will retain a hint of them. It will remember them long after they are gone.

This is the way of Newport. For almost four hundred years sailors, merchants, mill-barons, and commoners walked its cobblestone streets; and the streets, like a rock in a stream, absorbed the flow and feel of the people.

Some rocks are stronger than others; they resist the change for thousands of years. Other rocks quickly comply with the pressure and they change. Newport is of the latter. It eagerly accepts the heartbeats and thoughts of the people that crossed it. And it remembers them.

It is a place of mystery, a place where the very threads of people and time meet and have an affect on each other. The fabric of life here is very thick and this fabric settled easily into the fertile soil.

He eased the car into third and the tone of the engine changed to a deeper pitch. He glanced over at Arabella and she smiled at him. They had the road to themselves for the moment.

In the late afternoon everyone was still locked in what they were doing. Everyone that was out was still at the beach or perusing the shops in town. But in another hour or two, when dusk starts to creep in, everyone would pack up their beach chairs and head to the restaurants and clubs for seafood dinners and jazz. He looked at Arabella again. Her hair fluttered gently in the salty air. He loved her hair. It was long and straight, very thick and dark brown. He brought his eyes down to her legs. She was wearing her favorite jeans, the ones with rips in the thighs and knees. This went out of style in America in the late eighties, but in Spain, where she grew up, it was still fashionable. Most Europeans proclaim distaste for America and everything American, but secretly they all pine for the glamour that Hollywood portrays.

He took his hand off the shift, slid it right into the hole at her left knee and said "Gubra da lee." He pushed his hand further into the rip and cupped it under her knee. She gasped gently at the surprising contact, gave him a knowing glance, and without saying anything she closed her eyes and laid her head back on the rest.

She rarely spoke. Her English was not very good and he had forgotten most of his college Spanish but it didn't matter. She didn't need to talk. She communicated everything she felt and thought with a glance or a touch, or an innuendo of breath.

Without opening her eyes she reached her hand across, ran it gently over his head, brushed his ear, and then gently brought it to rest on the back of his neck with a soft squeeze.

His head was shaved completely bald and she enjoyed the feel of it.

A man should shave his head so the world can see the machine that changes the world but a woman should grow her hair long to show her connection to the earth -the colors of autumn leaves or the gold of wheat and honey.

The tempo of her rubbing his neck changed and he looked back over at her. She was staring at him, her brown eyes showing a bit of teasing. She wanted him to pull the car over so they could go out on the beach. He grinned. It wasn't just the touching. Newport did something to her. She loved the beach and she loved the sun. She loved the sound and the smell of the ocean but she never went in the water. The raw tactile power of the ocean attracted her but the enigma of its controlled and patient power scared her.

He coaxed the car to go faster. They were racing upward now. Thick slabs of granite bluffs were on each side of them and they were fast approaching the final curves and the top of the bluffs. In a few moments they would be over the top. The granite would fade away and gentler topsoil would dominate the landscape for the final few miles to the city.

A hundred yards ahead a figure stood by the side of the road and watched them approach. Storm saw him as they got close and turned his head to get a longer look at him as they passed him. It was a man, a large man, and he was dressed in a long dark coat. His hair and his eyes were dark and he was holding something in his hands. It looked like a large Axe – the type with blades on both sides.

Storm turned his attention back to the road and glanced in the rear view mirror at the man who just stood still and watched them as they passed. Arabella turned all the way around in her seat and looked back at the figure. Under his black coat his clothing was a dull metal color; almost like some type of armor.

Arabella touched his arm. Storm couldn't tell if it was concern for the figure or worry for their safety. That was some character he thought. There are lots of Theater groups in Newport. Maybe it was some actor in uniform whose car broke down on the way to a play. He watched the road ahead; looking for a broken down car. Tough place to break down. That guy is exactly at the mid-way point between the city and the beaches. You could flip a coin. It was a walk of a couple of miles either way. It didn't really matter which way you went. It was barren and underpopulated here because the granite bluffs and the river made it impossible for anything to be built. So this few miles was just a no-mans land. Funny though how the man didn't wave for help. He just stared at them as they passed. And while he was carrying what looked like a pretty nasty looking axe nobody was going to stop and help him.

They rounded another curve and Storm took one more look in the rear view mirror to be sure they had the man well behind them.

When he brought his eyes back to the road something dark and about the size of a large dog darted out in front of them.

In the perplexity of the last two minutes of driving Storm hadn't decelerated the car at all. His right foot had been locked in the same position and the car remained in third at too high a rate of speed. His reflexes took control of him before his mind could override him and he jerked the wheel sharply to the left and slammed on the brakes.

His body filled with adrenaline and the whole world went into slow motion. The tail end of the car turned out to the right and Arabella's side of the car slammed into a granite outcropping. This turned the car completely around and it launched itself backward down a slope between outcroppings and a scant moment later into the river. It was a moment that seemed to last forever. It happened so quickly yet it took so long to complete -but it did complete. They hit the water with a deafening crunch. And for a few seconds everything was quiet until the water started rushing in and Arabella screamed.

The sound of it went through his head like a spike. This was a sound he never thought he would hear from the woman that never talked. He unbuckled his seat belt then reached over and unbuckled hers as the water level inside the car quickly rose. They couldn't have gone that far out into the water but five feet deep would be enough to totally submerge the car.

Arabella was in a panic now. She was grasping at her legs somewhere down below the water level. She screamed again, but this time it wasn't a scream of shock, it was one of pain. He followed her hands down her legs as the water turned red.

When the car hit the rocks it had crumpled her side of the car and now her feet were trapped. He pulled on her knees and she moaned. The water continued its rise, now up to her chest and he dove his head under to look. She had a very bad gash on her thigh and it hurt him to see it. He choked back a gasp. The water was red but clear enough to see that her feet disappeared into a dark mess of metal.

He popped his head out of the water and grabbed her head in his hands. "The water here is shallow. Breathe deeply! Take deep breaths!" Recognition registered on her face and she started breathing in a long rhythm and just as fast as it started it seemed to end.

The car jolted and with the water at their necks it came to a stop. They forgot about their breathing and paused. Then like a knife, reality came back to him. The panic of the moment was gone. Up until now everything was reaction. The moment of crisis seemed to be gone and now he had a small amount of space to think.

He assessed their situation. The car launched itself into the river backward and now the rear end was the lowest part of the car. The current of the river was brisk -rushing quickly by them and through the car. Their position was precarious at best. The force of the river could move the car and send them deeper into the froth. Or maybe it was now settled into it's final resting spot just awaiting a tow. Difficult to know which way things would go.

Arabella's face was getting pale. She was losing blood.

He took off his belt, dove back under the water and tied it tightly around her thigh above the gash. The red water quickly turned clear. The belt stopped the bleeding but if it stayed too long she would lose the leg; and there was no telling the condition of her feet. She may have lost them already.

He put his hand on her cheek. "Help is probably already on the way. Try to stay calm." Terror showed in her face. Maybe this was the reason she never went in the water. Yet, the water still found her. It was something that sought her out and she had no control over it. No matter how careful she was for her whole life, never going in the water, never even taking a bath -only showers; and yet the water still found her.

"I am going to climb out the window, swim around to your side and try to open the door." He waited for her to respond but she just leaned her head back and closed her eyes. He turned and grabbed at the steering wheel so he could wedge himself by it and a shock of pain hit him. He pulled his left hand out of the water and held it up near his face. His thumb was broken and dislocated. The largest thumb-bone, near the palm of his hand had snapped, probably against the steering wheel at some point during the accident. With the adrenaline of the situation he hadn't been aware of it but when he reached for the steering wheel to get out, his thumb wasn't where it was supposed to be and he jammed it hard.

He closed his eyes and calmed himself. If he passed out in this position he could slip under the water and drown. And if he tried to reset the bone now he could pass out so he left his hand alone, just floating in the coolness of the water.

After a very long minute the pain subsided to a manageable level and he opened his eyes. Through the cracks of the windshield he could see the shoreline from where the car launched. There was a figure standing there and his heart, again, raged into action. He took a quick look at Arabella then scrambled for the window, quickly squirted his way through, and when he surfaced outside of the car he screamed for help.

"My wife is trapped inside and She's hurt. Did you call for help? Is help on the way?"

The figure didn't move. Maybe he was mistaken, maybe it was a tree. Storm shook the water out of his eyes and looked again. No mistaking it was a man. He wasn't very far away – only about the same distance as if he were standing on the sidewalk across a four lane street. Storm got a very good look at him and he shook his head again. It was the man in black. The man they had seen just before the accident and he was carrying an axe; a big nasty looking double bladed axe. And it didn't appear to be a prop. It looked like iron. The man's long black overcoat shimmered in the windy torrent of the river's edge. A hint of gold gleamed around his neck and the clothes he wore under the coat were of a strange make. The fabric at his chest and legs shimmered with a faint rainbow hue. His pants and shirt were made of what looked like overlapping scales of some large fish. He just stood and stared at Storm.

Sitting by the man's side was what at first looked to Storm like a dog with a dark black coat of fur –In its sitting position it was enormous – coming to over the mans waist. But it was no dog, its head and jaw were too big for a dog and its shoulders were enormous. Framing its face was a mane of black fur. It was almost a cross between a big dog and a lion.

"Go get help! There's someone still in the car."

Storm grasped an edge of the car with his right hand to steady himself and waved his left arm above the water, his thumb wagging at an uncomfortable angle. He beseeched the man. But he and his pet just stared back.

Storm swam around the car and popped his head into Arabella's window. She was still breathing but she looked terribly pale. The cold water was helping with the blood flow but she was clearly in shock. He frantically grabbed at the door handle with his right hand and pulled. It was a futile move. The door felt like it had been welded to the car. The accident had closed it securely in place. He looked in on her again and she turned her head to look at him. "Your head." She whispered. He brought his right hand up to his skull and felt around. A flap of flesh on the right side of his head over his ear screamed at him when he touched it. He leaned his hands and his head on the top of the car and looked over at the man on the shore. The man raised a hand and pointed at him. The creature at his side, as if being commanded, took two long lunges and launched itself into the water. When it surfaced it's head made a wake that pointed directly at Storm and Storm looked on in horror as it growled and its yellow eyes fixed on him. 'What the fuck! This wasn't good. What the hell is going on? Who is this man and what is this creature?'

He took one quick look at Arabella through the window and she coughed some water out of her lungs. Again his heart started to race but this time it was labored. There was very little adrenaline left in his body. His reserves were exhausted, his thumb was broken, he had a nasty cut on his head, and who knows what else. And head wounds tended to produce a lot of blood. That isn't good but maybe all that blood in the water wasn't Arabella's, maybe it was his. In some peculiar way the thought made him feel a little better. But then again maybe it was the blood loss affecting him. He fought off the instinct to run his hands down to his legs to see if they were even there.

He brought his focus back out to the water and the scene around him.

The yellow-eyed creature was halfway to him now and malice was clearly in its eyes. It growled in a timbre that sounded like no creature on earth.

Storm tried to assess the situation. The thing was big, maybe a hundred pounds and most definitely strong. It couldn't be too mobile in the water though. It would need all four of its legs to stay afloat, but the jaw, that was a weapon to be afraid of and it looked like it could snap an arm with very little effort.

It drew quickly closer and the sound of its heavy breathing rose above the water noise. It was laboring in the water and a few feet from Storm it veered, and with a scratching noise it hoisted itself out of the water and onto the hood of the car. Its nails clicked as it walked across the windshield then took a lunging bite at Storms head. He pushed himself away from the car and watched in horror as the weight of the creature tilted the car. Inside Arabella struggled to keep her mouth above water.

Anger rose up in Storm. Up until now everything was like a surreal dream, cloudy and out of focus. But now everything was sharp, it wasn't just the coincidence of things that happened, now it was a tangible threat, something that he could focus his energy against –the creature.

The car shifted and creaked as the thing shuffled around on the windshield. Storm had to get it off the car. It's weight was shifting the car around. It could sink the car deeper or turn it in a way that caused it to go further out, and presumably deeper. And if it went into deeper water Arabella would drown.

The hound was uncomfortable in the water and maybe Storm, with that fact and his weight advantage, could capitalize. With two strokes of his arms he moved back in against the car and put his already damaged left arm up to protect his face. The creature immediately attacked by clamping its powerful jaw on his forearm. The pain was like a lightning bolt to his head and he almost passed out again.

He curled up his legs in the water then pressed his feet against the car and pushed with everything he had. The force of his kick propelled him away from the car and it took the creature off the car and into the water. He wrapped his other arm around its neck then rolled in the water so he was on top of it. Its legs kicked furiously but it wouldn't relinquish the grip it had on his arm. Storm took a deep breath then dove himself down into the water. The two of them went down, locked in a death grip. One of them would die right here and the other would return to the surface.

The instinct of the creature was not suited for this type of a fight. In it's life it would latch onto its prey with its powerful jaws and tear and pull until the other creatures in its pack could find a killing bite to the neck or throat. But its pack mates weren't here and it couldn't bite and tear for the few minutes it usually took to wear down its prey because it had very little air and very little time. With a final gesture of its stubbornness and a shaking of its head that sent renewed sparks of pain through Storm it exhaled its air, breathed in the cold water and with a jolt it went quietly to death.

That was a lot easier than he thought it would be. The damn thing practically gave up without a fight but its jaw was still locked onto his arm. He surfaced, gasped for air, shook the water out of his eyes, and with his good hand pried the thing off. It floated down and away. Storm turned back to the car then turned again, and again in the cold water and for the fourth time his heart leapt. The car was gone. He couldn't have gone far down stream. He looked to the shore. The man with the axe was still standing right there. Storm swam toward the shore, now in a panic and he bumped into the car. It was submerged only a few inches below the surface. He dove and darted his head in the window. Arabella was holding her breath and looking at him. He motioned for her to exhale, she did and he placed her mouth on hers and gave her what was in his lungs. He darted back up and screamed. "Get Help! We need help now." Taking three quick breaths he submerged again, popped his head in the window again and gave Arabella another breath. He continued this pattern. Each time he surfaced he called for help then submerged again. Everything started to get gray and blurry. The rhythm of his breathing became a metronome of pain. Up to the surface, then back down to the car. He was hyperventilating but still not getting enough oxygen and had lost a lot of blood from his head and even more now from the bite on his arm. There were just a few inches of water between Arabella's life and her death.

He pushed himself harder and broke the surface again and sounds came to him out of a blur of numbness. Was something happening? There was a commotion on shore. He thought it might be voices. It could just be the blood pumping weakly inside his head. He dove again and now he couldn't see the car -the water had clouded; or was it his vision that clouded? Where was he in his rhythm? Going up or going down? Oh yes -going down. But he couldn't see her anymore so he felt for her, grabbed her face, kissed her and again breathed into her. He broke the surface again. Were those voices? Were people coming? Or was it his ears? Where was he in his rhythm? Going up or going down? Oh yes. Going down. He dove and a voice told him that he didn't get air so he looked at what he thought was up and he saw light. He moved toward up and the light turned to gray then the gray turned to black. The last thing he heard before the blackness was a strange sound in his skull. It was a "click click". As if a clock somewhere between his ears somehow managed to count out a single second.

Prologue

"When you gaze long into the abyss, the abyss also gazes into you."
- Friedrich Nietzsche

Blackness unfolded around him like a small room. He was laying down on something – maybe a bed; and the dark was so complete he couldn't tell if his eyes were open or closed so he brought his hands up to feel. Yes his eyes were open.

Awareness slowly came and he opened his mouth and croaked weakly. The sound he made was muffled as if he really were in a small room. He put his hands back down and the coolness of sheets met his touch. Other sensations returned slowly; the pillow, the sheets, and the nearby walls all came into his awareness. There was an open window to his right and it let a light breeze blow over him. All his senses worked but his eyes saw nothing.

A cuckoo clock broke the darkness with a single chirp and he startled -Not from the sound of the clock but from the awareness of what it was. He knew this place. It was the bedroom of an old apartment he lived in. The window was at his right. And in the far-left corner, past the foot of the bed, would be the door to the living room, and in the living room was where the cuckoo clock hung on the wall. He remembered the place well. It had been a cozy apartment that he had lived in and he had been happy there until he had a bad experience and moved out.

There was only one reason why he had chosen this apartment. It was close to the public library. He could see it from the window of the kitchenette. There was a comfort in that for him and every evening after work he would walk across to the big granite building and spend hours rummaging through the racks of books.
He chose books almost indiscriminately. The subject of each one almost didn't matter. There was a joy in the discovery of a new subject or author. He spent hours in the reading room and when the library closed he took the books home for more reading.

The library was a hundred-year-old remnant of the times when little New England towns were powerhouses in the textile industry. All of its racks were wrought iron and all its shelves, walks, and stairs were glass; a smoky hand blown glass that distorted the light that passed through the over-sized windows. A hundred years ago they went to great lengths to protect the delicate paper from the threat of fire. In just a few minutes flames could race through an entire library and destroy everything.

At the top of the library, off the stairwell that led to the clock tower, was a room. They called it the uncatalogued book room and it was where over the course of a century odd books found a home. This was the place for the books that defied the Dewey decimal system, were too large to fit into the shelves, or were somehow just forgotten about. And it was Storm's favorite room. He would often spend hours in there just sitting with his back against the racks and a book in his hands. It was in this room that he found the book.

It was a dusty old book, oversized, hand bound –and quite possibly the strangest book in a room full of strange books. But it caught Storm's attention. "The Papyrus of Ani – The Egyptian book of the dead." It didn't have a catalog number so he wasn't supposed to take it home but with a little persuading he managed to get the head librarian to let him check it out. That night he took the book to bed with him and read it by the glow of a lamp until his eyes were too heavy to go on. He put the book down on the nightstand and fell into a restless sleep.

The cuckoo clock proclaimed four times and it startled him awake. His heart was racing and something was in the room with him. The window to his right let no light in. This was a night without a moon.

Something was standing in the far-left corner past the foot of his bed where the door to the living room met the corner of the bedroom. It was a presence. He couldn't see anything at all there; but something was there. The corner was simply blacker than the rest of the room.

He lay in bed paralyzed, his breathing labored, his heart racing. Time passed very slowly. The dark thing didn't move, and it didn't speak. It was just there. Storm couldn't move and he didn't dare try to speak. He just stared into the darkness and waited for daybreak. It lasted for two hours until the sun started to pour the faintest of light through the window. For these two hours Storm promised himself to never forget this and to never let the memory of it fade as time passed. This thing came to his room and it was real. He looked into it but couldn't ascertain its intent. Was it good? Was it evil? There was no hint for Storm. He was scared so maybe it was evil. But the only thing he was absolutely sure of is that it was there. And as the room lightened the presence faded -and after the sun had brightened his room for an hour Storm finally climbed out of bed and slowly walked toward the dreaded corner of the room.

He fought back the impulse to stand where it stood. Instead he carefully opened the bedroom door and went through the living room and into the kitchenette to make a cup of coffee.

He sat down at the window overlooking the library and took a sip of his coffee. Damn strangest thing that ever happened to him. It wasn't a dream. It really happened. There was a mystery here. While he lay in bed for a couple of hours just staring at it he swore to himself over and over that he was awake and this was real and that he wouldn't forget it.

After his cup of coffee he went back into the bedroom to dress and he spotted the tattered book on the nightstand. He wondered if that was what brought the dark thing to him. After work he brought the book back to the library without opening it again and by the end of the month he had moved out of the apartment. Sometimes a man faced something that was simply beyond his comprehension. This angered Storm because the most powerful drive he possessed was his need to understand everything.

2 – The Rising Hunter

"To be or not to be, that is the question "
- William Shakespeare

Light came to him again. This time it wasn't the soft and smoky memory of a time gone past, it was a lightning crack of pain that sometimes accompanies the never ending now.

He opened his eyes and pain screamed at him from his arms, his legs, his head, and his lungs. He gasped for air and the world reassembled itself around him. He was floating face up in shallow water and his head rest in the muck of the river bank while the rest of his body splay out into the current. He gasped at the pain, turned himself over, slowly crawled out of the water and pushed his face heavily into the mud. Choking on the thickness of it he rolled over onto his back and gasped again as the stars leapt out at him – beautiful in a myriad of colors and a brightness he had never seen before. The blackness of the sky was deep and rich. There was no light pollution drowning out the stars and each one shone with a joy of color.

How long had he been out he wondered. It shouldn't be this dark. Where was the washing light pollution from the highway and the city lights? He scanned the horizon by rolling his head from side to side and everywhere there was complete darkness without a hint of the city or the highway. He tried listening for sounds of the city or sounds of automobiles but his ears were clogged with mud. He couldn't hear anything.
He lifted his head for a better look and nausea washed over him and the blackness came again.

After a time uncounted he was once again dragged back into the never ending now. The stars welcomed him back and the nerves in his body resumed their complaint. He had been through so much. The accident and Arabella and the dog and the man with the axe had all happened to him in the span of just a few minutes. And in that short period of time both his body and his spirit had been strained beyond normal tolerance.

He just lay there thinking about the pain in his body and the failure to rescue her and he couldn't move. His thumb sent a shock through his arm and he lifted his hand to look at it. His left hand was deformed. The thumb was dislocated and broken. And it pointed off at a peculiar angle. He couldn't touch it, it hurt too much. He lay his hand back down and turned his head. There had been too much for him. Arabella was out there in the river somewhere and he failed to rescue her. The pain he felt was nothing compared to that. He had built his life around her gentle spirit and now she was gone.

He remembered again the first time that he had seen her. That first glance had hit him like a thunderbolt. Clear and simple. There was nothing he could do about it. It was simply love at first sight. He always thought it was just a saying but it was true. It really did happen. And when it did happen it changed a man's life forever –if he were courageous enough to act.

He gathered himself up onto his knees testing his arms and his legs. He had a few cuts and the dog bite burned viciously but there didn't seem to be any broken bones other than in his thumb. Standing up slowly he waded back out into the river.

"Arabella?" he barely whispered and waded out further. Everything seemed different. The water wasn't the same, the shoreline was different and now there were trees. There were no trees where the car had gone into the water. Had his body floated downstream while he was unconscious?

He looked around. Everything was different. The air, the smells, and the water seemed warmer than it had been.

This was all too much for him to handle so he waded his way slowly back to shore and falling first to his knees the last of his energy left him and he fell flat on his face in the mud. Gagging on the filth he turned his head just a little to the side so he could breathe.

This was it he thought. No more strength and no more desire.

A comfortable calm came over him and he decided to rest. The thought came to him that this was sort of like carbon monoxide poisoning. The gas crept slowly into you and you just got tired and soon you were glad to just give up and go to sleep. It seemed like a good idea. Maybe he should just give up and go to sleep.

He opened one eye to take a last look at the stars. Lying face down in the mud with his head turned to the side he could only open one eye, the other was buried in the muck.

He looked down along the length of the river. It cleared a wide path through the trees and he could see the horizon off in the distance. The darkness of the sky was so complete that it reached all the way to the horizon line. No light pollution faded it near the ground. A bright and deep red star peeked slowly into view and he stared at it. Not too many stars like that. The deep red color and the brightness of it made him think it was Betelgeuse. But that was a winter star in the constellation of Orion. No chance of Orion showing up in the middle of summer. He just lay there and watched it as the minutes passed and it slowly climbed higher. Soon another very bright star rose up. This one a brilliant white. Damn if it didn't look a lot like Rigel –another star that was in the constellation of Orion.

Slowly Orion made itself visible and he thought about it.

Every winter Orion, the mighty hunter, threw one shoulder over the horizon and slowly climbed up. He had been doing this since the beginning of time.

Orion proclaimed himself the mightiest hunter that ever lived and he vowed to hunt and kill all the creatures on the earth. And for his folly the gods sent a scorpion to poison him and now he was cursed to eternity in the sky.

There comes a point in any crisis where the body no longer has control. It has been totally exhausted of its normal strength, and its reserves. But this isn't the absolute stopping point. The will has a say in the matter and the will can either agree with the body or push forward.

Storm lay there in the mud, totally spent, his body exhausted -beyond exhausted -and broken, but looking up at Orion his will took over. This would not be the end for him. If the mighty hunter could climb up over the horizon every winter for eons then Storm could rise one time.

He pushed his arms against the mud and rose to his feet. The blood he had lost through the slash on his head made him dizzy but he stood erect. This was not his time. There was still too much to do. He had to find Arabella and he had to understand what had happened to him.

Putting one foot in front of the other he walked toward the trees and entering the darkness of the forest he turned and looked at the river, hoping to see the car. But he saw nothing.

As he stepped into the treeline the smells and sounds assaulted him with a beauty that almost brought tears to his eyes. The smell of the soil, the leaves and the trees was beautiful. The sound of the insects was like music. He walked on and gained some strength from it. The crisis had passed now he just needed to get some help.

A flicker of color entered his line of sight and he focused on it. It was orange-red like fire. Instinctively he headed straight for it and as he walked it darted in and out between the tree. After a few minutes of walking, and covering maybe a hundred meters, he entered a small clearing to see it was a campfire and sitting around it were three men. They were eating around the fire and they sat and stared at him with food in their hands and in their open mouths. He croaked some indistinguishable words at them and fell to the ground and to another bout with the darkness.

3. The Rite of Passage

"Every seven years a man makes a transition into a new stage of his life. Some are not aware of this. But those that are have gained an insight, a clue as to how their life will unfold"
- The book of Varheit

He opened his eyes to daylight and a figure standing over him spoke.

"Well, looks like you have come around. You gave us quite a scare. There are a lot of nasty creatures running through the forest at night and for a moment we thought that you were one of them. My son almost shot an arrow through you. He has very quick reflexes."

Storm didn't respond. His throat was too dry.

The man stared at Storm, paused for a moment, then continued talking.

"Can you understand me?"

Storm nodded and the man grunted an approval.

"You have been in a bit of a fight and you had a tangle with the river. The damage of it isn't too bad, no broken bones except your thumb. I've sewn up the cut on your head. It isn't serious but head wounds do bleed a lot. The rest of the cuts aren't serious but the poison gave you a battle. Whatever bit you on the arm was festering with a nasty blood taint. It was touch and go for a couple of days but it will pass."

Storm registered shock at the statement. If he has been out for a couple of days then what happened to Arabella? And what was the poison that he had gotten? Did he get it from the dog creature?

He sat up slowly and it made him dizzy. "Could I get some water?" He rasped through dry lips.

The man smiled and walked over to a pack near the ashes of the campfire and after rummaging around in it for a moment he returned with a skin of water.

"My name is Bherin." He handed Storm the skin and continued with his talk.

"Lucky you chanced upon us. Not too many people venture into the dark forest around the Rhyme. Village folk never come up here except in the time of the Testing."

Storm managed a smile. "I thank you for helping me but why didn't we go to a hospital? Do you have a cell phone? Where's the nearest road?"

He paused to catch his breath and Bherin stared at him.

"These things you say are strange. Maybe the poison is still strong. The delirium may still be with you. You spent many hours ranting strange things in your sleep."

Now it was Storm's turn to stare. What the hell was going on here? He formed more questions but before he could fire them at Bherin two figures joined them in the little camp.

Bherin turned at the sound of the approaching footsteps and spoke to the two.
"Well met. He smiled. It looks like our wanderer has awoken from his sleep."

The men who entered the camp each smiled broadly at Storm.

One was an older man, maybe in his late forties or early fifties and the other was a young man no more than seventeen or eighteen. He carried a bow on his back and the two of them carried several small animal carcasses. They dropped the carcasses near the remains of the campfire and approached Storm and Bherin.
Bherin pointed at the older of the two. "This here is our village elder. His name is Rimner. The man's smile broadened and he slightly bowed his head at Storm. And this here is my son Ty. He is the reason that we found you out here alone. We have brought him out for his Testing."

The four of them sat under the tree talking for a while and Storm explained to them what happened with the car crash. They didn't understand what a car was but they did understand that Arabella had been lost.

After Storm finished with his story Bherin offered some help. "Let's you and I go back down to the River and have a look around. Today is the second day of the testing and Ty and Rimner have much to do. I cannot help Ty in any way but I can help you. Maybe we can discover something on the bank of the Rhyme."
It had been more than two days but it was worth trying so the two of them, lead by Bherin, went down to the river. It was only about a hundred paces from their camp and soon after they started Storm could hear the sound of rushing water.

Nothing looked familiar to him. He looked up at the sky in the hope that Orion could help him but there were no stars in the afternoon sunshine. They walked up and down the shore for a hundred paces in each direction and several times they waded out into the water. After a time they returned to the spot on the shore where they had first started. Storm sat down on a log and Bherin sat beside him.

He couldn't bring up the subject of Arabella again. He felt like he had already failed and this futile search was just a continuation of that failure. He changed to another subject. "You said that you were out here for the Testing. What did you mean by that?"

Bherin studied him carefully. "You don't know what the Testing is?" Storm shook his head and Bherin grunted in amazement.

"When a boy is on the verge of manhood he must undergo the Testing. It determines whether he has to leave the city and his people, or stay as a man." Storm stared at him blankly so he continued.

"When a boy reaches seventeen years he must prove his worth to the community. He must prove he has mastered two valuable skills and has the devotion to live among those he loves."

"What kind of skills?" Storm asked.

"There are many skills that a young man can contribute -pottery making, farming, combat skills and others. Ty, like myself, has chosen hunting and cooking."

Storm could see the pride in Bherin. The man was visibly proud and glad that his son chose the same path as he.
After the brief pause he continued with the explanation.

"The Testing takes six days. The first two days we travel to here." He waved his arms to encompass the general area they were in. "On the third day an elder tests his chosen skills. For Ty that would have been two days ago. Your arrival has thrown us off." He smiled to indicate the delay was not to be of concern then he continued. "Rimner has approved that today be Ty's third day. And Ty has chosen hunting and cooking so today he has hunted and Rimner tested him. He has done well. They returned with everything they needed so this evening Ty will prepare a meal and if that goes well tomorrow we will go to the judgment stone for the final test. If he passes that test he will receive his new name and for two days we will journey back. And on the seventh day the city will welcome him home."

This seemed to Storm to be a beautiful thing. Nowadays a young man went off to college for very much the same reasons. He would spend those valuable years learning a craft and if he passed the variety of tests he would return to his community with the ability to contribute. He even had his name modified if he pursued his chosen career to the doctorate level. It wasn't that much different than this but there were extra dimensions to this situation. Bherin and his son must have spent many days and nights together over the years hunting and cooking. It was an apprenticeship between father and son. The bond between them would be very strong if not unbreakable. And unlike college he didn't go off and get a degree in some obtuse skill. The hunting and cooking skills directly translated into a way that he would contribute to the well being of his community.

"What about the Judgment Stone? What is that all about?"

Again Bherin stared at Storm but this time it was a very long pause.
"This thing we do not talk about. Every young man faces it once and if he has sons he must face it again with each one of them. But to talk about it is not a comfortable thing. If Ty passes his cooking test then we will go to the Judgment Stone tomorrow and you will see for yourself."

Storm was satisfied with this answer but his curiosity was piqued. Based on what he had learned so far these people had built for themselves quite a beautiful life. It was direct and in contact with the simple things in life. The two of them talked for the rest of the afternoon and when the first shadows of dusk crept over the river they returned back to the campsite.

Ty was hard at work preparing the meal for his testing and Rimner hovered over him watching everything very closely but saying nothing.

"What is he cooking for his Testing?" Storm asked Rimner.

"He is a fine cook and he has chosen something most challenging – The Mothers Blanket." When this elicited no response from Storm Rimner assumed he didn't know what it was so he explained. "The Mothers Blanket is a meal that must be carefully prepared and very slowly roasted over the fire on a spit. He must clean a quail and stuff inside it an egg then stuff the quail inside a cleaned hare. This then goes inside the wild boar with vegetables and spices. Then he carefully and very slowly roasts it over the fire, keeping the heat very stead. It should be finished late this evening and we will see if he has passed the test, then we will eat."

Storm rubbed the broken thumb on his left hand. While he was unconscious somebody had set the broken bone and wrapped splints around it. It felt sore but it felt like it was set correctly. It should mend well. He was really hungry and didn't want to wait until midnight to eat but he didn't say anything. He watched Ty in his preparation for a while then as Ty had completed the preparation of the food and he placed it on the spit and began the arduous task of slow roasting. Rimner and Bherin relaxed and sat down with Storm. The three of them talked as Ty tended the food and the fire.

Rimner started the conversation.

"It is a puzzle how you came here. Your clothing and speech are very strange. Do you have the strength to talk some more of it?"

Storm mustered up the strength and told them his story from where it began with the car ride to Newport. He made everything generic so they wouldn't get caught up in details they didn't understand. Trying to explain an automobile was not possible. He finally settled on it being like a cart made of iron that traveled of its own power like a sort of magic. They accepted this and he continued.

He saw a slow look of horror dawn on their faces as he described the big dog-like creature that attacked him.

Rimner broke into his story. "So this thing bit you?"

Storm just nodded his head. It seemed like a small detail. Rimner looked at Ty and Ty spoke. "This would explain the poison." But this explanation made the two of them uncomfortable.

"I don't understand. What is so significant about the dog?"

Rimner spoke up. It sounds like a GegenHound. They roam the wastelands to the north. Always travel in packs, always attack humans, and have a poisonous bite. But you say that this hound belonged with the man? They were companions?"

"That's definitely right. They stood together and watched me. Then the man pointed at me and the hound attacked."

Rimner continued with the explanation.

"The GegenHounds are a corruption. They have been twisted to the powers of darkness. Many generations ago they were companions to men. But they were poisoned and brought to evil and their purity has been lost. They now hunt not just for food but for sport. They take pleasure in the killing. Often they will bite their prey and torment it while the poison sets in. It is a potent poison and truly remarkable that you have survived both the bite and the battle. This warrants further insight. Your plight is a mystery. Whence and how you came is beyond our questions. And the further perversion of the GegenHound makes me wary."

He gave Bherin a look and Bherin nodded.

Storm noted how the two of them seemed to be well synchronized. They almost didn't need to talk. It was like they were twins that spent their whole lives together. They just knew how each other felt. He didn't think it was specific to Bherin and Rimner he thought that maybe these people, as a whole, were just in tune with each other. They had a harmony that gave Storm reassurance.

After the pause Rimner continued. "We should have a meeting tonight. We will have the Gether when the moon reaches its peak." They both stared at Storm and waited for him to ask about the Gether but before they could continue further Ty approached them and announced the meal was ready.

Storm didn't realize that they had been talking for hours. He had forgotten all about his hunger but now it rushed back at him. The three of them stood up and moved over toward the fire.

Ty carefully removed the spit from over the flames and placed it on a bed of rocks. He removed the spit then cut open the boar. Both Rimner and Bherin watched intently. It seemed to Storm that there was more to this test than just a good tasting meal. Ty continued cutting. He severed the boar in half then continued on by cutting through the hare and then through the quail. He paused here and the tension in the air thickened significantly. Storm watched as

Ty reached carefully into the meal and pulled out the egg.

He laid the egg gingerly down on a leather pouch and the four of them hovered over it in anticipation. A minute passed by then two minutes and just as Storm was about to speak he heard a clicking noise. They focused more intently on the egg and Storm could see a small piece of it break away. The baby chick was hatching! He watched in amazement for ten more minutes as it struggled its way completely out of the egg. When it was fully out Ty gently picked it up and transferred it to a nest he had made of straw. Bherin clapped him on the back and Ty beamed in pride.

"Let's eat."

Storm reflected on this. It was quite a feat. The Testing was more than just the creation of a menu. He had to keep the heat very finely tuned so it slowly seeped into the meat, cooking it all yet hatching the egg. And about the egg itself; he must have brought it with him. It would be nearly impossible to find an egg in the wild and expect it to be within a day of hatching. Ty must have raised the bird that laid the egg and timed it very carefully to be ready to hatch today. He brought it with him and today he put it through the test and didn't fry it. He warmed it enough to encourage it to hatch and when it came out and cooled that is exactly what it did -it hatched. Or maybe in this world there were different rules when it came to chicks hatching from eggs. He had thrown Ty's schedule off by a couple of days.

The four of them sat down and Ty served them proudly. The feeling among the group was palpable. Ty had passed a significant milestone in his life and they all felt it –even Storm.   Tomorrow would be, according to what Bherin had told him, Ty's final test – The test of Judgment.

The food was delicious. Everything was fully cooked and the meat had absorbed the flavor of the vegetables. Ty really was a great cook. His father deserved to be very proud.

The whole situation overwhelmed Storm with a warmth that made him sleepy. He hadn't eaten in days and his strength was low. His thumb had been aching the whole day. But this food had an effect on him. He could feel its warmth working its way through his system. Gently healing all his hurts. It felt like an egg inside him had incubated and hatched. It was an egg of warmth and health. It didn't soothe the confusion and pain he felt at the   situation he was in but it did soothe his body.
He walked to the tree where he had first awoken and with the sound of a baby chick chirping a click click that resonated in his skull he lay down and fell into a restful sleep.

Storm woke to someone calling his name. He was not laying down, he was standing, in a fog, and a voice was calling him forward. He walked toward it and the fog cleared. Bherin, Rimner, and Ty were standing on a small hill under a tree.

The tree they stood under was large and beautiful; very old and very majestic. Its long sweeping branches extended far around the trunk and curved down almost to the ground. And it was some kind of fruit bearing tree. Every branch was heavy with large bulbs that looked like onions.

Storm walked toward them and as he neared the tree he turned his attention back to the men under it. They just stood smiling and waited patiently for him to draw near.

A feeling of awe and wonder overcame Storm. The three men looked very different. They were all naked and their skin was slightly transparent. The only article that any of them wore was a pouch on a long leather strap that Ty had draped around his neck. At the pouch, which lay against his stomach, was the baby chick that he had hatched. It peeked through a hole in the leather.

As Storm got close enough to speak he could see that their skin hid almost nothing. Through their chests he could see their hearts beating. With each beat a ripple moved out of their chests and distorted the air. It was like a raindrop in a still pond. When the drop hit the water a ripple extended gracefully along the surface. When their hearts beat a ripple extended gracefully out through the air.

He looked at his own heart. It was beautiful, not the ugly thing you see in horror movies. He could see that his own heart was something more than just a muscle. It was a receptacle for something else. It contained his life force and with each beat it proclaimed its joy.

He joined the three men under the graceful branches of the tree and they all bowed but never took their eyes off his heart.

Rimner spoke first. "It was very difficult finding you. You have never been here before?" Storm shook his head to indicate no. "What is this place? Am I dreaming?"

"This is the Gether and you are sleeping but you are not dreaming." Rimner replied paradoxically. "This place, under this tree, is a place between the real world and the dream world. It is a place where a man can talk and think differently. We sometimes come here when the puzzles that life place in front of us are unusually difficult to understand. We brought you here to try to understand your dilemma.

Ty broke into the speech. "Why does his heart not beat with ours?" Storm looked down at his heart, then at the hearts of the three men. Their hearts all beat exactly as one -the little ripples spreading out from their chests at the same time, and mingling in the air. He could almost hear them as a gentle tingling of bells. Even the tiny heart of the baby chick at Ty's stomach beat in synchronization with the men. Then he looked down at his own heart. It didn't beat in the same rhythm as theirs. It followed its own course.

"Maybe because he doesn't come from this world." Was Rimner's answer. "Maybe his heart still beats in the rhythm of his world. Maybe he will need time to come into harmony with everything that is around him."

After a long pause with them all staring at Storm's heart Rimner began what seemed to be a ceremony.

"We have before us several questions. This man here has been placed in circumstances that are strange to him. His appearance here is also strange to us." Bherin and Ty nodded in agreement. "The first question is from whence has he come?" The three men all looked off the hill and out into the distance. Storm followed their stare and in the fog off to his left another hill appeared. It rose from the darkness of the fog. In the middle of the hill a plant sprouted. Storm watched in awe as the sprout grew into a sapling then developed into a full-grown tree. It grew leaves, then blossoms, then it fruited with a thousand bulbs that looked like apples made of glass.

The Gether was truly like a dream world. The normal rules of life didn't apply here. It had a logic of it's own.

They all watched as the fruit ripened then as a single glass apple fell from the tree to the soft earth at its trunk. They walked through the knee-deep fog and climbed the hill under this new tree. Bherin picked up the glass apple and they all looked into it. He didn't see anything with his eyes but impressions of his world rushed at Storm. He saw his house, his work, his city and impressions of the world he lived in. These impressions came to all of them.

The other men were confused by the images. This type of world was alien to them. They couldn't understand the complexity of it. Storm lived in that world, and he couldn't understand the complexity of it.

Bherin dug a hole in the soil under the tree and buried the apple then asked another question. "Storm has endured a terrible ordeal with his wife Arabella. What has become of her?" Storm choked back a lump in his throat. He was afraid that the next apple would show him that she is dead.

They all looked up at the tree and waited for another apple to fall but nothing happened. Storm looked from apple to apple hoping for a sign of something. Each apple shined with a glass beauty but none gave a hint of revealing anything. His anxiety doubled. He was afraid that he would get bad news but getting no news was even worse. Not knowing is the worst possible thing.

Seeing they would get no answer to this question Rimner asked another one. "What is the purpose of Storm being here?"
Again they all looked up up at the tree and as an apple fell to the ground with a thump something wailed in the distance. It sounded like the baying of a large wolf. The voice was very deep.

They looked off into the distance and saw that another hill had appeared. On it was a dead tree and under the tree were several big dogs. They looked just like the one that had attacked Storm in the river. Storm glanced at the apple where it lay on the ground then he looked back at the big dogs. Ty lost some control and in a trembling voice exclaimed "GegenHounds!" and as if on cue the hounds on the other hill all sprinted directly at them. Storm watched in horror as they entered the fog that was knee high for him. The hounds cut through it quickly with muscular intent. It only went as high as the underside of their bellies. That meant they were big - about waist high to a man. Storm looked at Rimner. Could these things hurt him here in the Gether. He saw horror on the man's face. This was definitely not normal. He glanced at the apple shining in the dim light of the Gether. There it was, as simple as that, the answer to the question of why he was here.

He glanced again at the GegenHounds. They had covered half the distance to the hill he stood on and in a few moments they would be upon them. His thumb began to ache as if the presence of the hounds had reawakened traces of poison still left in him.

"Run!" It was Bherin who screamed. "We can't leave from this tree. We must return to the tree that brought us." They all made a fast break through the fog for the first tree –the bowing graceful tree that they had first appeared under.

When they reached the tree Rimner began to chant and Storm turned to look at the hounds. The hounds converged on the hill with the glass apple tree and paused. One of the hounds sniffed at the glass apple that had fallen and with one sharp movement grabbed it in its teeth, tilted its head upward and swallowed it. Rimner continued his chant as the hounds turned to look at them. With the purpose of a single mind all the hounds broke into a run directly toward the men but before they had completed the sprint Rimner completed the chant and Storm woke up under the tree where he had fallen asleep.

***

He sat up with a start. His body was covered in sweat. He ran his hands on his body to make sure everything was in place then looked over to the burnt out embers of the fire. The other men were also sitting up and laboring in their breathing. They all looked around warily as if they were afraid that the GegenHounds had followed them back from the Gether. But there was nothing -no sounds of baying and no hint of hounds. It was early morning and the sun was starting to burn off the evening's dew. There was no sense in going back to sleep. So they went about cleaning up the camp. Today was the day of the Judgment stone and they thought about that rather than about the implications of what had happened in the Gether.

Storm helped with the clean up as much as he could but his thumb hindered his ability to do anything. After they had packed up everything and buried the remnants of the fire they started on their hike to the Stone. It was a beautiful morning and they made good progress. Just doing something/anything lifted his spirits.

The four of them had remained silent for the whole morning as they followed the banks of the Rhyme River toward the north. The chick in Ty's pouch was mostly quiet but occasionally it would chirp and the group would stop for a few minutes so Ty could feed it.

By mid morning the freshness of the air and the simple exercise of walking lifted all their spirits and they started to talk although they avoided the subject of the Gether and the Hounds.

In early mid afternoon they took a break and set up a mini camp. Ty broke out large chunks of meat left over from the previous days evening meal and Bherin started a fire. Rimner sat down and opened a conversation with Storm.

"We are close to the Judgment Stone. We will camp here for a bit then move on to the Test. If all goes well we will camp here again for the evening and tomorrow we will head back to the city."

Storm looked Rimner in the eye. "What is the Testing?"

Rimner paused for a moment. "This is something we never talk about. Ty will undergo his final test of manhood soon and he will pass or fail. You will see that, but you must understand something. Things are not always as they seem and you must under no circumstances interfere with the process. Do you understand?"

Storm nodded his head.

Rimner reiterated his point. "Whatever happens will be what happens. You must not interfere. You have not undergone the testing so you don't understand what it is. This evening, if all goes well we will talk about it." Storm nodded his head again and let it alone. He resigned himself to the wait.

Bherin and Ty were noticeably nervous. Storm watched them as they unpacked and set up camp. The meal they ate was hardy but Storm imagined that to the others it was bland. When something weighs heavily on your mind it is difficult to enjoy the simple things like a meal. You end up just eating for sustenance or go through the motions just to distract yourself from what's to come.
They finished their meal and quietly packed up their camp.

4. The Testing

"The biggest challenger a man faces is himself"
-The book of Varheit

They wound their way through the woods and the light brush turned to thick fauna. Their progress was taking them to lower ground. It was a slow and leisurely sloping down, and the further down they went the thicker the flora got. The gentle forest they had been walking through turned into a jungle and their progress slowed.

After a few hours Rimner, who was leading, stopped and announced that they had arrived. Storm looked around. They were standing in front of a stone entrance into the earth. Two slabs of granite lay on the ground about six feet apart and between them was a stone staircase that led down. It was tangled with a mass of vines and undergrowth but still passable.

Ty removed his pack, took some torches out, and striking some flint he lit the torches and handed one to each of them. They moved down the staircase and into the earth without a word.
They were in a tunnel that slowly graded downward and after a few steps they were through the vines and undergrowth and were walking on bare stone.

It was some kind of underground complex. The walls, ceiling, and floor were all stone and every ten paces was an iron holder on the wall – probably for torches. They crossed several intersecting corridors but they maintained their straight-ahead path and after only a short period of time they entered a large room where their torches cast only dim shadows a short distance into the darkness. The air felt different and the sounds of their footsteps hinted that the room was very large. Storm raised his torch and looked around. He couldn't make out the ceiling of the room. It might have been just out of reach of the torchlight or it might be considerably further off. He could make out the vague images of the walls of the room. Vague hints of vertical columns lined both the left and the right. It felt like he was in a church with marble columns along the right and left. And standing where the altar should be was a large object.

As they moved further into the room. Storm looked at the large object in the place of an altar. It was a large boulder and about the size of an elephant. It rested on a pedestal of granite about six feet across and a foot high. They walked over to it and Storm touched it. Its surface was pebbly and it looked as if someone took tens of thousands of pebbles and squeezed them together until they stuck, creating a large boulder in the rough shape of a human heart - sort of spherical but not quite. Rimner watched Storm inspecting it and explained a little to him. "This is called the testing stone, but it has many names. Because of its shape it is also called the heart of the mother. Many, many generations ago, possibly even before the time of man it was placed here in this very spot by sheets of ice that slowly moved across the world. It was a time of great coldness. In time the earth warmed and the coldness receded to only the far north and far south of the world. But the things they brought remained. This is one of them. It has remained perched on this very spot since that time, and this complex was built around it."

While he listened to Bherin's story Ty and Rimner busied themselves. They took off their packs and removed a dozen more torches and as each torch was lit Ty carried it to a section of the room and placed it in a torch holder against what were now clearly the walls of the room. As the room lit Storm gained a clear picture of it. It really was like a church. A dozen marble columns lined the walls to the left and the right and on each one of these now burned a torch. The columns climbed up to reveal a second level to the room and on the second level there were dark spaces between the columns that appeared to be alcoves or maybe open doorways.

After the torches had all been placed Ty and his father sat down together in front of the Testing stone. The orange torchlight cast flickering ghosts on them and on it. Rimner took hold of Storm's shoulder and led him ten paces back toward where they had entered the room. "We will sit here." He motioned toward the ground and both he and Storm sat down and faced Ty and Bherin who sat cross-legged on the floor facing each other, their foreheads touching as they whispered back and forth. After a few minutes of this Bherin placed one hand on the back of Ty's neck and with an affectionate tone said "You are ready."

The two of them stood up and Bherin took several steps away from the Testing stone while Ty approached it and turning around he placed his back against it and with his legs started to push against it.

To Storm it seemed like an impossible task. The stone was very large and must weigh several tons, unless it was delicately balanced one man would never be able to move it. He looked at Rimner and Rimner, enjoying the role of guide, gave him an explanation. "There are two strengths that every man possesses. An internal strength and an external strength." Storm furrowed his brows not understanding what this meant so Rimner continued. "External strength comes from those around you. If you are born into a family and a community that is filled with love and a bond of the blood that is true then your strength is combined with the strength of others.

This strength is formidable and from it can be derived the determination to weather the many obstacles in a man's life. Internal strength is different than this. It flows out of a man. Only he knows the true depth of it. And the intensity of the first strength can fuel the fires of the second if a man is pure. The Stone tests the first strength. If the blood that runs through Ty is pure and those that he followed are pure of heart they will help him to accomplish this part of the testing." Rimner fell quiet and Bherin began to speak to the room in general."

"This here is my son. He has come to make the testing. I proclaim that I have taught him the ways of truth and strength to the best I am capable. He is at the moment just a boy but he wishes to take the steps necessary to become a man and we ask for your help."

Ty continued to strain against the massive stone. And it appeared to Storm that it was about the same as leaning your back up against an elephant's leg and trying to push it over. The elephant stone didn't budge in the least. It didn't even feel the push but Ty continued to push. His face turned red and beads of sweat rolled off his forehead, down his face and neck. His effort was substantial and his desire was earnest. But the stone did not relent in the least.

Tension increased in the room. Storm could feel it. Something was either going to happen or it wasn't. He looked at Rimner and saw the tension in his face. Bherin with his arms by his sides and his palms facing out was imploring something to happen and Ty continued to push against the stone as the atmosphere changed. A slight hint of cool air brushed against Storm's face. He looked at Rimner who was now smiling and looking up to the second floor of the room. Storm followed his gaze toward one of the black areas between the columns and something moved.

A man stepped forward out of the darkness then stepped off the ledge on the second floor and drifted down to their level. He was wearing a leather tunic and Storm started at the fact that he could see right through the man. He was a ghost and he shimmered as he moved. Storm watched transfixed as he walked over to Bherin and said in a hollow voice "Hello son." Bherin fought back tears and replied. "Hello father." It appeared to Storm that Bherin was fighting back the urge to clasp his arms around his father in a mighty bear hug of warmth.

The ghost looked over at Ty who struggled against the stone and he smiled. Then on feet that didn't really touch the ground yet still mimicked the fluid motion of walking it pressed its hands against the stone and began to push.

Bherin continued to look up toward the second floor of the room and a second ghost appeared in another dark alcove. This one too came down to their level, approached Bherin and spoke. "Greetings Grandson." Bherin replied to this one as well. "Greetings Grandfather. Thank you for coming." This ghost smiled at Ty and also approached the stone and began to push. This procession continued and more ghosts came out of the darkness –each one an earlier generation. Each one greeted Bherin and then pushed against the stone. After six generations of ghosts were pushing against the stone the weight in the room began to noticeably shift and the stone rolled forward a quarter revolution.

It revealed a small shaft in the ground about the size of a small doorway. Ty stopped his pushing against the stone and climbed down into the shaft. Bherin grabbed a torch from the wall and followed him down. Rimner clapped Storm on the back and grabbing two torches from the wall he gave one to Storm and climbed down in after Bherin. Storm, alone for a moment looked at the ghosts who continued to hold the stone away from the shaft then climbed in.

The shaft turned into a very narrow corridor that sloped sharply downward. He followed behind Rimner who continued on with his explanation of what happened. "Ty has passed the first half of his test. His blood has come to support him in his quest and it bodes well for him. Six generations came to his aid. That is a strong number. His blood is strong and his family is good. No doubt that Bherin is very proud of the turnout for his son and this will help him face the final half of the test."

They entered a circular room. Their torches easily illuminated the walls and the contents. Storm judged it to be twenty feet in diameter. In the center of the room stood a square stone dais about six feet in length and waist high to the men. On the other side of the dais, opposite from them, stood a man with closed eyes.

They all stood huddled about the doorway just inside the room not wanting to press further in and Storm scrutinized the closed eye man. He was big -well over six feet tall and probably around six feet six inches. His frame was very sturdy and well muscled with the type of muscle that comes from hard work. It was the real strength that a man could attain through either a life on a farm or a life on the battlefield. He stood as still as a marble statue and there was no hint of life or breath in him. His massive arms crossed his chest and they cradled a large and broad two-handed sword. It was nearly four feet in length and the blade at its thickest was nearly eight inches wide. On the blade near the shaft was a long rectangular hole. Storm could see the man's steel breastplate through it.

Carved on the blade was a distorted face, its jaw was elongated and the hole in the blade was its mouth. He looked intently at the face on the sword and its eyes opened and looked at him then spoke. The hole on the blade moved as a mouth and words came out: "Anwat hirt drisnan." Storm stepped back against the wall in shock as the big man opened his eyes and looked at them. His head was reeling from what the sword spoke. But before he could fully wrap his mind around it the big statue-like man holding the sword spoke.

"Who has come to be tested?" He asked in a deep voice.

"I have." Replied Ty.

"And who will stand in for him?"

Bherin spoke this time. "I will."

The tall man looked at Bherin then gestured toward the Dais. Bherin quickly removed the pack from his back and handing his torch to Rimner he lay down on the cold stone of the dais. The tall man took a step forward and with one hand he suspended the massive sword over Bherin's heart and looked through the oblong hole in the blade. With his other hand he pointed at Ty. "Come forward and be tested." Ty took several steps toward the Dais. Both the tall man and the sword watched him carefully.

The tall man gripped the sword with both hands then hefted it directly over Bherin's supine body on the dais. It pointed directly down and with the point of it only inches from Bherin's heart he peered through the blade hole and spoke to Ty.

"What is your name?"

"I am Ty Hilltracker, son of Bherin Hilltracker and grandson of Thekis Hilltracker."

The face on the sword spoke. "Es Var." The tall man grunted in approval and asked a second question. "Why do you come here?"

"I seek the test of manhood so that I may be deemed worthy of a place as a man among the people I love." Again the sword spoke. "Es Var."

Again the tall man grunted and tightened his grip on the sword, readying himself to plunge it through Bherin's heart.

"Are you willing to give your life for the safety of your people?"

Ty paused and looked at his father prostate on the dais then stuck forward his chin in a gesture of certainty. "Yes I am."
The tension in the room became palpable as the face in the sword also paused, scrutinized Ty then replied. "Es Var."

Rather than Bherin being cut through, the tension in the room was cut. Everyone exhaled the breath they were holding and the tall man lowered his sword and took a step back away from the Dais. Bherin quickly climbed off and retrieved his backpack and torch. The tall man spoke to Ty.
"You have passed the test. You may return to your people as a man. Your new name is Ardan Hilltracker, son of Bherin and grandson of Thekis."

Bherin and Rimner rushed to Ty and embraced him. Clapping him on the shoulder Rimner spoke. "Welcome Ardan Hilltracker!" They all smiled and embraced for a few moments while the tiny eyes of the sword watched, then they packed up their stuff and quickly shuffled out of the room and back into the corridor. Storm shot one last look at the tall man standing again as a marble statue with his arms crossed as they were when they first came into the room. The sword looked at him and spoke another word "basool" then closed its eyes. The word it spoke sent a shock down his spine.

They climbed out of the shaft, backed away from the testing stone, and watched as each of the six ghosts looked at Ardan, smiled and returned to his dark doorway on the second floor of the room. When the last ghost removed his grip the stone rolled back into place over the shaft to the lower room.

Storm was in a daze. This was something totally unexpected in a world full of things that were unexpected. The sword spoke the language that he and Arabella created. How could it do that? How could that possibly be? They made up that language. It came out of their heads and they only spoke it with each other. Was he hearing things? Or did the sword really speak their language? He shook his head and the only thing that came to mind was "Es Var" as if in answer to his questions.

5. The Return to the Town

"A man explores the world, not to explore the world. But to arrive back home a better man." - The book of Varheit

They traveled for several uneventful days and during these days Storm's companions were mostly quiet. In general they were not a talkative group. This gave him plenty of time to contemplate and puzzle over what had happened to him. And it gave him a little bit of hope that Arabella was still alive. If he had survived the ordeal in such a crazy manner there was no reason why she couldn't have survived it also.

During the daylight hours of their travel they walked. And during the late afternoons they hunted for game and gathered vegetables. Each evening they would make a big fire, cook a big meal then after feasting they would retire for the night. This created a wonderful rhythm that soaked into Storm with a gentle feeling of health. His thumb stopped its incessant aching and he thought that soon he would be able to remove the splint for good and regain use of the hand.

On the morning that he removed the splint and bandages from the thumb of his hand they were topping a grass hill and saw in the valley, an hours walk away, a beautiful town. It had about a hundred small stone houses all squatting around a larger circular building in the center. Their spirits lifted higher and their pace quickened and within an hour they had arrived at the outskirts of the town.

They entered a small stone hut on the outskirts of the town and they removed all their gear. There were several cots and each man claimed one. Storm thought this a little funny. Why didn't they enter the town to their welcome. Ardan's mother and siblings would no doubt be very glad to see him.

Bherin left the hut and Storm posed his question to Rimner. "Bherin has gone off to see his family and announce the addition of a new man to the town. This evening there will be a festival and a welcome for the new man." With that he shot a smile at Ardan who stuck out his chest and smiled back.

After an hour Bherin returned with a certain amount of pep in his step and announced all would be ready. He had a sack with him and he emptied it on the table. It was a variety of food. Ardan started a fire in the fireplace and by mid afternoon they sat down at the table for a light meal and conversation.

"Who was the tall man with the sword that tested Ty, err.. I mean Ardan?"

Rimner took the question enthusiastically. "That was Anfang. He is the founder of our way of life." He lived many, many generations ago. He set for us the rules by which we guide out lives and he remains with us to test each man as he quests for passage into manhood."

"
So he just lives there like a statue and comes alive when someone visits?"

"No, he has long passed into another life. But he has ties with us, and his love for us remains strong. His body remains here, and through the strength of Varheit he returns when he is called."

"Varheit. That's the sword right?"

"Yes that is the sword of telling that he carries." And seeing that Storm had more questions about the sword Rimner answered before he could ask. "Varheit is an enigma. No one knows, mayhaps even Anfang doesn't know from where Varheit came. It is believed that the sword speaks the old language. The language that was born when the world was born. And it is believed that Anfang too knows this language.

"So that was the strange words the sword spoke? The old language?"

"Yes, that is what we believe to be true. The sword see the truth or lies in a man's word and tells this to Anfang who passes the sentence. It is believed that the sword knows all truths and even knows what you will say before you say it."

A lump formed in his throat at the furthering mystery of this world. It was truly amazing. These people had a simple yet beautiful life. They were straightforward and honest and the rules that applied to their world seemed to be quite different than the rules of the world that he had grown up in.

"What if someone else were to hold Varheit? Does it just work for Anfang?" Rimner thought about this for a moment. "Varheit is an enigma and the only one that has ever held it has been Anfang. That goes as far back as we know. Maybe Varheit is much older and maybe there have been other carriers of it -I don't know. But one thing is certain. Did you notice how Anfang held the sword?" He stopped and stared at Storm.

"You mean the way he held it over Bherin?"

"No, I mean the way he held it with his left hand. Since the time of Anfang there has never been another that can wield a sword with his left hand. There has only been him." Storm stared at him hard. "Nobody in this village is left handed?"

Again Bherin answered in the negative. "No one is left handed, nor has anyone been born left handed for the past thousand years at least."

Storm rubbed the thumb of his left hand. It was sore but the healthy life of the past several days had healed it well. He flexed it and thought about being left-handed. There was a puzzle in this but he didn't mention that he was left-handed to Bherin, he just grunted in understanding. His frantic rubbing of his left thumb brought attention to it. Bherin stared at it then looked Storm directly in the eye. Storm thought that he might ask the question but after an awkward pause the moment passed and their conversation turned to food. Ardan had placed some of the bread near the fire and now that it was warm he broke off pieces and passed them around.

"The stew is almost ready."

This pushed all thoughts out of Storm's head. The smell of the stew filled the room and Ardan filled bowls for them and they all ate.

They all had one bowl of the stew and a small piece of warmed bread. This left Storm still hungry but he didn't say anything.

After they ate they cleared the table and wiped down the dishes. Rimner clasped a hand on Ardan's back and asked him a question. "Have you chosen an offering for the feast?"

"Yes, I will gather watergourds." Rimner smiled in approval. "You should be off then. Not much time until the feast. Maybe Storm will help you?" He turned and looked at Storm.

"I would love to help. I don't know what watergourds look like but I'll help."

Ardan grabbed a couple of backpacks and emptying them of their contents he handed one to Storm. "Let's be off. I'll show you watergourds. We must gather as many as we can."

The two of them left the small hut and walked back out into the fields that they came through. The afternoon sun was starting to soften and Ardan walked at a quick pace. Instead of heading back into the woods they had earlier arrived from they followed the sloping terrain and stayed in the grassy plains until they arrived in a section with plenty of lush underbrush but sparse trees.
This was the first time that Storm and Ardan had spent alone.

"Watergourds are about the size of your fist and green with yellow stripes. They are heavy and filled with sweet water. But we will carry many with the sacks."

"Bherin asked you what type of offering you would make for the feast. What does that mean?"

Ardan answered without slowing down the pace. He had grown accustomed to Storm not knowing much about their ways.

"It is traditional for the man returning from the Testing to bring a bounty of fruits or vegetables. It's just an offering in exchange for his being allowed a new place among the people. It's just an old tradition. I chose watergourds because they symbolize abundance. So with them I give my hopes that our people will always have abundance."

The baby bird in the pouch he had suspended over his shoulder chirped as if to accentuate the point that he had made. Ardan and the bird were constant companions. The two of them never separated and every few hours of each traveling day the group of four men had stopped to let Ardan feed it.

Storm stopped Ardan with a pointed finger. "Are those watergourds?" He was pointing at a large patch that sprawled along a large area of the ground. The leaves were the size of a man's head and the plants ran along the ground. Scattered throughout the maze of leaves at intervals were green fruits with yellow stripes.

"Good eye. Yes those are watergourds." And Ardan continued walking right past them and sensing the hesitation in Storm's step as they walked past he explained.

"We never pick a fruit or a vegetable, or kill an animal on the first encounter. The first one we see remains safe. This way we always insure there is plenty. We will find a second patch and from that one we will harvest."

Even though this was a small thing it hit Storm like a thunderclap. There was undeniable balance here. These people understood implicitly how closely they were tied to the earth; it's well being meant their well being. They only took what they needed and they maintained the balance.

They came across another large patch of watergourds and walked out into it. The two of them started picking them and the picking was easy. He walked among the plants peeking under the large leaves, plucking the watergourds as he spotted them and slid them into his pack.

For one of them he reached down and grabbed it and it squealed and scampered away. The surprise and incongruity of it caused him to fall back on the ground. He sat and looked in shock as the watergourd ran away. Ty started laughing. "Looks like you found a gourd-rat. They are rodents and about the size of a watergourd, when they feel threatened they curl up in a ball and look just like a watergourd. Sometimes things are not what they appear to be."

With that he laughed some more, but it was a kind laughing. He meant no real malice with it. Damn it all Storm thought to himself. Nothing in this world is as it appears to be. Dreams are real and real probably is a dream. And now rats that look like gourds. "gourd-rats" he thought to himself. "When something isn't what it appears to be." And this brought a thought and a chuckle to him. Some people that were like that. Not really what they want you to think they are. Yup, it's a good word, he made a mental note to remember it "gourd-rat."

They came across another large patch of watergourds and gently Storm picked the fruit and put them in his backpack. He almost felt a sense of guilt as he pulled each one from its vine. After they had gathered full packs they returned to the stone hut as the sun was fading from view.

After the sun had completely fallen and they had exhausted all topics of conversation Rimner announced it was time to begin the festival so they left the hut and walked down to the center of town.

The sky was dark and beautiful and everywhere in the town torches cast a red orange glow on the houses and streets. A large congregation of people had gathered in the Town Square and many tables had been set out. The smell of roasted meat drifted gently through the air and Storm's stomach rumbled in anticipation of the coming feast. Now he knew why they had only had a light meal earlier in the day.

As they came into view of the townsfolk all the conversation stopped and everyone turned to watch them. Several people came to greet them before they crossed an imaginary threshold into the square and one of them spoke.

It was a tall man with a large belly and large black beard spoke to them first. "Ahh! Rimner and Bherin! Welcome home!" He glanced at Storm and continued. "I see you have brought a companion." He stared harder at Storm -looking him up and down carefully. "He is of strange dress."

Rimner responded to this observation.
" We have found him by the river Rhyme and have brought him along on the Testing." At the mention of this the man raised his burly brown eyebrows in surprise.
Rimner continued. "Of this man we must talk further but for now a new man has come to join our town." Storm was unexpected for the feast but the large man pushed it aside and regained his sense of their purpose. He continued on with what seemed like a scripted play.

"A new man come to our village?" What is his name?"

Rimner pointed at Ardan and introduced him to the burly townsman. "This is Ardan the son of Bherin and the grandson of Thekis. His ancestors have graced him with a blessing and Anfang himself has tested him."

Ardan smiled and stepping forward he presented his hand to the burly man.

"Pleased to meet you Ardan. I am Grame. Welcome to our town." He smiled a great big smile then clasped Ardan in a bear hug. Even though there was a ceremonial introduction Grame could not forget the fact that he had known "Ardan" all of the boys' life. He clapped Ardan on the back and pushed him forward toward the throng of people. They all watched in anticipation as Grame, in a booming voice, made his announcement. "Townsfolk of Mainz we have a new man among us and his name is Ardan." The townsfolk all cheered and moved forward.

A handsome woman in her forties rushed forward and grasped Ardan in a warm embrace. Storm guessed it must be Ardan's mother. Somewhere at the back of the square a group of musicians began playing a cheerful tune and amidst the laughing and cheering they all moved into the square -and the festival began.

As the moon rose the feasting came to an end and the drinking began. They cleared the tables from the center of the square and to the sound of the music many of them broke out in dance. With a mug of brew in his hand Storm found a place to sit and watch the Townsfolk in their merriment. The sight of the women and girls dressed in brightly colored sundresses, many of them with flowers wrapped in their hair gave Storm a twinge. The beauty and the magic of this place was overwhelming. He felt like for the past days he had been in shock -his mind was too occupied with trying to understand what was happening in each moment to think about what had happened to bring him to this place. But now, with a little bit of time to reflect, and a little bit of the brew inside him everything came unwound like the spring of a clock, and his thoughts went to Arabella.

Would he ever see her again. Did she too survive the ordeal in the river? And who was the man with the dog and what part did he play in this?

As if he had sensed Storm's change in mood Rimner sat down beside him. "I have talked to Grame and several of the council members about the mystery of your arrival. I have told them to the best of my understanding what has befallen you and I have also described to them what happened to us in the Gether when we tried to probe into these questions. It has brought concern and they have many questions for you. Tomorrow they will send for the council heads of several nearby cities and when they arrive we will meet in a grand council and discuss your plight and what action we should take."

This lifted Storm's spirits. He needed to do something about his situation. Just waiting and doing nothing weighed very heavy on him. Maybe they could find some answers.

It was with a lighter heart that Storm spent the rest of the evening enjoying the festival. A woman with beautiful brown eyes and bright yellow flowers in her hair even asked him to dance but he declined. That was something he could not do.

Before the festivities had ended Storm returned to the little stone cottage on the outskirts of the town. He made his way to his bunk, lay down, and let his thoughts go to a memory of Arabella.

***

They had been together about a month and he was starting to get comfortable with life in Spain. He had quit his job but still had a pretty hefty savings so he wasn't worried about his finances. He was just taking his time and getting to know Arabella.

One night had a profound effect on him in a subtle way. Sometimes profundity can be subtle. All of the various women in the family were going out one evening. It seemed to be a big thing but he really couldn't understand what it was all about.

They were in a club of sorts in the coastal city of Cadiz. It wasn't a loud club like we typically had in the states. It was different, the people were more relaxed. But at one point, it was as if on cue, as if they all knew when it was going to happen. A man picked up a flamenco style guitar from the corner of the room and stood beside a woman. He began to play and she began to sing. Some kind of beautiful flamenco style music. It was heart filling. But the remarkable thing about this whole scene was that all the women got up and began to dance.

He was shocked by the utter beauty of the scene –all the women dancing some kind of flamenco with their hands over their heads. And watching them he realized that it was a very even mix of women – About half of them were in the forties and late thirties while the other half were young women in their teens and early twenties.

There was something happening here. It seemed that the adult woman were reveling in their own beauty and sensuality. They were celebrating themselves and their joy of being alive. And they were passing some of it down to their daughters. He was stunned by the beauty of it. It was a chain of life that had been going on through the generations for who knows how long. Storm would never know if this was a planned thing or just a spontaneous occurrence but it didn't matter. To the observer there really isn't much of a difference between the two.

***

The next few days passed slowly. Each day Storm wandered the town and talked to people. It was a pretty typical town. The townsfolk were happy and busy. He spent some time in the Market Square each morning and throughout the days he spent time with various craftsmen.

The blacksmith particularly intrigued him and after watching the smith for an hour the smith offered for him to have a go at hammering by handing him a hammer. He took the hammer and had some fun with it. All he did was hammer out some hot iron. It didn't form any particular shape but it felt good to just manipulate something with a little bit of physical exertion. He got a little overzealous with the hammering and it seemed to make the smith uncomfortable so he gave the hammer back, thanked him then spent a few more hours watching the man forge various metal objects from hinges to nails. He noted that a good portion of a blacksmith's day was devoted to repairing items. And he never saw the smith so much as forge a single sword or knife.

He spent his evenings in Rimner's home where they would eat a hardy meal, talk about things for a few hours, then retire for the night to a bed where he felt the absence of his wife.
Each day he would ask Rimner when the council would meet and discuss his situation. The response, each day, from Rimner was the same. One or more councilmen had arrived that day and when they all arrived, which would be soon, they would meet.

Toward the evening of the fourth day there was a palpable tension in the air. Something was going to happen, he could feel it and while he and Rimner sat to dinner he had the feeling that this evening there would be a council meeting. Rimner didn't say anything about it. Nobody talked about it at all. Storm just had the sense that it was going to happen. These people had an uncanny synchronization about them. It was a kind of group-think. They all had the feeling that tonight was the night for the council meeting and in some way, after spending a few days among them, Storm had got the feeling too. There was no need to set a day and a time. There were no clock-induced constraints on them. When the time was right, the time was right, and they all knew it.

It didn't feel to Storm like it was some kind of psychic link. It was just the result of a group of people living in harmony together. Storm thought about the way a large flock of birds effortlessly makes large flowing circles in the sky. These people were human but they hadn't lost that connection with the world around them or with each other. In the Gether their hearts beat in unison. He wondered if they also beat in unison here in the "real" world.

The absurdity of the thought of this being the real world made him grin. The Gether is a reality wrapped in this reality further wrapped in the reality of his previous life. The thought brought up the meal that Ty/Arden had cooked for his testing. Was Storm the chick in the egg? Was he at the center of it all? For that matter was everyone at their own center?

He had spent many years working within the confines of a cubicle in that other "real world" but the thread that tied him to the earth and the rest of the natural world hadn't been lost; it was just asleep and now it was coming awake.

When a man's shadow was three paces long the sun was getting ready to set and people started to converge in the main hall of the town. The hall was a single room structure, circular in shape with a domed ceiling. It was like a planetarium and there was no furniture, just a fire-pit in the center. And directly over that was a circular hole in the domed ceiling. A young man busied himself with starting a fire. It would keep away the chill of the oncoming evening air. And the hole above would let the smoke out – the curved ceiling guiding it up and through the hole.

He looked at the gathering men and women. There were about twenty of them and they mulled about the room quietly greeting each other. They all wore weapons of various types. Most had swords but some had axes and some had battle hammers. As the fire in the pit grew so did the urgency of the group. One by one they took a seat on the stone floor around the fire.

When they all were seated a man directly across the fire-pit from Storm stood up. He was in his fifties with a gray beard and a look of long practiced patience about him. The scabbard of his sword scraped along the stone as he stood. He looked directly at Storm and with an unreadable expression he stared for several long moments. The fire licked orange shadows across his face and with a quick underhand motion he threw something at Storm. It arced over the fire and Storm, acting on instinct, put out his hand and caught it. The seated people around the room gasped and some of them stood up.

The man who had thrown it grunted. "The smith was right. It looks like he is left handed." Storm, embarrassed by the attention, looked down at the object in his left hand. It was a glass apple much like the ones he had seen on the tree in the Gether. The man had thrown it directly at his right shoulder so the natural instinct would have been to catch it with his right hand. But he was very strongly left-handed and his natural instinct was to reach across his body and catch it with his left hand.

The group continued to chatter in small islands of conversation for several minutes.

After several minutes of the chatter they sat back down one by one, and as the last one sat down Rimner stood up. The room quieted and they all turned their attention to him as he recounted the events of the past few days. He described to them how a man wearing strange clothing stumbled into the outer edge of their camp and collapsed. At the mention of strange clothes he had pointed at Storm and all eyes turned to examine him. He went on to describe how they had sought answers in the Gether and as he described the appearance of the GegenHounds many of them shook their heads in disbelief.

When Rimner was done with his story Graybeard stood back up. "For the past several months there have been reports of cow and sheep disappearances in the north-lands. Maybe the GegenHounds have returned to the land and this is unsettling. But for them to have also penetrated into the Gether is unheard of. They alone do not have the intelligence or the spirit to pass into it. Something or someone must have drawn them into it.

As he spoke several young women came into the hall carrying large trays of food and drink. They worked their way around the room passing it out. The men and women all began eating without interrupting the flow of the meeting.

Graybeard, still standing, continued with his thoughts on the matter. "Storm, our guest, poses a puzzle to us and the disturbing occurrences of the past few months, and within the Gether, are also a puzzle. Maybe these things are linked together?" He paused and slowly looked around the room.

"A story has also come out of the far north-lands, from the base of the mountains that a body of a Grim has been found."

A spark of electricity ran though the group around the fire and some of them stood up in shock. Graybeard raised his hands to calm them down and they slowly sat back down as the chatter from the shock of the news subsided. "I had thought it to be a rumor with no substance but it may be true. Strange things are happening and if the Grim have returned to the land then there will be much trouble. I suggest there are a couple of things we must immediately do. First, this evening we should bring a war party into the Gether to examine its corruption, second we should get word out to the cities to prepare for trouble. We haven't had war with the Grim for many generations but if they are returning then we must be ready.

As the evening grew darker and the fire grew higher the group in the Hall continued to speculate and make plans. And at some time during the late evening, as if on cue, being all synchronized as they were, they unrolled furs and cloaks and lay down to sleep.

As each one lay down, he or she unsheathed his weapon and held it firmly in his hands. Rimner handed Storm a sheathed sword and grunted when Storm took it with his left hand. Then he and Rimner also lay down on some furs and the room full of people drifted off to sleep ready for a potential battle in the Gether. The last thing Storm heard before he drifted off was one of the serving girls picking up a tray. She jostled it and something on it made a click clicking sound.

6. Battle in the Gether

"All that we see or seem is but a dream within a dream."
-Edgar Allan Poe

Storm woke to a hand on his shoulder; Rimner was shaking him vigorously. "You are a difficult one to pull through."
Coming into the Gether was much like coming out of a deep sleep while staying in a deep sleep.

He sat up and shook his head to chase away the grogginess. A chill wind was blowing with a faint whistling sound. People were gathered in small groups around him and he looked them over. He was definitely in the Gether. Everyone had the thin veneer of transparent skin that exposed glimpses of their insides; the beating of their hearts sent colorful little ripples into the air. His awareness broadened and he took in his surroundings.

The ground was bare dirt and scattered around the group was a collection of large boulders. It was a barren environment and coupled with the chill in the air Storm felt as if he were on the top of a mountain.

Rimner lead him over to a group of townsfolk standing on the edge of a precipice. They were on the top of a ridge about a hundred feet high and everyone was staring down into a valley.
A lush green carpet of vegetation, trees, and plants, covered the valley. And a fog was blanketing the whole valley except for one area a few hundred yards from them. It was an open area of the valley with no fog -a perfect circle of clarity where something was happening and they were all staring and watching it.

It was like the valley was completely covered in a fog but someone had taken a round cookie cutter and cut out a piece of the fog. And in the middle of that opening was a small hill with structures on it and it is there that a battle was taking place.

They were too far away to make out the specifics of the battle but they could see groups of figures embroiled in fighting.
Graybeard, who had been a leader of sorts in the town, took control here. Stepping up onto a rock he spoke to them.

They all turned their attention to him and none of them saw as a group of figures broke off from the battle below and made a direct line for them standing on the ridge.

"Terrible things are happening here." Graybeard paused and looked the group over. A blight has come over the Gether and it is battling for its health, if not for its very existence; and while this battle rages the Gether can offer us no answers. We have come prepared for the possibility of battle and now the question is put forth for us. Should we return to our lives or should we go down into the valley and find out what is taking place?"

The question was moot. It was answered for him. The group that had split off from the fray below had made a panting sprint for them among the dirt and the rocks and had been quiet until they sprung upon them with snarls and roars.

The group of snarling Vile smashed into the knot of people with their bladed weapons swinging and several men and women had been sliced before they knew what was happening. But they responded quickly and after the first few moments were lost in surprise the situation turned quickly into a pitched battle with Vile and humans vigorously swinging weapons in a fevered maelstrom.
Storm was too shocked to even move. He stood still and just watched the unreal situation. The creatures were humanoid in shape and size; roughly five feet in height and very slender with unusually long arms. Their skin was a pale gray and their eyes a bright red. They shouted and snarled as the battle raged. It sounded like some kind of a guttural language but Storm couldn't be sure.

The townspeople outnumbered the creatures so the battle quickly turned to their favor and the pitch slowed down. And their philosophy of battle was significantly different. The villagers helped each other, blocked and parried blows for each other. There was a camaraderie to their fight. And just as their hearts beat in synchronization so their weapons and shields did in a similar manner. Soon many of the creatures had more than one person attacking it and when it became clear to them that the goal of overrunning and killing all the people was out of reach one of the larger creatures shouted louder than the others.

Storm, from his viewpoint of not engaging in battle focused his attention on that larger one. Unlike the other creatures it had a sturdy frame and was easily fifty pounds heavier than the rest of the onslaught. And it appeared to be barking out commands.

This wasn't just a group of wild creatures acting with a pack mentality. They were acting like a chaotic military unit. They weren't very disciplined but there was some control to their chaos. And the big one seemed to be in charge.

Storm watched in shock as the big one raised an arm, pointed its index finger directly at him and barked commands to the group.

For the second time in the battle the group of town-folk were taken by surprise as all the Vile disengaged themselves from their separate battles and spurred on by their leader they launched themselves in a suicide fashion directly at Storm.

When a real threat at your life comes you either respond or you die. If you die then it was fate and you surrendered to it. But for Storm this time wasn't fate and his reflexes took over his body and his thinking mind fell to sleep. He became a thing of action and reaction. This was something that he had practiced in the dojo for many hundreds of hours and all those hours came to his rescue now.

When the first Vile thrust its sword at him he parried it easily and someone else thrust a sword through the neck of the Vile. Several more made swings and thrusts and Storm danced, swinging his sword and making counter strikes.

The thing that saved him was the fact that he hadn't yet engaged in battle. He had been watching in a sort of trance, almost detached from it all. So, every one and every thing around him had been slowed by the fatigue of battle. He was still fresh. His quick responses and dodges preserved him and gave the people around him to enough time to realize he was now the sole target of their strikes. And they reacted accordingly. They parried the creatures away from him and struck at exposed limbs when they swung at Storm.

Out of the corner of his eye and in between the thrusting and parrying Storm watched the big creature as it rushed toward him. It had started out thirty yards away and although it wasn't fast of foot it had closed the distance in the first few seconds. Someone stepped into its path and with a long, slow and powerful arcing of its arm it brought its sword down. The person had brought his sword up to parry but the force of the blow from the beast was so powerful that its sword just pushed right through the block and down on his head. The man was gored in his face by his own sword.

The creature hadn't even broken stride. Another ten yards closer and another man stood in its way and with the same technique it brought its sword down in a great arc and with a tremendous slashing it broke through the blocking sword and sliced into the mans face.

It had only one technique and brute force to carry it through. Its goal was Storm. Several people slashed it as it passed but the slashes didn't dissuade it. With the thunder of its feet hitting the ground it lifted its sword again and just as it got within reach of Storm it began the powerful downward arcing of its arm but instead of lifting his sword in an attempt to block it Storm reacted differently.

When something was as powerful as this thing was you couldn't just meet it with brute force, you had to use its power against itself and this is what he did. Instead of bracing himself and bringing his sword up to meet the tremendous blow Storm launched himself directly at the creature. He stepped in toward the creatures midsection and turned so his back was against it. He hooked his right arm under the sword arm of the creature and in a standard judo move he twisted his hips and threw the creature right over his back and onto the ground. He used the strength of the beast against it.

The arcing of its powerful blow took it right over Storm and its forward momentum took it right over his back and flat onto its own back on the ground. As it passed over his shoulder he smelled the raw putrid rank of its hot breath. It was so potent that he tasted it. For one long moment Storm just stared down at it and it stared up at him. The move was so unexpected that the beast was shocked. It didn't seem to be possible to shock something such as this. Maybe it was only disoriented but before it could regain its orientation, and its feet, a sword plunged into its stomach and it grunted it pain.

The one-second pause was enough time for Graybeard to capitalize on the situation. It was his sword plunged in the stomach of the beast and with a relish he twisted it and the beast capitulated.

Still alive it just stared at Storm, it's red eyes still a menace. The battle around them had stopped. Most of the Vile had been killed and the remaining had run off when the big one fell.

It breathed in guttural gasps but continued its stare at Storm and with the sword still in its stomach it laughed a vulgar laugh and spoke to him. "He will not be denied. You will do his bidding."

"Shut your foul mouth." Graybeard twisted the sword again and this time the creature uttered one last breath and was silent.

Greybeard pulled out his sword, pointed it at the dead creature, and looked at Storm. "The smaller ones are Vile. This big one here, it's a Grim. Nasty creature. Quite a bit stronger than the Vile. Quite a bit angrier too."

Storm watched as the body of the Grim faded and disappeared.

He looked around the impromptu battlefield and there were no dead bodies anywhere. There were no dead creatures and no dead people. As they died their bodies had disappeared from the Gether just as the Grim had.

Graybeard sized up the situation then brought his attention back to the battle that was taking place in the valley. There were still a dozen town-folk standing about and panting. "Follow me." Was all he said as he head down into the ruckus. Storm and the remaining battle weary people followed him down into the valley.

They descended off the ridge and into the tree line. The trees eclipsed their sight of the battle but before they could veer too far off course the sounds of the battle came to them. They corrected their direction and after a scant few minutes they broke out of the tree line into the open field.

Graybeard raised his hands bringing them all to a stop so the situation could be assessed. They looked on the scene. The battle was about a hundred yards away and it looked like a handful of men in some kind of uniform were engaged in a pitched battle with more of the creatures they had themselves just fought. Storm saw a man fall under the blade of a Vile and after a few seconds he died and disappeared from the battlefield. The battle was not going well for the soldiers. They were fighting valiantly against numbers larger than their own and in a few minutes they would be over-run.

Graybeard made a hasty plan and giving Rimner a look he spoke. "You stay here with Storm. He is of interest to them and we don't want to get him into another difficult situation. The rest of you follow me. They look like soldiers from Vorgard and they need our help. This time we have the element of surprise and we can turn the tide of this battle quickly."

He led a charge across the grass toward the battle and the rest of the group followed, leaving Storm and Rimner behind just on the edge of the tree line.

Storm watched the men crash into the melee. They took the dark creatures completely by surprise and in the first few seconds six or seven of their tainted dark bodies had fallen and disappeared.

The soldiers had been almost surrounded by the creatures and Graybeard didn't move his force directly in to help them. He brought his men up to the backs of the creatures and this caught them in a deadly pincer grip between him and the soldiers. When the creatures turned to defend themselves the Vorgard soldier hacked them down quickly.

From his vantage point across the field Storm could see the whole situation clearly. Their help was turning the tide of the battle and it looked like some of the soldiers would be saved. If they had joined a few minutes later it would have been too late and seeing that there was now hope the soldiers fought with an increased intensity.

He watched in awe as the bodies of men and creature swirled in furious strokes. The sounds of clanging metal and crashing wood echoed across the field and into the forest.

To the left of the battle, just inside the tree line a shimmering of color caught Storms attention. He squinted and focused on the tree line. There was something moving in there. He could see splotches of red between the trees as it moved toward the battle.

He gasped as a figure moved out into the field. It looked like a man but much taller –maybe seven feet or more. He was wearing a long blood red cape and the hood was pulled up over his head so you couldn't make out any of his face. He walked slowly but walking is a poor term for his motion because he didn't walk like a normal man. It was as if something were different about his legs. They didn't flow smoothly.

Storm looked over at Rimner. He was staring at the figure too. And they both were transfixed as the figure stopped its gait toward the men and creatures of the battle and turned to look toward them. Storm swallowed hard. This could not be good. The thing had an other worldly feel about it. If it meant them harm it would be difficult to defend against.

It didn't move in a normal way so it probably couldn't be defended against in a normal way. Storm felt his pulse start to rise as the thing started walking toward his end of the field – right at him and Rimner.

They unsheathed their swords and waited impatiently. As it got closer more details about it could be made out. It's robe was a blood red color and it had an unnatural feel to it –almost as if it were alive and the color was real blood showing just below the surface. The hood completely covered the head and folded partially over the face of the thing, and inside nothing could be made out as if the face of the thing refused to let any light inside the hood. In its hand it held a black sack that looked like it contained something about the size of a human head. The blackness of the sack was the same as inside the hood. It had a dull luster to it as if it were not allowing any sunlight to touch it. It was like a small tear in reality. The blackness was like a hole that peered into an evil place.

It walked slowly toward Storm and the sounds of the battle faded and were replaced by a ringing in his ears. He was getting nauseous. The presence of the thing was overpowering and the closer it got the worse he felt. He wasn't sure if he could stop himself from vomiting. The red cloak shimmered dully as if the color were bleeding off into the air around it.

He stared into the blackness inside the hood looking for a face, features, anything that would make this thing real but all he could see was the nothingness. It was more than just dark inside the hood. The blackness was something more than that. It was an emptiness –devoid of anything, even air.

It came to within three paces of him and stopped. Storm's head started swimming in the nausea. He felt like he was on a small boat in a vicious sea. Waves of red shimmer beat at his head and tried to gain entrance. The thing was looking for something inside him – prying away at his mind.

He fought back with an adamant "no." This thing could not have at his mind. He felt it laughing and through the nausea he saw the sack in its hand wriggle. There was something alive, or not alive in the sack and maybe it was laughing too.

If this were the first time he had ever faced such a darkness he may have succumbed to it. But it wasn't. He had faced a darkness very much like this one many years ago in his little apartment near the library. Maybe that was enough to help him find the strength to not give in to the thing. If this were his first encounter it may well have been his last. Whatever the thing was looking for inside his mind, if it could, it would have taken it and left just an empty shell. But Storm resisted. He had enough inner strength, or maybe it was stubbornness. It didn't matter. He resisted long enough for help to arrive.

The melee between Graybeard, the town-folk, the soldiers, and the creatures ended abruptly. None of the creatures fled. They all fought to the death. And each one disappeared as it died.

After pausing a minute to gain their breath and assess their wounds one of the soldiers pointed across the field toward Storm, Bherin, and the red caped creature. "Something amiss there. Are they with you?"

Everyone turned to look across the field and after an initial assessment Graybeard again started a run across the field and this time everyone, including the soldiers followed.

Storm and Bherin were locked in some kind of a trance with the red robed creatures three paces away and staring at them. One of the younger soldiers was first to arrive and without even breaking stride he swung his sword and crashed it down directly on the creatures head. The sword didn't plunge through the hood of the cape. It didn't make any physical impression at all. It bounced right off and the young soldier crashed into the creature and he too bounced off.

It turned its head slowly, rotating it in an unnatural way so it went all the way around facing the oncoming attackers while its body still faced Storm.

The spell Storm was under was broken when its head turned and he came back to clarity. The battle inside his head abruptly stopped and he felt free to think.

The onrushing group of attackers all came to a halt several paces from the thing. They were unsure as to whether an attack was of any use. It hadn't caused any bodily harm to Storm or Bherin. They stood and waved their swords at it tentatively. Maybe they could just scare it off but it didn't seem that swords were much use against it.

Over its shoulder, through the shimmering red bleed-through of its cape into the air Storm could see that the men were also getting nauseous. It wasn't just fear. It was something more. This thing was a blight on the world. It was a sore that hurt the air and the earth and they all felt it.

One of the soldiers spoke to it in a loud voice. "I am Barmen A captain of the army of Vorgard and personal guard to the lady Petra. I have seen creatures more vile than you and in the good name of the lady I tell you to be gone. You will hold no council here."

They all paused to see if the captain's words had any effect. Nobody was even sure that it would understand spoken words.

It answered this question by speaking itself. It rotated its head back around and faced Storm. The blackness under the cape redoubled his nausea but it didn't try to penetrate his head. A low inhuman voice issued from inside that blackness. "Do you know if your lover still lives?" The black sack in its hand wriggled as if in delight.

The question hit Storm like a blow to the stomach. It took his breath. But before he could recover from the blow the thing asked another question. "Do you know why you are here?" The low raspy voice set nails against his ears. "If you find out why you are here do you know whether you will succeed or fail?" The sack in its hand wriggled at a more furious pace as if it were saying that it knew the answers but it wouldn't tell.

Storm tried to form a question but nothing would come. In the course of a few minutes the thing had assaulted his head and his stomach. And now with the mention of Arabella, and the thought that maybe she was still alive, it assaulted his heart. These things were too much for him. He just couldn't speak. Maybe it knew whether she was alive or why he was here but he couldn't ask the questions. He remained dumbfounded as the thing cackled and turning away began its slow non-walk toward the tree-line with the sack wriggling almost gleefully in its hand. Nobody tried to stop it and nobody followed it. They were glad to be rid of the vile creature and the sickening nausea that it brought.

They all watched intently until the thing had passed out of sight into the trees and the Captain of the Vorgard broke the silence. Battle was familiar to him and he was quick to recover from the violence of the situation.

"What brings common town-folk into the Gether armed for battle?"

Graybeard responded. "We have heard of trouble stirring in here so we came prepared for anything." He pointed at Storm. "This stranger, along with three of our folk, encountered what we believe to be GegenHounds here. We came to see what is amiss. It seems that things are growing even worse." He paused and looked over the group of soldiers.

"Something similar has brought soldiers of Vorgard here?"

The Captain scrutinized Storm, looking him up and down very carefully and responded to Graybeards question but never took his eyes off of Storm.

"The Lady Petra had a vision that a darkness was falling over the world and the Gether would be first to see its blight. In her vision she saw a man strange to our land and ways, dressed in strange clothing. It is her belief that this man holds secrets to the dangers we are now seeing. She has sent me and my guard here into the Gether to learn what is amiss and to find this man."

He walked over to Storm and put out his hand. Storm shook his hand.

"You must be the man the Lady has seen in her vision. You are no doubt a stranger to our land and ways, and your dress is truly strange. The Lady Petra wishes to hold council with you. You must travel to Vorgard immediately."

He stared at Storm; intently waiting for a reply but Storm was dumbfounded. He didn't know who this man was, who the Lady Petra was or even where Vorgard was. He wasn't sure if he wanted to be pulled around like a rag doll.

Graybeard broke the silence. "The man is truly strange to our land. He knows not of the gift of the Lady, or of the oracle. But he does have many riddles of his own that need answering. Mayhaps the Lady can help him to sort out his own questions. If he so desires we will send him to Vorgard with an escort and will leave in the morning."

This answer satisfied the Captain of the Guard. "Very well then. I shall give word to the lady that he is found. What town do you all hail from?"

"Our town is Mainz." Said Graybeard.

The Captain grunted. "Tis a long journey. I will tell the lady to expect him in a fortnight." With that he turned and motioned for his soldiers to follow and Graybeard interjected a quick question at the man's back.

"Mayhaps the lady would meet us here in the Gether?."
The captain stopped and slowly turned.

"The lady refuses to enter the Gether anymore. She says it would be her death."
He turned back around and his group walked off toward the place across the field where the battle had been fought and where they had entered the Gether.

Graybeard did the same and without a word they all turned and walked back to where they had also entered the Gether.

**

Storm didn't return to sleep. He immediately woke up in the council room to the sounds of commotion. He was probably the last one to return and everything was in disarray. People were tending to the wounded and the dead were being carried outside.

It had been a question in his mind as to whether what happened inside the Gether carried over into reality and this scene answered that question. If you were killed there you were dead here. If you were wounded there you were wounded here. He wondered if he were killed here in this world if he were dead in his "real" world. Not that he couldn't be sure he wasn't already dead. And it occurred to him that it might go the other way too. If he were killed in his world maybe he was dead in this world too. It lightened his load just a little to consider the possibility that neither he nor Arabella drowned in that river. After all, he was still alive here. Maybe she was still alive and here.

There was quite a bit of blood and people were passing around white cloth and treating a variety of wounds. He looked over his own body carefully. A soreness in his shoulders was all he could find. It came from throwing that overweight creature. The things armor had scraped him on its way over his shoulder. Otherwise everything seemed to be undamaged.

Rimner grabbed him by the sore shoulder.
"As you are slow going in you are also slow coming back out. We are already making plans for your departure."
Storm stood up and followed Rimner out of the building. They walked through the town and into another building.

It was a tavern they stepped into and it was just as busy as the meeting hall. Graybeard was sitting at a large wooden table and a woman was sewing closed a nasty gash on his right arm. He was talking to Bherin and Ardan and the three of them were poring over a map spread out on the table.

Graybeard spotted them coming in the door and waved them over. Storm and Rimner took a seat at the table and a woman brought them some food -large slices of bread and bowls of stew.
When the woman finished stitching his arm Graybeard moved it around vigorously to test the strength of the stitches. He dug into his stew and talked around big gulps.

"While we were away there was a bit of a ruckus here in town. A hunting party was out to the north and spotted a group of what seems to be the same creatures that we had encountered inside. Luckily they were upwind of the things and returned to town safely but guards have been posted and the town is locked down. The journey ahead of you may be a dangerous one. If those things are roaming the countryside there is no telling how many there are and where. But if they have come this close to inhabited farm lands it's a good bet that there are plenty more of them in the more dangerous parts of the land."

He paused and stared at Storm and Storm wasn't sure whether the man was questioning his ability to make the dangerous trip or his desire to even try.

"The Lady Petra is a strange one. They call her the sleeping oracle and her ability to see things is something that has not been seen by anyone in all of our recorded history. They say she has even spoken with Anfang." He paused to let that thought sink in before continuing.

"We have made plans for your departure. You should leave at first light and Bherin and Ardan will go with you."

Graybeard softened up his approach. Storm had become a very important part of a radical change in his whole world and the man didn't know how to treat him. He changed his tact from simple commands to asking. "Will you be going?" The words came out of his mouth awkwardly. It was as if the man was unfamiliar with asking for things.

Everyone at the table paused and stared at him. He wasn't questioning whether or not he should make the journey. It was a foregone conclusion to him. Things were moving in a certain direction and almost taking him along for the ride. He had questions to ask and maybe the lady Petra could help him find answers.

Their stares brought him out of his reverie. "We leave in the morning."

The men at the table all exhaled in unison and Graybeard finished off the evening for them.

"Finish your meal. Bags are being packed for you and if all goes well it should take a fortnight to arrive in Vorgard."

With that they all finished eating and then they left the tavern and retired to Bherin's house where they slept. But it was an uneasy sleep for Storm. Things were happening and he felt like he had very little control over the events. Maybe he had no control. The image of a rag-doll with his face on it came to his mind.

7. The Journey Begins

"We don't receive wisdom; we must discover it for ourselves after a journey that no one can take for us or spare us." -Marcel Proust

A knock on the door woke Storm from his restless sleep. Bherin entered carrying a small oil lamp that threw shadows of yellow into the early morning darkness. "We will break our fast then leave within the hour. I have got a pack and some new clothes for you. The journey is rugged and what you are wearing won't hold up." He left the room while Storm got out of bed and stretched the kinks out of his sore muscles.

Even though it was a restless sleep he felt good. The simple life with plenty of fresh air, clean water, good food and a tranquil community agreed with him. He never realized how much the burden of long work days, horrible commutes, morbid newscasts and the stress of always pushing for more had taken a toll on him.

That had all been broken like a rubber band when his car had taken a turn off the road and into a river.

He looked at the thumb of his left hand. It had healed well. He flexed his fist in amazement. He would have had his hand in a cast for six weeks. It would have taken antibiotics, plenty of aspirin, and a miserable time at work trying to work at his computer with only one hand.

He was familiar with having breaks; he had broken a bone in each of his hands over the course of many years of training. Sometimes you can't be sure about a broken bone in your hand without an x-ray but a break was almost always accompanied by a low fever and a feeling of nausea. Well, here he was with his thumb healed with no x-ray and no cast.

Bherin and Ardan, each carrying a load of stuff, entered the room. They laid it all on the bed and by the yellow light Bherin went over it.

"Here's some clothes and here's your pack; it's a bit heavy but you are a big man and should be able to handle it." He reached down, grabbed a dagger about the length of a mans hand and pulled it half way out of its sheath to reveal a shiny blade. "Bit of a utility knife. Sturdy and clean. It comes in handy in a tight spot." He put the knife back on the bed and picked up a sword. He drew it a few inches out of its scabbard. "good length to it, strong blade and a simple hilt. It should serve you well should you need it." Storm reached for the sword and Ardan and Bherin stared at his hand then glanced at each other. After a pause Bherin handed it into Storm's outstretched left hand.

"Change your clothes then join us for a quick breakfast. Then we will grab our packs and be off." They left Storm alone with the assortment.

He looked over at the clothes and personal effects he had neatly placed on the wooden table at the other side of the bed then quickly changed into his new gear. Bherin was right, it was sturdy and very utilitarian. There were no frills about it. A pair of soft leather pants, a cotton shirt, a leather vest and a pair of sturdy leather shoes with a thick layer of soft wool inside. There were no socks or undergarments but he left his underpants on. The leather would chafe.

He went through his personal stuff and grabbed his keys, his wallet, his wedding band and his watch. His new pants didn't have any pockets but the vest had a large pocket on the inside with a button that kept it closed. He put the wallet and the keys inside it and buttoned it up. He slipped on his wedding band and his watch and left the room to join them for breakfast.

The three of them, Storm, Bherin, and Ardan set off after breakfast and the morning of their first day passed pleasantly. They made good time. The sun came up brightly and they were heading east as if straight for where it had broken the horizon. They stopped on the top of a small hill when the sun had reached its zenith and had lunch.

Bherin took a map out of his pack – it looked like the one they had been poring over with Graybeard.

He pointed out some landmarks. "No roads go directly from Mainz to Vorgard so the going would be slow. There is a lot of dense forest between here and there. Vorgard is northeast of us. We will travel east for several days until we come to the Mid river. We will cross it then travel further east until we come to the road that travels north-east from Speyer to Vorgard. Speyer is a major trade city and the road to Vorgard is a main trade route. Once we get on that road the traveling will go quickly; there are plenty of Inns and places to stay along the way.

The afternoon was more relaxed for them. When they had set out in the morning there was a determination about them. They had an important mission ahead and they were anxious to be on with it. But in the afternoon the pace had settled into a brisk walk and the realization had set in that they would be at this for maybe two weeks so they relaxed a bit and struck up conversations as they walked.

Ardan was curious about the life Storm had lived in another place and he asked a lot of questions about Storm, his clothes, his home, his watch, and anything else he could think of. Storm had the feeling that Ardan probably didn't understand most of it, and the answer to each question just brought up two more questions. How do you explain an automobile to somebody who had never seen any type of transportation? And as far as Storm could tell there weren't any horses in this world. He asked Ardan if there were any horses but got a blank response. Storm couldn't tell if there were no horses here or if the word "horse" was strange.

Their first day came to an uneventful end. As the sun went down they found a good spot to camp in a thickly wooded area, made a fire, had something to eat and with the stars shining brightly they quickly went off to sleep.

They had walked from sunrise to sunset and had taken only a couple of small breaks along the way. The terrain was hilly and not overly covered in thick woods. Storm figured they had made a good first day of it and with that he ignored the aching in his legs and feet and he fell immediately to sleep. Plenty more days like this was his last thought.

Over the next few days their travel remained fast and comfortable. The aching in Storm's feet and legs had passed and the three of them had found a rhythm with each other. Bherin lead the way, Storm followed him and Ardan was behind him.

They had become attuned to each other and body language was all they needed to communicate the subtle shifts in their progress. Storm knew when it was time to take a break and could accurately predict how they would traverse the hills, copses, and forested sections along their path.

On the fourth day of their journey, toward late afternoon, the rapport Storm had built with his traveling companions had brought him to a silent stop. Bherin had been acting different. His steps were quieter and he raised his head to look around more often. Something was troubling him and when he came to a complete standstill so did Storm and Ardan.

He turned around and motioned for Storm and Ardan to come forward.

"For the past several hours I have had a funny feeling. Nothing I can specifically identify; just a feeling that something is amiss." He looked around at the surrounding woods. "I haven't been able to find any tracks and I haven't gotten the scent of anything. The only thing I can think of is that we are being followed."

Storm resisted the temptation to turn around and look.

Bherin pointed northeast of where they stood. "There's a pretty steep slope in the terrain there. As we approach it we will spread out, leaving more distance between us. When I reach the cover of the hill I will circle around it and come back out behind you two. When you two reach the bending of the hill, continue on in a northeast direction without me. I should be able to come up behind whomever, or whatever it is that is following us.

An hour later they had rounded the sloping terrain and whomever it was that was following them would have lost them in the curve around it. Bherin made a sharp left turn to follow the foot of the sloping landscape and Storm and Ardan continued on in a northeast direction.

After a half hour of walking Storm and Ardan found an area that was particularly thick with trees and brush and they started to make a short camp. It would give the appearance that they were going to have something to eat. Whoever was following them would have to get real close to realize that it was only the two of them.

Storm was in the middle of tearing off a piece of dark bread when Ardan jolted. It was as if an electrical pulse had run through his system. Storm just stared at him. Ardan just stopped moving; his mouth open, a large piece of dark bread showing between his teeth.

"My father is in trouble." Was all he said as he unsheathed his sword and ran off in the direction they had earlier come.

Storm paused another two seconds and unsheathing his own sword he ran off after Ardan.

The young man could run fast and he got further and further ahead of Storm; He navigated through the dense trees easily and Storm struggled to keep sight of him.

Storm lost sight of him but kept running in as straight a line as he could. He burst open into a small pocket of clearing in the dense wood and he saw Ardan kneeling on the ground holding the limp body of his father.

He slowly walked up to Ardan and tried to focus between heavy breaths. Bherin was a terrible mess, there was blood everywhere. His midsection had been torn out – he had been disemboweled. His dead body was laying in Ardan's lap and Ardan was embracing his head and rocking him slowly. There was no sign of whatever it was that had done the violence to him.

Storm swung around and rotated quickly in circles looking for signs of danger. He peered into the trees in every direction then looked back at Ardan who just continued rocking his father. Bherin's sword and dagger were both still in their sheathes. And whatever attacked him had taken a big slice out of his stomach which means it had come straight at him and not from behind. It must have been very fast –or very elusive. Bherin probably had very little time to react.

He looked around into the trees again then sat abruptly on the ground. Dizziness was overcoming him. He tried to regain control of his breathing and he fought off the blackness of passing out while Ardan cried softly.

Storm just sat up against a tree while Ardan mourned the loss of his father. It was several hours before Ardan spoke.

"We will make camp here. I have to prepare my father for burial."
"We should return to Mainz." Was Storm's response.
Ardan stared at him blankly – the color had run out of his face.
"No. It took us four days to get here. To carry my father back would take us a week. That would set us back far too long and there are very bad things happening. We must make haste."

"What about your family? What about your mother?" Storm choked on the word "Mother."

"She already knows."
Storm didn't question this. Ardan instinctively knew that his father was in trouble. He supposed that distance didn't make a difference and his mother would also know that something dire had happened.

"Tonight we rest and tomorrow we will have a funeral for my father and prepare him for burial." It was a statement but really more of a question. Storm felt as if Ardan was asking for permission to do this because it would set their mission behind by a day. Storm just nodded his head and looked at Ardan.

It was such a short time ago that Ardan was Ty. He just became a man and now he had to face this. Even though the circumstances were grim Storm had to admire the young man. He was shouldering the load with courage. Ardan was handling the circumstances. They would bury his father then continue on with the mission.

The two of them removed their packs and made camp. Storm never relaxed. During the whole time he kept looking over his shoulder and peering into the trees. He couldn't shake the feeling that he was being watched. But for him it was just a feeling – he couldn't tell if it was just his imagination. Would he be just as quickly disemboweled? Was there nothing he could do about it? No doubting that Bherin had better sense of the world than he did. How could he possibly defend himself when Bherin couldn't? Maybe it came out of the tree tops? He glanced up. But didn't see anything. Or better said, he couldn't perceive anything. There was no doubt in his mind that Ardan knew whether or not they were being watched but Storm didn't ask him about it. Ardan would warn him. He trusted that. Even though Ardan was in mourning he still seemed to be in possession of his senses. He just left Ardan in quiet to mourn in privacy.

The night was plagued by strange sounds and a restless sleep. Bad dreams insinuated themselves into his head but when he woke in the morning he couldn't remember any of them.

Storm looked over at the body of Bherin hoping that he had magically come alive and that maybe all of this was just one of the bad dreams he had that night. But no, Bherin's supine body lay exactly where they had left it; under a blanket that Ardan had placed over him before they went to sleep.

Ardan was fully dressed and preparing the fire so they could have something to eat. He probably didn't sleep at all.

He looked over at Storm. "We will break our fast then we will search for some passage root. I have much to do but we will finish everything today and set off again tomorrow morning. This will set us back only one day."

He looked at Storm as if he were stealing a day from him. He almost seemed to be asking permission to take the day off.

Storm had watched him change from a boy to a man and so soon was this thrust upon him. He had a new name and had passed the testing but he was still very young and without his father he looked to Storm for guidance.

Storm just nodded his head in approval. It would have been alright with him if they took a week to mourn the death of Bherin. Damn, for all he cared they could just give up the whole quest and return to Mainz. Let the queen come to him. Why should Ardan and his family have to pay such a high price because she wanted to talk to him?

The day dragged on slowly and by mid-afternoon Storm had given up the ghost of looking over his shoulder. The feeling still nagged at him but he ignored it.

While Ardan prepared his fathers body Storm dug a hole in the ground. Ardan had dug a small shovel out of his pack and Storm took the task with enthusiasm. It felt good to do something. The physical exertion was an expression of his respect and admiration for Bherin.

Ardan stitched up Bherin's wounds, washed him and redressed him. He made his father as presentable as he could and when Storm finished digging the hole they set off into the woods in search of passage root.

As they walked Ardan spoke to Storm. "We have to travel into the darker parts of the forest. The passage tree does not like sunlight and it can often be found under the shade of larger trees."

His speech was mechanical but it was good for him to talk. He had always enjoyed explaining how the world worked to Storm. He would make a good father some day.

It made sense to Storm that they called it passage root and that it came from the passage tree; having its relationship to some kind of ritual in the passing of loved ones.

"What does a passage tree look like?"

They continued their walk toward the darker parts of the forest.

"It is small as far as trees go. About the height of a man and its leaves are sparse and tend toward purple in color. On one day each summer it blossoms black flowers. It is said that the Passage Tree does not like the sun because it does not draw it strength from it. Its strength comes from elsewhere."

He stopped walking and looked around. Then regaining his bearing he head off in a new direction.

The forest was getting denser and in a few minutes they were standing under the canopy of a massive tree that looked much like a willow. The long thin branches wept down almost to the ground all around them. It formed an enormous tent that enclosed them. The main branches of the tree were ten or twelve feet above them and the hanging branches and leaves formed an inverted bowl that was twenty feet from the trunk in all directions.

As his eyes adjusted to the darkness Storm could see the Passage tree. It was about five feet high and was standing several feet from the trunk of the Willow.

Even though it was five feet high it looked like it was at least a thousand years old. The bark was very old and the branches twisted and turned. There were only a few purple leaves on it. It looked like a bonsai tree. If Storm squinted his eyes he could imagine that it was fifty feet tall. It had the proportions of a large tree. That was the effect that bonsai growers tried to achieve.

Ardan moved back out of the canopy and Storm followed him.

"Was that a Passage Tree?

"Aye"

"No good?"

Ardan looked at him and smiled.

"It was fine but as in all other things we never take the first."

They head off in a new direction and an hour later they found themselves under the canopy of another large tree. This one wasn't a willow like the last one. This one had a massive trunk and its leaves were very large –twice the size of a man's hand. A dozen of these trees stood together forming a knot that blocked out all of the sunlight.

As with the other Passage Tree one was here too in the shade and several feet from the trunk of the large tree. They liked the darkness that large trees brought but didn't like to get too close to the trunk. It almost looked like the large tree leaned away from it as if in fear.

This one posed just as the other one did. It huddled in the dark cover like an overgrown bonsai and stood about five feet high; its sparse purple leaves drooped gently toward the earth. There was no reaching for sunlight with these leaves.

Ardan walked around the small tree and choosing a spot several feet from its trunk he began digging with his hands.

About a foot into the ground he uncovered what he was looking for and he motioned for Storm to look. Storm could see in the hole the root extending toward the tree. It was purple in color and about as thick as a man's wrist. There were several nodules on it about the size of a mans eyeball.

Ardan unsheathed his dagger and cut one of the nodules off. He wrapped it in a piece of cloth and placed it in his pack. He then pushed all the dirt back into the hole and patted it down gently.

They had wandered several hours away from where Bherin lay and when they returned it was getting to be late afternoon.

While they walked Ardan explained the Passage Root.

"When a person dies their spirit remains in their body for a period of time. If they lived a long and happy life, are surrounded by a loving family and their death is expected and prepared for they will pass quickly into the next stage of existence. But if the person is young, or the death comes as a shock and they haven't lived the experiences they were meant to live, the spirit will remain for possibly several days –sometimes even longer. The spirit needs time to accept the change. The Passage Root will give a temporary sort of half life to the dead and reunite the spirit with the living. We can talk about what happened and bring peace and acceptance for the dead and the living. My father died an unnatural death, in the midst of a quest. His spirit will have a sense of incompleteness. He will want to talk to us. We will help him accept what happened to him and maybe he will help us understand how it happened."

Storm wondered how all of this would feel from Bherin's perspective. Was it possible to ask Bherin about the afterlife? There evidently was something after death. The spirits that appeared at the testing stone taught Storm that. But, did they not exist until the moment they were called? Or did they exist, and know it all along? Would Bherin be aware that he was dead for a couple of days? Was he experiencing something right now? Could Storm ask him about it? Just as always, each question about the mystery of what happened next brought up two more questions. It was like a Fibonacci sequence where the questions just gave birth to new questions at an exponential rate. And to make it all worse Storm himself was stuck somewhere in that sequence not being in his "real" world but being here in this one.

And he wasn't so sure he would want the root to be used on him after he died. It did seem very strange.

Storm just went with the flow and made them something to eat and as the sun started to set he had the feeling that the time was right.

The sky turned deep red with the loss of the sun and the forest was coming alive with the sounds of nocturnal creatures. Ardan unwrapped the swaddling he had put his father in and Storm stoked the fire in anticipation.

The two of them sat in silence beside Bherin's body and Storm used the time to contemplate the spirit of Bherin. He was a good man and he always treated Storm and Ardan with a fatherly respect. Storm remembered how proud Bherin was when Ardan successfully completed the Testing.

Ardan sat, as if in he were in a trance, and holding the wrapped piece of passage root he spoke in a soft and long cadence. It was some kind of a funeral rite.

Ardan carefully unwrapped the Passage Root and using his dagger he cut an incision in it in the shape of an X. Storm watched in shock as he placed the side of the dagger between Bherin's teeth and with a twist of his wrist and a snapping sound he popped the dead mans mouth open. The sound made Storm nauseous. He might have broken Bherin's jaw. Not that it really mattered -Bherin felt nothing.

Ardan held the root nodule over Bherin's open mouth and squeezed it. Several drops of purple fluid dripped from the root into Bherin's mouth.

Storm recoiled and fell onto his back in horror as Bherin abruptly sat up. He stared in disbelief and horror as Bherin's eyes opened. They were a milky white as if they had already begun to rot.

Bherin rotated his head with a sickly slow motion and brought the milky white gaze on Ardan who sat quietly beside him. He didn't move like he had come back to life. He moved as if he were a puppet being tugged on badly tangled strings.

"Welcome father." Ardan said in a low tone.

Bherin twisted his mouth into an unhealthy grin. There was something very bad about this; everything about these people and this world had a feel of beauty to it. Storm got glimpses of this all the time -but not this time. He got the sense that there should be a beauty about this too but there wasn't. The Passage Root was something these people used with good intent. It was an opportunity for a family to speak with a loved one for a final time and in the case of an unexpected death it could bring closure. What family, having suddenly lost a loved one, wouldn't want one last chance to talk?

This also would have a dramatic effect on the psychology of crime within the community. A murdered person could be brought back with the Passage Root and he could describe what happened to him; and possibly who murdered him.

But it didn't feel right and the little hairs on the back of Storm's neck stood up. It wasn't just the reanimation of Bherin's corpse. There was something more at work here. If this was Bherin's spirit reunited with his body it should have a sense of Bherin about it. This corpse didn't have that feeling. It felt alien; like it wasn't Bherin. It looked like Bherin but didn't feel like him. The red orange flickering of the campfire cast hideous shadows on his face giving him a horrible look.

When Storm fell back he had pulled away from Bherin but Ardan remained sitting on the ground beside the now sitting body of Bherin. After greeting his father he bowed his head, closed his eyes and continued with the low chanting of the ceremony.

Time slowed for Storm as he watched Bherin fumble for something at his waist with his dead puppet hands. The blood rushed to his face and his skin went cold as he watched the disconnected and awkward body of Bherin pull his dagger out of its scabbard then lunge slowly and awkwardly toward Ardan. All of the energy had been drawn from Storm. He had no strength to make his lips move. He couldn't scream a warning to Ardan. He just watched as Bherin plunged the dagger into Ardan's throat. For a brief few seconds they all maintained this pose as if it were captured in a dark oil painting.

Ardan snapped his eyes open and stared into the possessed face of his father who held the dagger all the way up to the hilt in his throat. Their faces were only a foot apart. Ardan held a look of shock and Bherin held a look of broken-jawed glee. Bherin pushed on the dagger with an awkward thrust and Storm watched the shiny tip come out the back of Ardan's neck.

The pose of the three in the horrible orange flickering of the campfire, and the spell of the painting was broken when Ardan fell backward in a dead heap –the knife hilt still protruding from his neck.

Storm pushed violently backward with his legs and landed on his palms and his heels. He scrambled for his feet on legs that quivered in fear and shock as Bherin brought his gaze and his gleeful broken-jaw smile onto him.

The body of Bherin also stood up on unresponsive muscles and awkwardly removed the dagger from Ardan's throat then without a word moved slowly toward Storm.

Alarm bells went off in Storms head. "Move damn it." He willed his unresponsive muscles into action and the spell was broken. Adrenaline hit his system and he was moving without the hindrance of thinking. He sprinted several steps away from the oncoming Bherin and he reached for his sword but it wasn't at his waist. He glanced around and saw it laying on the ground near the rock circle of the campfire, but Bherin was directly between him and it.

The slow walking Bherin advanced closer and Storm turned and bolted in a burst into the trees, and the darkness.

He had run fifty yards through the tangle of trees and brush before the force of exertion slowed him and he glanced back to see if Bherin was following him.

There was a quarter moon so he wasn't engulfed in total darkness but the forest was perilous; every step was an opportunity to fall and an opportunity for the corpse to catch him. There was no sign of pursuit so he stopped to regain his breath and after a minute the sounds of Bherin stumbling through the trees came to him and he watched in horror as the jerking body of Bherin appeared then disappeared between the columns of trees.

Bherin was coming straight for him and he was carrying the dagger. Storm could see it glinting in the weak moonlight. His body moved awkwardly through the trees and he spotted Storm with his milky dead eyes and grinning an ugly grin he broke into the semblance of a run and fell to the ground. He had limited control of his body and he couldn't navigate well through the trees. Maybe it was the milky covering over his eyes that were impeding his process. Storm watched carefully as it stood back up and continued its walk. There was a danger here; he was going to plunge that dagger into Storm just as he had done to Ardan but he was going to have to get close first.

Storm thought the situation out. He was alone now. There was nobody to help him on his way.

Just two days ago everything was fine and he and his companions were making good progress toward a future with some promise. But now everything had turned sour; His companions were dead and something wanted him to join that group.

Doubt crept into his mind. He had run off with nothing, in the dark, with only a faint moonlight to guide him. He didn't have his sword or his pack.

He would have to return to the camp and retrieve his things -and the map. If he could even find the camp. It would be very easy to get totally lost in one minute of running. Hopefully the campfire was still burning bright enough for him to see it from a distance. And after that he had two choices. He could either return to Mainz or continue on with the trip to Vorgard.

He started walking to his right. He would make a circle around and return to the camp and retrieve whatever he could. Bherin adjusted his path and turned toward him. He didn't seem to project that Storm was heading in a new direction he just turned to follow whichever way Storm headed. Storm picked up the pace and passed about ten steps to the right of Bherin and back to where he hoped was the camp site. Bherin hissed and tried to speak and again tried to lunge at Storm but again he fell.

Until he figured out what to do about Bherin he should be able to stay out of arms reach.

In less than a minute he spotted flickering orange through the trees and the brush and he adjusted his direction and head straight for it.

He got back to the camp and hastily gathered up his stuff. He strapped on his sword and opened all the packs. He found Bherin's map and stuffing it and some extra food into his pack he shouldered it, and as the corpse of Bherin approached him he set off in the direction he thought they were heading in before all this had happened.

He walked out of the glow of the campfire and into the pale glow of the quarter moon that peeked between the trees and in a few minutes he had put enough distance between him and the corpse so that he couldn't hear it stumbling through the brush.

He walked for what seemed like an hour and feeling comfortable that if the corpse were still following him it was far enough behind that he could take a few minutes to figure out what he was doing.

He unshouldered his pack, leaned it against a tree, and rummaging around in it he brought out Bherin's map. He unrolled it and moved around under the trees to find a spot where the moonlight came straight through a gap in the foliage. It was no use. The moonlight was too dim. He could only make out vague impressions on the map so he put it back in the pack and re-shouldering it he continued on with his walk in the direction he thought was correct.

After several hours of walking and no sign of the walking corpse the sun started to lighten the sky. The adrenaline of last night had long since worn off and only fatigue remained. He had gone the whole night without sleeping and he would eventually have to sleep. But if Bherin were still following him would he walk right up to him and stab him in the throat while he slept?

If Bherin were still following him he would have to do something. Now that he had his sword he was confident that he could best the walking corpse. It moved extremely slow and he could make fast work of it. But this option was distasteful to him. It still looked like Bherin and he wasn't sure he could plunge a sword into him.

Maybe he could find a safe place to sleep – up in a tree or some other isolated place. He had to do something; he couldn't just walk for days without sleep. And if he got lost he could be wandering around in the forest for weeks.

He continued on at a brisk pace until the sky had lightened enough to read a map so glancing around for any sign of the corpse he opened his pack and took out some dark bread and dried meat. He ate this while studying his map.

Mainz was clearly marked on the map and that was their starting point. To the north-east was Vorgard so he seemed to be heading in the right general direction. He scrutinized the map for more details.

The river Rhyme flowed from the north and passed close by Mainz. That was where he first appeared in this world. Another river flowed from the mountains to the north and through most of the map almost half way between Mainz and Vorgard. This river was marked as the river "Mid." If he kept in a general easterly direction he would eventually get to that river at some point along it. He could follow that south to Speyer. Hopefully there he could enlist some help in getting to Vorgard. He, Bherin, and Ardan had been on their journey several days and had predicted the journey would take two weeks so if he kept the pace up he should come to the river Mid in just a couple of days.

He walked in solitude for the remainder of the day –taking short breaks to eat and drink water. The landscape was easy to navigate and he made good progress. He fought off his need for sleep until the sun started to set.

There had been no sign of the walking corpse throughout the whole day but the thought nagged at him. Bherin couldn't walk fast as a corpse but if he could somehow follow Storm eventually he would catch up to him –and most likely while he was sleeping. And he really needed to sleep. It would be a deep sleep and probably a good ten or twelve hours in length.

He stopped and looked around. There had to be someway to protect himself. But he couldn't find any inspiration. The only thing he could think of was to climb a tree. The walking corpse wasn't very coordinated and the decaying muscles probably didn't have a lot of strength. It probably couldn't lift itself into a tree.

Storm made his plan and hunted around for a really big tree and finding one suitable he opened his pack and took out a length of rope. He climbed the tree and when he was about twenty feet above the ground he felt that he was high enough to be out of danger but low enough so the limbs were strong enough to support him comfortably.

He found a comfortable spot on a thick limb right where it met the center column of the tree. He lashed the rope around it then threw it at a forty-five degree angle to another limb. He wrapped it again around the limb he was sitting on and threw it again. He now had two lengths at a comfortable angle about two feet apart. He lashed the rope back and forth across these two lengths as far up as he could reach and at intervals of three or four inches. When he ran out of rope he had a nice half hammock. He could sit on the limb with his legs dangling over but he could lean back and rest comfortably.

He leaned back slowly and everything felt good. Nothing settled and the weaving of rope held tight. It had taken him some time to accomplish this and he hadn't noticed that it was getting pretty dark. He climbed back down the tree retrieved his sword and his pack and climbing back up he settled back into his half hammock with them and this time when he rested his head back he could see small patches of dark sky with glimmers of stars. As he wondered if Orion were up there somewhere he faded off into a deep sleep.

An irritating scratching noise worked its way slowly into his dreams. He was in a small rowboat with a group of rats out in the middle of the ocean. The rats were frantic for freedom. They looked over the edge of the boat and deciding that was not a good option they started to dig at the bottom of the boat with their claws and teeth. They spoke to each other in an almost human tone. He listened intently but couldn't make out what they were saying. He wanted to tell them that what they were doing was not a good idea. They didn't realize they were sealing their doom, and he had no way of telling them. He just watched and listened to the clawing sounds and their mumbled speech.

He woke with a start and he was back in the tree. The morning sun was shining brightly and burning the dew off of everything. The dream of being in a rowboat was gone but the sounds of rats scraping and mumbling to each other remained.

He sat up in his half hammock and looked down. And there was the animated corpse of Bherin, moving awkwardly, scraping at the trunk of the tree with his dagger and uttering incoherent sounds from rotting vocal chords.

Storm was instantly awake and fully aware. He expected the corpse to somehow find him and sure enough it did. He had hoped that it wouldn't be strong enough to climb the tree and sure enough it wasn't. Maybe he wouldn't have to "kill" Bherin again. Maybe he could just continue on, traveling during the day and sleeping in trees during the night. Eventually the decomposing corpse would be unable to follow and he would be free of it. Well, at least that seemed probable. But he didn't really know.

He dropped his pack and his sword down to the ground; swinging them as far away from the trunk as he could. Bherin didn't notice the action. He untied the half hammock and coiled up the rope then swung himself down to the lowest limb he could get to and still remain out of reach of the corpse. It continued to hack away at the tree with the dagger as if it were going to somehow fell it.

Storm walked himself out onto the limb until he was about ten feet away from the trunk and as the corpse stopped hacking at the tree and looked up at him he jumped to the ground. He rolled and in three quick strides he snatched up his pack and sword and trotted away from the tree and the corpse.

About fifty yards away he stopped and waited. Within a minute he heard sounds of the clumsy corpse moving through the brush and another minute later he could see it.

It was moving more slowly than it had on the previous day and it had a host of flies buzzing about it. Bacterial rot was setting in and soon it would probably be consumed by maggots. Storm wondered if that would stop it. Once all the flesh was eaten away would the skeleton continue to follow him? He was no expert in anatomy but he was pretty sure that a lot of the bones would separate once the ligaments holding them together rotted away.

Even though he had nightmares he still had a good night sleep and felt good so he continued on his walk in an easterly direction – directly toward where the sun had risen. In a couple of hours he would be far enough ahead of his dead stalker so that he could take a break and have something to eat.

The morning went well for him. The sun quickly burned away the dew and the tree cover kept the temperature down. By mid afternoon the terrain had changed to lighter brush and the forest had thinned considerably. He walked through more and more grassy areas and by late afternoon he had come to the edge of the river Mid.

He turned to the right and continuing his pace he followed the bank of the river, now traveling south. This should lead him all the way to the city of Speyer which was located on the other shore; but if the river became shallow enough to cross at any point between now and then he would cross.

The Mid river wasn't a fast flowing river. It traveled many hundreds of miles from the mountains to the north and cut its way gently through the whole of the land which tamed it by the time it was half way to the ocean.

At the point where Storm was along its shore it was pretty wide though – maybe a quarter mile, so wading across it was out of the question.

There would probably be bridges at intervals along the way but as a minimum there should be a bridge at Speyer.

8. The Clockmaker's Obsession

"There is a relation between the hours of our life and the centuries of time.... The hours should be instructed by the ages, and the ages explained by the hours."
-Emerson

His first day along the river was a pleasant one. Pleasant if you don't consider that he was in a strange land, possibly lost, and being followed by a dead rendition of what used to be his friend.

The walking was brisk and the weather was good. He was constantly looking ahead to judge the terrain and the thought struck him that he was getting in tune with the world around him.

He had spent most of his adult life driving an automobile. One of which had got him into the river near Newport and into this baffling situation he had now been in for several weeks.

But now that he was walking he was more aware of the world around him. Now it mattered what the terrain was like. The sloping of the landscape made a difference. The condition of the weather made a difference – day and night made a difference. The types of plants around him mattered. And whether or not they bore fruits or berries mattered very much.

Coming from the world he used to live in none of these things made a difference. A hill was meaningless. The artificial muscles under the hood of the car didn't care, and it had no effect on him whatsoever. Night was of no consequence. Everything was well lit so day and night blurred together.

These things now mattered very much to him. If it rained that changed what he did. Clouds in the sky were watched very carefully. Everything was important from the type of vegetation to the type of rocks and the presence of wildlife.

But the thought that came to him wasn't the fact that all of these things had an impact on his progress but that he was becoming a part of them. He was connecting with the world around him. He was starting to feel a little bit like the people that lived here.

This feeling of being connected was something new for him and he tried to embrace it –experience it more fully. He concentrated on being more sensitive as he walked.

He walked with the river on his left and the woods on his right. All along the river there was a thin stretch of land maybe fifteen to twenty feet wide where the river and the woods had found a compromise -the ground was sandy and rocky with sparse vegetation. For thousands of years –even tens of thousands of years the river had brought up sand and slowly deposited it on the shore. This sand controlled the vegetation –leaving a long stretch that was a natural path for him to walk along. It was a line of demarcation between the two environments and it made for easy walking. He would make good progress.

The sounds of the river came to him along with the sounds of the shore around him. Birds and other creatures went about their way and he heard them.

The world became sharper as he focused on actually "seeing." This place really was quite beautiful. The plants displayed a wonderful variety of greens and everywhere there were blossoms in many different colors.

The strip of land between the water and the woods wasn't barren. It too teemed with life but of it's own particular variety.

He looked far ahead along the river and came to a stop. He spotted a figure walking along the shore.

It was a man and he was doing something. He kept bending over and walking back and forth between the river and the tree line.

Storm wasn't close enough to get a sense of the man so he re-started walking forward and as he got closer he could make out more detail.

The man seemed to be old. His hair was gray and he had a scruffy gray beard. His clothes were gray and tattered but he had an energy about him. He moved with a wiry agility between the water and the woods; bending down often, and a couple of times he got down on his knees to look at something.

Storm thought that when he got to a comfortable distance from the man, not too close so as to startle him, he would call out to him.

But before he could get that close the man had disappeared into the line of trees.

Storm picked up his pace. All his worry about whether the man was friendly or dangerous evaporated. Now the man turned into a lost opportunity.

After several minutes he arrived at where the man had been focusing his attention.

A wooden sluice about a foot wide stretched from the bank of the river and followed the gentle slope down into the woods. It looked like the kind of thing old time miners used to pan for gold. A vigorous stream of water flowed into the sluice from the river and down the length of it into the woods. This is what the old man must have been looking at so intently.

It was well made and all the wood was hand cut. It drew a perfectly straight line from the river down the slope of the bank and into the woods. There was some kind of hand mechanism at the point where it met the river. Storm turned it and a slice of wood, like a door slowly came up and blocked some of the river flow. The stream down the sluice decreased. He turned it in the other direction and the stream returned back to its original flow.

The old man might have been adjusting the flow of the water. He looked off into the woods for him with a little more confidence. He probably didn't lose the man. All he had to do was follow the sluice and it would probably lead right to him.

He set off into the woods. If he got lost or found nothing he could always follow it back to the river and continue his journey to the south toward Speyer.

He also had a hunch that if he stopped the flow of water by closing the sluice gate the old man would soon show up to investigate what happened. He did seem very intent on inspecting and caring for the sluice.

After a hundred yards the sound of the river faded and was replaced by the sound of creaking wood. Paired with the melody of water flowing down the sluice it felt like he was on board some kind of ship.

He walked another hundred yards along the straight as an arrow sluice and   found its destination. It poured itself right into a hole in the wall of a stone and wood cottage; A large cottage -maybe fifty feet square.

There was no sign of the old man. He must have gone inside. And that was where the wooden creaking noise was coming from. Storm walked further down the slope and around to what appeared to be the front of the cottage.

The front area was a large and bright yard. The trees had been cleared away for fifty feet forming a neat circle. At one end of the circle was the cottage and at the other end was a pond. The water from the river went into the cottage at the back and out through the front. The sluice continued through the yard and down to the pond.

The yard was dotted by several dozen small structures; some were wood and some were stone. Most of them were about waist high and looked like bird baths.

The scene evoked a sense of disorientation in him. The little hut, the yard, the flowing water – it was idyllic. It felt like he stepped out of the horror he was in and right into a different world.

It seemed that knocking on the door of the hut was the "appropriate" thing to do and the thought struck him as very strange. Here he was, out in the middle of who knows where, being followed by a corpse, on a quest that he didn't even know why, and he would pause to knock on the door of a hut. It just seemed absurd. Should he brush his clothes clean first. Maybe comb out his hair so as to be presentable? This made him chuckle. Although the sound of it was strained and weak.

Before knocking on the door he walked around the yard. He looked closer at the first bird bath. It wasn't a bird bath. There was no water and it had a small vane on it. The top was carved with circles and lines and the sun cast a sharp shadow of the vane on the surface of it. It was a sun dial. He looked to the other structures in the yard. Most of them appeared to be similar to this one.

In the center of the yard was one large structure, about the same height as Storm and as wide as his outspread arms. The sluice ran right under it on its journey between the house and the pond. It clicked with a semi-regular beating rhythm. The water probably drove some kind of mechanism within it. He looked it over, and walked around it but couldn't figure out what it did so he turned his attention back to the cottage and walking over to it he knocked on the door.

The sound of the knocking was lost in the quiet symphony of water flowing through the sluice and the rhythmic wooden creaking coming from inside the building. He knocked again louder and a voice responded from the other side of the door.

"Who's there?"

It was an old voice –most definitely belonging to the man he had seen at the river. Storm paused for a few seconds. This was too unexpected. What should he say? I'm a man that almost died in an automobile accident, nearly drowned, and woke up here. Oh and by the way a dead man is following me.

He gained his wits and opted for something simpler.

"I'm a traveler. I was heading for Vorgard but have lost my way. Now I am going to Speyer."

He waited for a response from the other side of the door.

"Count to ten aloud." Was what the old man on the other side said.

"Huh?"

"I want you to count from one to ten."

This was a bit puzzling. The old man was probably a hermit and maybe a bit eccentric but he indulged the request and counted out loud from one to ten in a slow even cadence.

After he finished the door slowly opened and the old man peered at him.

He was old, but he was strong and healthy. His frame was straight and well filled out. His hair and beard were iron grey, well maintained and neatly trimmed. His clothes were clean and very utilitarian.

Storm broke free from his gaze and peered past him into the cottage. It had the feel of a workshop. Storm could see several tool laden work benches as if maybe the man were a carpenter.

"Your counting is very strong and extraordinarily even."

It seemed like the man was complimenting him so he thanked him. But this had to be the first time anyone ever complimented him for being able to count from one to ten –since kindergarten anyway.

"I didn't even look at my watch." Storm pointed to his watch and smiled at the joke.

The old man stared at him intently then looked at his watch; his face wrinkling into a frown.

"A watch? Is that some kind of counting device?"

He took a step forward and peered intently at the watch on Storm's wrist. The curiosity had given him the courage to forget about how much of a risk Storm might pose.

Storm brought his wrist up to face height showing the watch to the old man.

"It's a time keeping device. It marks off the hours in the day."

Shock registered on the old mans face and he stared at Storm, his mouth wide open. He stepped forward and grabbing Storm's wrist he brought his face close to the watch. He stared intently –mesmerized by the motion of the second hand as it swept its way smoothly around the face of the watch.

"What do the numbers mean?"

"A day is divided into twenty-four equal hours. The watch counts to twelve twice. From midnight to noon are the twelve hours of morning then another twelve hours from noon back to midnight."

"This is truly remarkable." The old mans voice rose in pitch. "How does it get its power? Is it magic?"

"No, it has a battery." Was Storm's response but he could see that the old man didn't understand this.

The gap in understanding made a pause in their conversation and the old man used it to change the subject.

He opened the door wider. "Please come in. Maybe you need a rest from your travels. All of a sudden the old man was very motivated to have a guest.

Storm stepped through the door and looked around the cottage. At the rear wall was a large water wheel much like what you would see on the outside of a flour mill. The sluice from the river powered it from high up on the wall and the water flowed over the wheel, turning it, then continued through the cottage and out the front where it probably finished its journey in the pond.

The water wheel moved with a smooth creaking which was what Storm had heard before he entered the cottage. And connected to it was a variety of wheels and pulleys that slowly moved an assortment of wooden contraptions around the room.

The rest of the single room cottage was cluttered with benches that held tools, books and wooden objects in varying degrees of completion. It appeared that the old man had been hard at work at something for a very long time. In one corner of the room was a cot that he slept on and along one wall was a fireplace and a table cluttered with dishes and mugs.

The old man moved to the table and motioned for Storm to follow.

"Sit, I will find us something to eat."

Storm removed his backpack and sat at the table. While the old man rummaged for food Storm took a closer look around and tried to understand what the man was building. Everywhere there were large and small wooden mechanical devices that turned and creaked –powered by the flow of the water and the turning of the wheel. He couldn't make sense of any of it. Everything just seemed to move for the sake of moving but there was a beauty about it all. There was a gentle cadence that thrummed through the walls of the cottage.

The old man placed a large plate in the center of the table. It was full of bread, salted meats, and vegetables. He sat down and they ate heartily, talking between mouthfuls.

The old man introduced himself as Uhr and told Storm a little about himself.

He had grown up in the prairie far to the south and when he had come of age and gone to take his testing he had intended to be a carpenter just as his father was but when Anfang had held Varheit over his father and he passed his testing Anfang spoke to him and told him that he had another calling. He told him that it was his quest to understand the rhythm of life. He had placed a vision in Uhr's head. It showed millions of stars swirling in a pattern like a whirlpool and Anfang told him that this was as it always would be and every twelve billion years it completed its cycle. Then Anfang showed him more cycles from the changing of the seasons to the beating of his heart. Everything follows a rhythm he told him. And that it was his quest to see and understand these rhythms. He told him that humans follow these rhythms just as everything else. Some human rhythms are obvious like the rhythm of a life from birth through childhood adulthood and death. But there are larger human rhythms that we follow and do not see; rhythms that span more than one generation.

Uhr paused and stared at Storm. His brow wrinkled as if he was trying to determine whether Storm believed what he was saying and whether or not he should continue. He glanced at the watch again and continued.

"Anfang told me that there is also evil in the world and it too follows a rhythm – one closely tied to us as a people. This evil awakens every forty generations and it challenges the place of humans. He told me that the time of the next awakening was soon to come and that I should prepare myself by following the quest he had given me."

His brow furrowed deeper and he took a large bite of bread.

"Anfang told me no more. So I built this cottage here as a place to follow my quest to the best I can. I spend the days building things that beat to the rhythm of the water and the earth. I watch and try to understand the sun and how it moves. And during the night I watch the stars and try to understand them, how they move, and how their rhythm affects us.

The man's speaking was almost mesmerizing. His words fell into a gentle cadence that followed the rhythm of the water and the wheel. After spending years, maybe decades in the cottage with the thrumming everything about him had fallen in step. He probably walked and moved in rhythm with the wheel even when he was far enough away from the cottage that he couldn't hear its drone.

The old man fell quiet and Storm took this as a cue to tell him about himself. He unstrapped his watch and handed it over to Uhr who took it gingerly and examined it. He then reciprocated by telling the story of how he came here and all the things that happened along the way up until his knocking on Uhr's door.

When he had come to the part about Bherin being brought back from death with the passage root Uhr took his eyes from the watch and when Storm had completed his story Uhr questioned him about Bherin.

"Does it still follow you?"

"I don't know for certain that it is still following me but it was very determined even though it was slowing down. If it is still capable of walking then it is still following me and will arrive here eventually."

The two of them glanced nervously at the door then Uhr returned to his examination of the watch. It seemed to Storm that Uhr was looking for a waterway through it. Everything for him was powered by water and he probably thought that you had to flow water through the watch to make it work. He probed at this with a question.

"Do you use water to power everything?"

"Well yes. The force of the river moving through time and ever flowing is the source of power. The watch doesn't use the power of water?"

Storm thought about this for a moment. "No, it doesn't use water. It uses stored energy in the form of a battery. It's a chemical reaction."

This wasn't going to help Uhr much so he tried a different tact.

"There are many forms of energy that you could use to power your machines and your time pieces." He paused and thought about this for a moment then he opened his backpack and brought out his rope.

"Where I come from we have a long history of building mechanical time pieces without batteries –grandfather clocks, cuckoo clocks and all kinds of mechanical devices" He moved over to the fireplace and pulled out of the pile of cold embers a stone about the size of a loaf of bread.

"Do you understand the force of gravity?" He bluntly asked Uhr but Uhr just stared blankly at him so he continued by holding the rock out in front of him.

"What happens when I let go of this rock?"

"It falls to the ground." Uhr responded.

"So the earth is exerting a force on the rock."

He let the rock drop to emphasize his point and it clunked loudly on the floorboards of the cottage.

"There is no force, it just fell down as all things do."

Gravity was too ubiquitous. Uhr wasn't getting the point. It was so obvious that it was impossible to see.

"No, it really didn't fall down; it was pulled down."

Uhr nodded his head as if he understood but it was tentative. Storm could tell that he really wasn't getting it. He tied one end of the rope around the stone then he tossed the other end of the rope over a rafter in the ceiling. He pulled on the rope until the stone was suspended three feet in the air then he handed the rope to Uhr.

"Can you feel that Stone pulling on you?"

Uhr nodded his head again.

"What you are feeling is the force of the earth pulling on the stone. Feel the tautness in your muscles? The larger the stone the greater is the force. Now let the rope slowly slip through your hands.

Uhr complied and let the rope slowly slip through his hands so the stone slowly moved toward the floorboards.

"That is motion and it is just like the flowing of a river. We can harness this power to make very accurate time pieces."

Uhr was getting visibly excited. He pulled the stone up quickly and lowered it slowly several times. He had building mechanical devices for many years and Storm could see that he was already thinking about how he could harness this "new" power.

Storm walked back to the fireplace and dug out a twig that was charcoal burned on one end and using it as a pencil he drew some sketches on the wood floor of the cottage. Earlier in his life he had been very interested in mechanical clocks and he had built several grandfather clocks from kits and he had a particular love for cuckoo clocks. He had even traveled to the Black Forest in Germany to see how they were made and he brought several back to the States with him. So he had a good understanding of how mechanical clocks were made.

"The most important thing you have to accomplish in the making of a time piece is accuracy. You have to get the mechanism to move at a very steady rate. This is done by a mechanism called an escapement and it is attached by a pendulum."

He continued to draw sketches on the floorboards and the two of them spent the next hour going over the building of a clock. Uhr listened almost gleefully to everything. His enthusiasm grew so large that Storm had to stop every few minutes and watch him pace about the room making wild motions with his hands and muttering to himself. It seemed as if the old man had grown twenty years younger in the past hour. This was a major breakthrough for him and he could now set off in a totally new direction and bring himself closer to his goal however vague of a goal it actually was.

It was late afternoon when the conversation had finally waned and Uhr had picked all of the information that Storm could offer him he brought up the subject of his having to get to Speyer then Vorgard as soon as possible.

This snapped Uhr into a new train of thought and he shifted into a helpful mode –being very grateful for all that Storm had taught him.

"Your plan for getting to Vorgard is sound. You have chosen an easy path. You will not get lost. If you follow the river south it is a one day journey from here to Speyer and there is a well traveled road between there and Vorgard. You should stay here for the evening and set off in the morning. By tomorrow eve you will have arrived in Speyer. There you can find an Inn to stay the night and on the following day you can set off for Vorgard."

"There is the problem of the corpse that is following me."
Uhr thought about this for a moment.

"Yes, there is that. I think it would be better to rid yourself of this problem as soon as possible. It wouldn't do to have this abomination following you all over the countryside. We should devise some kind of a trap."

He opened the door and ushered Storm outside. The two of them looked nervously around -talking about the walking corpse heightened their awareness of their surroundings. It could just spring out at them from anywhere and at any moment. The thought of it "springing" out at them brought Storm's thoughts to the concept and usefulness of springs. He made a note to spend some time talking with Uhr about the use of springs when it came to clocks. A spring replaces the weight in a clock. Uhr would like that. Because springs made clocks portable.

Because there was only one entrance into the cottage –the door, and no windows, that would be how they would capture it. Uhr formulated a plan for making a cage that would sit up against the door and he drew out a quick sketch in the dirt. The corpse would walk into the cage in an approach for the door and Uhr would release a rope that would slam the entrance to the cage shut. Then they could drag the cage into a fire and immolate the abomination. Fire, Uhr explained would be the best way to insure that the animated corpse was completely dis-animated.

Uhr set to work on the cage and trap door and he set Storm off to gather firewood for a bonfire.

They spent the rest of the afternoon working on the task and by dark all their preparations were complete. The wooden cage, about six feet square, sat firmly against the door and the open side, which the corpse would enter, had a trap door that was raised up into the air by a rope and tied off to a branch in a nearby tree. It was a make-shift but sturdy portcullis of sorts.

Uhr climbed the tree and released the rope; the trapdoor slid down and sealed off the cage with a resounding thud. Storm handed him back the rope and he pulled the trapdoor back up to its raised position and tying off the rope he climbed out of the tree.

"Okay we are ready. You go inside, have something to eat then get some rest. I will wait out here in the tree and if that thing shows up I will trap it in the cage then we will drag it over to the bonfire and your problem will be solved."

They moved the cage about a foot away from the door so Storm could slide in and enter the cottage. Once inside he pulled on the cage while Uhr pushed and they set it tight against the doorway. And satisfied that everything was in order Uhr just waved a goodnight to him across the cage and Storm closed the door.

He busied himself making something to eat while he thought about Bherin. That was his friend and he had been hesitant to do anything about him. And even though it was clear that Bherin wanted to kill him he couldn't bring himself to do anything about it other than run away. But Uhr didn't have any such hesitations. It gave Storm a mixed feeling of comfort and unease.

After he had eaten he snuffed out several of the oil lamps and leaving only one burning he laid down on Uhr's cot.

He lay listening for what seemed like a long time. The room thrummed to its own rhythm. The water flowed through the sluice, the large water wheel squeaked along at its even pace and a variety of wooden mechanisms churned out little sounds in the dim light. He was just waiting for the sound of a corpse banging against the door, or maybe the sound of the trapdoor on the cage slamming shut. And he wondered if he would hear it over the background noises in the room but that sound never came and he drifted off into an uneasy sleep as the water-driven wood-hewn machines around him click-clicked in a methodical rhythm.

Storm had a dream that he was standing on the wooden porch of an old log cabin. He could hear water sounds coming from the nearby lake but his attention was on a set of wind chimes hanging from a rafter on the porch that clinked softly. He just looked at them. Several hollow bamboo shafts just swayed in the wind and clattered against each other. Their hollowness didn't sound right. They should have a pleasant sound he thought to himself. But these just sounded inert like dull thuds, almost like they were bones clattering against each other.

He woke with a start. The thought of the wind chimes being bones brought him immediately awake and alert. He tried to look around the small cottage. The oil lamp had burned itself down to a very dull light and he couldn't see anything well in the room –just vague shadows.

The sound of dead wind chimes that was in his dream didn't leave with the dream. It continued with a clicking and clacking as if somebody were shaking a bag of wooden blocks.
He got up off the cot and picked up the oil lamp. It was almost out of oil and was no brighter than a small candle. Soon it would burn out. He carried it around the room looking for another oil lamp to light.
He walked carefully to the wall near the head of the cot and started following the wall. He bumped into a table then a cabinet then he bumped right into the large water wheel that powered the whole room.

Storm held the lamp up near it. It wasn't turning. A small amount of water was trickling over the paddles but it wasn't enough to turn the wheel. Realization came to him that the room was quiet except for the click clacking that had awoken him. The sound of water flowing was now only a trickle and the variety of sounds that had filled the room was now gone. The water had stopped and this stopped the wheel and everything that ran off of it.
Before he fell asleep the room was vibrant with a variety of small clicks and squeaks as the mechanical contraptions went on about their business.

This had all stopped when the wheel stopped and the only sound remaining was the wooden blocks rattling in their bag.
He navigated his way around to the back of the wheel where the sluice entered the room and lifted the oil lamp high against the wall.

Two skeleton hands lunged out at him from the sluice and a bony skull chomped its teeth in a grimace of worms and rot. He fell back onto the floor and the oil lamp sputtered out leaving him in total darkness.

His heart hammered against the inside of his chest. The walking corpse of Bherin had continued to follow him and trying to get into the cottage not by the door where they had set the trap but by squeezing itself through the wooden sluice. It would have slid through then slit his throat while he slept but the sluice was too small and it had gotten stuck and was struggling to free itself. The sound of its struggle was what had filtered into his dreams —sounding like wooden blocks rattling in a bag. He might not have even heard that but its getting stuck in the sluice had obstructed the water flow and brought the water wheel to a stop and all the mechanical devices in the room had gone quiet.

He sat on the floor listening to the clatter of Bherin's bones as it tried to free itself from the sluice. The clacking pace had accelerated. It sensed he was near and worked itself into a frenzy.
The thing had no eyes, they were probably the first thing to rot away when Bherin died; but it still could follow him and still could find him. It probably didn't matter to it that the room was totally black and that left Storm at a very big disadvantage. If it got free of the sluice it could pounce on him without warning.

Storm stood up quickly and backed away from the clattering. He groped around in the direction he thought the door might be and after bumping into several items including the table he found a wall and laying his hands on it he followed it around the bed and to the door.

The clattering of Bherin stopped and Storm panicked —it must have freed itself from the sluice he thought.
The hair on the back of his neck stood up. He imagined Bherin plunging a knife into his back. He fumbled his hands along the door and finding the knob he wrenched the door open to a dim light.
The moon was in a quarter phase but the sky was clear so it cast enough light for him to see clearly.

He pushed against the cage and it slid away from the door – just enough for him to slide out of the cottage. As he slid out and fell to the ground he heard a grunt of surprise from Uhr in the nearby tree.

Uhr jumped to the ground and the two of them pushed the cage back up against the door then they stood and stared through it into the darkness of the cottage.

Several minutes passed with the two of them just staring and waiting until Uhr broke the silence.

"What happened?"

"It tried to come in through the sluice instead of the door."

Uhr just nodded his head.

"But the sluice is too narrow and it got stuck. It was rattling around trying to free itself and I fell and dropped the oil lamp then everything got quiet and I was afraid it had gotten free so I bolted for the door."

They stared at the dark doorway waiting for something to happen but nothing happened except that water sluice started to flow again in a half strength stream of water. The large water wheel inside the cottage began creaking in an attempt to get itself back into rhythm.

Uhr bent down and put his hand inside the waterway that led from the front of the cottage and poured out into the pond. "The water is flowing again but not at full strength."

Uhr grabbed for the cage in front of the door and pushed it aside –completely clearing the doorway. Now there was nothing between them and the skeleton of Bherin. Uhr listened at the doorway but nothing could be heard over the creaking of the wheel and the clatter of the various mechanical devices that had come slowly into action.

Storm noticed that the pace of the clicks and clacks were slower than they had been. They thrummed the previous day and through the night at a very measured pace and now that the water was flowing slower everything moved slower. This was a flaw in Uhr's work. He had to keep the water at a very even flow. The marching time of his machines changed with the flow of the river. If the water through the sluice varied, the marching of time varied. But all this would change now that Uhr knew about the technique of using an escapement and how it keeps an accurate beat. Uhr would be able to redesign his machinery.

He thought about the fact that the simple concept of an escapement had revolutionized his world. It enabled whole societies to beat to a common rhythm. It enabled everyone to get into a synchronization where eventually tens of thousands of people could show up to work at factories at the same time every morning. It was a critical component of the Industrial Revolution that changed the whole world. Storm wondered what kind of advancement, or havoc, it would bring upon this world.

Uhr walked right into the dark cottage and Storm, after a moments pause, followed him as far as the doorway. He couldn't see anything inside. It was total darkness.

Uhr lit an oil lamp and the inside of the cabin came alive with a dull orange light. He walked around the room and lit more lamps while Storm stared into the dark area behind the waterwheel. Storm walked over to it and Uhr, carrying a lamp, met him there.

They looked up at the area where the sluice poured out of the wall near the ceiling. Bherin's torso was still lodged in the sluice, its tattered clothes swirling in the flowing water. But his head was gone. One arm hung down and clattered against each paddle of the wheel as it passed. The other arm was missing. Other than the casual motion of the arm the rest of the corpse was lifeless. There was no more unnatural life in it. It was gone. Storm could feel that there was nothing left but the remnants of Bherin's corpse.

Uhr pointed to the sluice in the middle of the room. Bherin's head lay in the flowing water like a rock. As Bherin had tried to free himself and the water started to flow. The wheel turned and the paddles probably forced against his head. Being connected by remnants of rotted flesh it had separated, fallen into the wheel, gone up and over and fell into the sluice on the floor. The missing arm was on the floor near the wall. Its bony hand was still clutching at the dagger.

Uhr grabbed a large walking stick from a corner of the room and he pried the corpse from the sluice. It fell onto the water wheel in a series of thumps and rotating over the wheel each piece fell into the sluice. Both he and Uhr paused for a very long moment; watching to see if it would reanimate itself. Maybe it would get up and attack them without it's head. But nothing happened. It seemed to be gone. The bones were lifeless. Storm gently collected each piece and brought it outside.

After an hour of work they had collected all the pieces of Bherin into a pile of bone and clothing and as the sun broke the horizon Storm found a place near the pond and dug a shallow grave. While Storm buried Bherin Uhr left him to his solitude and went about cleaning up the mess inside the cottage.

It was still early morning when they had both finished what they had set out to do. Uhr made them a hot breakfast and as they sat to eat he broke the silence.

"How long had that thing, I mean your friend, been following you?" His obsession with time was complete. How long something took was always the first thing to come to his mind.

"This evening will be three complete days since Bherin was murdered."

Storm was just about to put a chunk of bread in his mouth when he stopped. Bherin was murdered. The thought just occurred to him. These several days had been a blur to him. He was in a strict survival mode. But this had all started because something was following them and Bherin had lay in wait to find out what, or who, it was.

He glanced over his shoulder at the doorway. His two day and two night ordeal with the following corpse had ended but what had been following them before? And is it still following him now? Uhr interrupted his thoughts.

"The Passage Root is a powerful thing. It opens a door between two existences; and this process is not well understood so it is used only very rarely. In my life I have only seen it used one time and it lasted but a few moments. Only a short conversation can occur before the effect wears off. And it can only be used once. Trying to use it again on a corpse has no effect. Whatever happened to your friend was brought about by something else. The Root was probably just the catalyst that made it possible. Maybe it created an opportunity for something with bad intent to capitalize on. And for your friend to be animated in such a twisted way, and for three days, there was some strong magic at work." He stared for a very long time at Storm as if trying to perceive something that wasn't obvious.

"You have very serious business to attend to and you should depart immediately. I will travel with you to Speyer. If we leave now we should arrive by mid day tomorrow. And there I can help you find passage to Vorgard."

They finished their meal and went about preparing for the days journey. Storm reviewed the materials in his pack and examined his weapons which now included Bherin's dagger. Uhr shouldered a light pack and selected a walking stick from the many that were standing in a corner of the room.

They walked out of the cottage and with Uhr in the lead they head around the back and directly along the sluice toward the Mid river.

When they got to the river Uhr went straight to the sluice gate and after pausing a moment to consider what he was doing he turned the crank on the gate and the flow of water stopped its journey down the sluice.

Storm had the feeling that cutting off the water flow, which stopped the machinery, was something that Uhr hadn't done in many years –possibly never. But Uhr didn't say anything about it. He just watched the water dry up then he head off south toward Speyer without ever looking back. Storm followed a few steps behind -It felt good to once again have a traveling companion.

9. The Cleric's Secret

"And a Storm will set itself upon the land."
-From the Book of Varheit

The old man was more agile than his years revealed and the two of them traveled quickly down the winding path of the river. He moved with a quick and strong motion always leading them along the river and toward Speyer.

On the morning of their second day the terrain changed. The river began to sink down into the land and within an hour they were walking along the side of a cliff that sloped steeply down to the water.

The River, over the course of countless millennia had cut a path into what was probably softer land here and it created a ravine – a canyon of sorts. But the river didn't really cut down into the land. The land was rising and they were walking slowly upward in the slope of it. But the river didn't follow this rule. It had stayed on the same level; it just denied the upward slope and cut itself a path right through it. Storm imagined that over the course of centuries, underground forces, maybe the shifting of tectonic plates had caused the area to slowly rise. And the river just ignored the rise and patiently cut away the land.

The total rise in land was only several hundred feet at this moment in time, and maybe in a hundred thousand years the hill would have slowly grown to the stature of a mountain. But it didn't matter to the river. It would patiently work its path and continue its journey.

After another hour of gently walking their way upward they broke through an area where the trees were sparse and they got a good view of the terrain to their front. Uhr stopped in the bright sunlight and tinkered with his walking stick.

Storm watched curiously as Uhr pulled a small wooden lever from the handle of the walking stick then holding the stick upright, its foot firmly on the ground, he rotated the stick.

The little wooden lever cast a shadow on inscribed lines on the staff and Storm guessed it must be some kind of timepiece. The man truly was obsessed with time. He had to always know what time it was, and how long things took.

"We have made good time." Uhr declared. Obviously satisfied by the reading he derived from his mobile sundial. Storm glanced at his watch out of habit but there was really no point in him doing so. Then he pointed a question at Uhr. "How do you tell the time after the sun sets?"

Uhr folded back down the little lever on the walking stick.

"I haven't figured that out. The moon is not the same as the sun. It changes from night to night. And some nights it isn't out."
Storm, unhitched the wrist band on his watch and held it out for Uhr to take. Uhr just stared in shock with his mouth open.

"This way you can also tell the time at night."

Storm's words broke the spell Uhr was under and Uhr reached gingerly for the watch. The whole interaction was a bit awkward. Not quite what Storm had expected. It was as if he was granting Uhr the sun and the moon themselves. To him it was just a watch. But to Uhr it was everything.

He showed him how to work the little buckle on the band and with a crack in his voice Uhr thanked him then spent the next several minutes looking at it, watching the second hand smoothly circle around the face.

Uhr came out of his reverie and pointed ahead toward the highest point of the land in sight. "There's old Speyer." It was a large outcropping of rock, barren of any trees or foliage and it stood up above the rest of the land. It was a barren promontory that stuck up above the rest of the terrain. It looked like the tectonic forces had forced one huge finger up through the earth that pointed toward the sky.
He looked more closely at it. It was flat on the top but the profile at the top was broken by small bumps. From this distance, Storm gauged it to be three miles away, the flat portion at the top of this granite pointing finger was probably several hundred feet across and if that was so then those bumps at the top might be buildings.
He asked Uhr if he was right.
"Yes, there are buildings on top" Replied Uhr. He squinted at the granite finger. "I can't make out anything though. Your eyes are younger than mine."
They continued their walk toward Speyer and the promontory. Uhr broke the silence by telling him about the city.

"That rock outcropping is called the finger of God." On top of it was where the original Speyer was built by Anfang. Those were difficult days and it was a good place to defend. But in the many generations since that time the land has grown peaceful and the city moved down into a nearby valley. Anfang built a church on the top of the finger and although much of what else was up there has now crumbled to dust the church still remains. It is the first temple of the land and a very holy place. People travel from every corner of the land to pay homage there."

After another hour they were at the foothills of the finger of god and they could see down into the valley where Speyer was nestled. It was a beautiful sight. The finger of god marked the end of the ravine they had been traveling along and the river broke into a valley that spread out in front of them for miles. The terrain was green and moved off into the distance in gentle hills. New Speyer sat peacefully in the bottom of a valley along one side of the river. A hundred buildings of different sizes were scattered around a large central area that Storm guessed was the market place. The whole scene was beautiful, the trees, the grass, the flowing of the river and the peace of the town that sat quietly in the valley struck Storm hard. This place was idyllic. It was the kind of place that he had dreamed of retiring to when the days of corporate life had gotten too hectic. It was like a sleepy little village in the south of France or in Tuscany.
This was the kind of place that Arabella would love. She would resonate with its simple beauty. She grew up in a town that was very much like this and she was happy there until Storm found her and changed her whole world.

Storm didn't remember one more step of their walk until they reached the outskirts of the city. He was lost in a painful memory of the first day he had met Arabella.

***

He had been on a business trip to a small town in the south of Spain called Cadiz and on a Saturday afternoon he decided to see the Bull fights. It wasn't really high on his list but all week the locals were building themselves up into a frenzy over it. So he went. It would be interesting to take in this aspect of the culture he thought. And it was there in the stands that he first spotted her. The sight of her hit him like a bull fighters sword through the heart. It was as simple as that. She was sitting two rows closer to the arena and she was with a girlfriend. There was something in the way she looked and the way she sat and he knew he just had to talk to her.

She sat quietly and would occasionally whisper something in her friend's ear. She was the exact opposite of her girlfriend who would stand up and cheer and chant things in Spanish to the toreadors and even the bulls.

When an intermission came between fights and they had carted the first dead bull out of the arena. Storm approached her and her friend wondering if they would be carting him out as they did the bull.

He stuck out his hand in a request for a handshake and simply said in English "Hi, my name is Storm."

Arabella looked at him and blushed a deep red. Her girlfriend tilted her head back and laughed.

He weathered the first few seconds and was still in the ring so he blathered a few inanities and eventually asked if he could sit down with them.

The three of them sat down with him on one side, Arabella on the other and the girlfriend in the middle. She could speak some English so she acted as a translator between Storm and Arabella.

Mostly Storm and Matilda talked and she explained a little bit about the history of the bull fights and the story about some of the matadors. She would punctuate various points by jumping up and cheering or shaking her fist at different points in the fight.

After the fights they went to a local outdoor cafe for coffee and more awkward translation.

Storm sat and felt the conversation through its changes. All the while Arabella sat quietly looking at him. The conversation started with the women cheerful and curious about the novelty of having coffee with an American. Then it slowly shifted to a more serious stance as he made it clear that he was seriously interested in Arabella. At this point the translation of his words that Matilda gave to Arabella seemed to take on a more serious tone maybe even a little skeptical. He couldn't understand the words she was saying but he could feel the tension.

The Spanish people are not like Americans. They take their time. The pace of their life is different. No day planners, no rush to the next appointment and definitely no rush into relationships. Storm was operating at one speed and the women were at another. Neither pace was right nor wrong -just different.

The conversation went on in its disjointed way for two more hours and Storm spent a lot of time just staring at Arabella over his coffee. The waiting for the translation, and wondering how accurate it was wore on him and at one point he smiled at Arabella and said "Rather than worry about English and Spanish what we should do is make up our own language." He waited for Matilda to translate. Arabella laughed as she heard the translation of this and responded through Matilda. "Sounds like a wonderful idea. What will be the first word in our new language"? He chuckled at the fun of it all and looked around. When his eyes settled on his coffee he pointed and said "Kaflae." Arabella clapped her hands, pointed at the coffee and repeated the word "Kaflae." Something clicked into place with that word and a new language was born. Throughout their relationship they would deepen this new language and use it almost exclusively. It was as if they each would give up what they were and embrace a new thing; a "them" complete with it's own language.

When a hint of red came into the sky announcing the first glimpses of sunset Matilda announced that they would have to be going. She looked at Arabella, said a few words and Arabella nodded her head in agreement.

The three of them stood up and as Arabella approached him she stuck out her hand in a gesture of a shake and said in English "goodbye Storm." It caught him totally by surprise. During the whole course of the afternoon she had never spoken directly to him. She had always spoken to Matilda and Matilda translated to him. Even then she had always whispered and never said more than three or four words.

Arabella and Matilda moved several steps away and time slowed down for Storm. He distinctly heard the change in sound as the women's feet moved from the brick of the cafe to the cobblestones of the road.

He watched as the two of them put their heads together in a small burst of conversation all the while Matilda keeping her eyes locked on him as if he were a hungry lion watching its prey.

Matilda glanced at him then the two of them turned and walked down the street. Storm watched helplessly as they moved further away and was shocked when Arabella glanced over her shoulder at him, smiled and in a gesture that meant more than goodbye she waved her hand.

Storm smiled a smile that welled up from his heart and then he laughed. He could hear Matilda launch into a tirade of expletives as the two woman turned a corner in the street.

He knew Arabella would come back tomorrow, he just didn't know when. So he decided he would just have to stay right there in that spot until the place closed and then come back very early in the morning.

***

As Storm and Uhr approached the town a feeling of ill ease set upon them. There was something in the air; a smell or a feeling. Storm couldn't put his finger on it but something just felt wrong. They quickened their pace and as they got closer to the town limit they heard faint screams and sounds. Something was going on in the city. It sounded like a riot or some kind of commotion. They were passing the path that led up the side of the finger of god, up to the abbey and church at the top, when a bell started ringing. It was coming from the church perched up there. They looked up and could see several figures waving their arms.

Uhr assessed the situation. "I think the monks are trying to signal us." Storm watched as two of the figures started running down the spiraling path that led to them. He and Uhr turned away from the city and hastened up the path.

After a couple of minutes of climbing the path they met the monks who were very animated. Even though their heads were shaven and they wore brown robes like monks their frames weren't that of monks. They were muscular –not what Storm had expected. Monks were supposed to be frail and thin. They spent their lives reading books, chanting, and hand copying manuscripts. These monks looked like they formed by a life of healthy living and hard work.

One of them spoke.

"You must not go into Speyer." He paused to inhale a deep breath then continued. "A great evil has befallen the people of the town."

Uhr looked up for the sun then fidgeted with his walking stick as if telling the time would clear up the situation –whatever it was.

The monk continued. "Come with us, do not enter the city." The two monks turned and headed back up the path to the church. Storm and Uhr hastily followed behind.

The path broke out onto the top of the finger and Storm gasped. The surface was solid rock, and very smooth and flat. The whole structure was almost like someone had taken a giant stone cucumber and slammed it halfway into the ground then cut an inch off the top so it was flat.

The total area at the top was about the size of a football field and in the center was a large stone building that looked like a church. Attached to it were several smaller buildings. The monks lead them to the big wooden doors of the church. One of the monks banged a fist on the wood and someone inside shifted what sounded like a large wooden latch then one of the doors opened. He ushered them all inside.

The inside was like a typical church. Six stone buttresses lined each side. Each with a complimentary one on the other side of the church that met it at the point of the roof down the center of the building. Stained glass windows were placed between each buttress. Wooden rows of benches filled the inside between them and the altar at the far end. Behind the altar was a statue. It was a figure of a man holding a sword out in front of him as if to ward off an attacker. It looked to Storm like it was Anfang –the figure that presided over Ty's passage ceremony.

As the monks walked them forward toward the altar Storm couldn't take his eyes off the statue. It stood one and a half times the size of a man. He guessed it to be about nine feet in height. It was very realistic and beautifully sculpted. The sword he held was a perfect copy, in marble, of the actual sword that Anfang had carried. As they got closer Storm could see the face on the blade and the hole where its mouth was. He half expected it to speak.

Half a dozen monks sat in various benches. Each one was praying or chanting -almost feverishly.
Another monk, wearing a goldenrod colored robe with a brown cord at the waist came out of a door in the wall behind the altar and greeted them. He was slender and muscular but his face was very round. His forehead had deep wrinkles as if he had spent many years puzzling over things.
"Uhr. I am glad to see you. You don't usually come until mid-winter. What brings you at this time of the year?" He looked at Storm carefully. It was as if he knew that Storm was the reason for Uhr's arrival.
"True, I am off my schedule." He twitched his walking stick at the thought of being off his schedule. "My companion here has dire need of passage to Vorgard."

The monk extended a hand out to Storm. "My name is Benedict. I am the caretaker of the shrine of Anfang and of all the brothers who live here."

Storm shook his hand and was shocked at how callused it was. The man had spent his whole life working hard at something and it left the skin on his hands very rough and thick. It made him wonder about these monks. They all seemed to be muscular and strong. It was very un-monk like. "I am Storm, stranger to this land."

He didn't know why he gave himself a title but it just felt right.

Benedict flinched and the lids of his eyes closed and opened several times in rapid succession as if he were blinking out a breeze of dust. There was an awkward pause and just as Benedict was going to say something Uhr broke the tension.

"What is going on in Speyer?"

This brought Benedict back from the thoughts he was having.

"There is an evil upon the town. People are running through the streets like mad-men. They are having visions and hearing voices; there is violence everywhere. They act as if they have lost their minds. I believe a spell or enchantment possesses the entire town. It has been foretold in the book of Anfang." With this last sentence he fell quiet and the wrinkles in his forehead gathered together as if a storm were brewing in his head.

Again Uhr broke Benedict's introspection with a question. "When did this start?"

Storm almost chuckled at the question. He knew this would be the first question Uhr would ask.

"It started last evening shortly after the supper bell. A young boy from the town, Than, ran up to us pleading for help. He told us that his parents were acting strange, and that others in the town were also acting strange. I dispatched two brothers down to investigate and they found this to be true. I was also very concerned about Brother Frederick. He had been down in the town for several days. We send a brother down to stay so he can guide people in their daily prayers. Many of the older people have difficulty making the climb up to the temple here. The Brothers I sent found the boys story to be true. The town was in a riot with people running through the streets screaming as if being tormented. It continued through the night and still continues through this day."

Now it was Storm' turn to ask a question.

"Did they find Brother Frederick?"

"Yes they found him huddled in a corner of the prayer room muttering incoherently. They bound him and walked him back up to us."

Storm perked up at this.

"So the Brother is here?"

"Yes, we have him restrained in his cot."

"And the young boy Than; Is he here too? He has not been affected by the affliction?"

"No, he is okay. And still is okay except for the fear of what has become of his family."

"Are there any others that haven't been affected?"

Benedict wrinkled his brow again. ""Umm… yes, there are several townsfolk that have come to us and they seem to have not been taken by the possession." He stressed the word possession as if to correct Storm for using the word affliction.

"Could we see them? Is Than here?" He looked around the room in hopes of spotting the boy. "Could I talk to him? Maybe there is something we can do to help?"

Benedict blinked rapidly again. This time it was a response to the rapid set of questions that Storm shot at him.

"The only thing we can do for them is pray. They have been possessed by something evil. It has been foretold by the book." He pointed over Storm's shoulder at the handful of monks praying at benches.

Benedict wrinkled his brow and smoothed out imagined wrinkles in his goldenrod robe. "We will talk to the boy, and any others that you wish to talk to." He nodded at Uhr. The courtesy seemed to be on behalf of Uhr. "You said you have urgent business in Vorgard? Let's have something to eat and we will discuss your plans."

Uhr nodded in approval. A part of him wanted to be released of the burden of Storm. The man brought a tempest wherever he went. Uhr had many years of solitude and peace until the day Storm showed up on his door. And Speyer had been a peaceful town until the man showed up.

"That's a good idea. Let's eat then, we can discuss how to best get this man to Vorgard."

Benedict nodded and waved an arm toward the door he had previously came through and the three of them went to the dining room.

The smell of the kitchen was intoxicating. Storm hadn't had a kitchen prepared meal since he left Mainz.

Within minutes of them sitting down they were all eating and Storm threw himself into the meal with zeal.

After taking a bite from a warm piece of bread Storm looked up from his plate. "This bread is delicious."

Benedict and Uhr were staring at him as if in a state of shock. He looked down at his tunic to see if he had spilled food on it.

"What?"

He looked over his shoulder to see if someone had come into the dining hall.

Uhr's face twitched. "You're eating with your left hand. Are you … left handed?" Storm looked at the wooden spoon in his left hand.

"Yes."

The thought of what questions would come next made Storm uncomfortable so he returned to his original statement.

"This bread is really delicious; and still warm."

Benedict, having spent his whole life maneuvering in the politics of an organization – the temple of Anfang, picked up the clue easily and smiling uncomfortably changed the subject. "Yes, we bake our own bread here." After a pause where he considered asking questions of Storm's dexterity he decided against it and continued. "We are self sufficient. We tend our own farm down on the outskirts of Speyer –grow our own vegetables. We produce or make almost everything we need. Anything we don't produce we barter for with the town folk. We don't hunt so we get all our meat from them."

There was a subtle shift in Benedict's behavior toward Storm. This new revelation changed Benedict's disposition toward him.

"You have urgent business in Vorgard?"

"The Lady Petra has summoned me."

Benedict's eyes grew wider and the wrinkles got deeper. Maybe he had misjudged the whole situation. "We should finish our meal quickly. We will make preparations for your departure immediately." He waved his hand for one of the Brothers. The two of them talked briefly then the other Brother rushed off.

"I want to first look into what is happening down in Speyer." He felt like he was name-dropping but if his mission had changed Benedict's outlook he had to test the waters and see how far he could push. And it seemed to be so. Benedict did a fast turn around as any consummate politician would. His years of training and growth in the temple had made him flexible. He could move with the winds.

"Anything at all. What do you think is causing this affliction?"

Storm was almost shocked by the fast turn around. He had used the word affliction in an attempt to please him. When not fifteen minutes ago he had insisted that it was a possession.

"You mentioned a boy that was in the town and isn't affected. Can we talk to him?"

They finished their meal and Benedict led them deeper into the temple. They passed through several rooms and a corridor that led them to a wide staircase down. It curved slowly around to the right. As they walked Storm rubbed his hand against the wall. "This staircase was carved right out of the stone?"

Uhr took the opportunity to fill Storm in on some details. "The Brothers have been hollowing out the stone for many generations. They dig ever downward. It is their mission and their obsession."

They stopped their walking down the steps at a platform on their right. A short tunnel in the wall led into what looked like a room at the end of the tunnel. Benedict took the opportunity to explain a little about the finger of god.

"The brotherhood was begun by Anfang some six thousand years ago. He and his men originally began the digging –but from the ground up. They began this staircase from the ground. It curves several times around until it reaches the church at the top. It took several generations to complete the tunnel. Then we began digging the rooms in the center which is now half hollow. It is a series of rooms one below the other for many levels with the exception of one level. Half way down the structure we dug outward.

This explained the physical condition of the monks to Storm. They spent their whole lives working with stone. It could make a man very strong. It puzzled him though as to why they would do it.

"Why go through all this work?"

"Anfang has directed us to do it. According to the Book of Varheit it is in preparation for the time of the breaking or the Wechseln."

"What kind of preparation?"

"Anfang didn't give us any specific instructions. It is just the preparation and we do the best as we know how. The first few levels from here are quarters for the monks. Then there are many empty levels then near the ground level is a cluster of used levels. They store food, weapons, lumber, a library, and plants. Whatever the monks fancy. We delve into all things in the world."

"What happens when you reach the ground level?"

"We reached it many generations ago and we continue to cut and quarry levels below the earth. The stone remains the same."

"This stone is remarkable." Storm took a close look at the wall near his head. "It is like granite but very smooth in composition. There doesn't seem to be any veins or impurities anywhere. It is simply solid stone." It brought to him the image of a glass blower blowing a long cylinder but instead of using glass he used molten stone. Twirling it slowly he worked all the impurities out of it, spun it into a cylinder and when it cooled he thrust it into the ground.

"I don't know about the preparations of the stone itself. It doesn't seem to make a whole lot of sense to me. It is a lot of work. Did you ever stop to think that maybe Anfang's goal wasn't to prepare the stone?"

"No, no, what do you mean? The book is vague in many ways but in this way it is clear. The cutting of the stone is the most important task in the land and each monk must spend half of every other day doing it."

The pieces fell together like a granite jigsaw. That's why these monks were so muscular and in such great shape. They lived a healthy life, simple living, good nutrition and strong physical labor but always with time to rest. He looked at the broadness of Benedict's shoulders. They were so not like what a monk would have.

Storm nodded at this. "Each monk spends half of every other day cutting stone for his whole life. So he gets stone working physical labor but always gets a day of rest. A day for his body to recover; I think that the preparation that Anfang meant was that of you monks. He meant for you to be prepared not the stone."

"Well yes we are preparing for the Wechseln as we should. The tower continues ever downward."

"No, not the tower. You are being prepared."

Benedict shook his head. He didn't understand what Storm was driving at.

Storm pointed the index of his left hand at Benedict's chest and because he used his left hand Benedict became quite uncomfortable with the whole conversation.

"Just look at yourselves. You spend your whole life digging at the stone, probably with just hand tools. And all of this stone is carried out by hand. Look at your chest and shoulders. Look at the strength in your arms. The face shows you to be in your fifth decade but your body is that of a much younger man; And a very strong younger man."

Uhr picked up the conversation with a blurt and wave of his hands. "They are an army. It all makes sense. Everything they do is to make them stronger." His voice rose in pitch at the revelation. "They work at what seems like an impossible task yet they persevere. And I have watched them dig. It is like a ritual. They don't dig in the most efficient manner —which has always boggled me. They cut the stone in patterns, swinging their sledges, picks and chisels overhand, underhand, side to side. It's very bizarre to watch but it all makes sense now. These are the same motions as made with a weapon."

He stared at Benedict with a sense of astonishment and appreciation. "You are an army!" His excitement was gaining control of him now and he turned back to Storm. "Every year each monk must go through the purification. For three days and two nights he must work at the stone without break and he must cut and remove a set amount. He gets no food, only water. The first few years it is a difficult task for them but soon it becomes easy. They can go days without food or sleep and all the while working very hard. They are a remarkable force —as strong as the stone they carve." The creation of the metaphor pleased him; he smiled and fell silent.

Benedict looked at Uhr with a stony glance. This was a secret that few but the monks knew. He made no comment about the whole situation he simply said "the boy and the others from the village are in here" and he turned and walked down the short corridor. Storm, after a pause, followed behind him. Looking at the broad muscular back in front of him Storm was amazed at how a plain robe and a rope belt could so easily hide what should be apparent.

The hollowed out stone room was large; about twenty-five paces across. And the ceiling stood at twice the height of a man and it had a slight tilt toward the far end so the thin smoke from the oil lamps was directed out. The whole complex had a network of tunnels and shafts to manage air and smoke. And none of the shafts or tunnels were small. The smallest shaft had to be wide enough for a man to dig it with hand tools. The entire structure was like a termite mound.

Five minutes ago the room would have looked like the sleeping quarters in any abbey or monastery. It was sparse and neat. Wooden cots lined the wall all the way around and there were a few simple wooden tables and cabinets. But now, after their conversation, and the insight it offered, it looked like a military barracks –a little too neat. There was a military precision to everything.

Two monks sat at a table engrossed in a board game as a boy watched.

Benedict called to the boy. "Wren?"

"Father Benedict!" He ran over to them.

"Wren these men would like to talk to you about what is happening down in the town. Do you think you could answer some of their questions?" He placed a big hand on Wren's shoulder and even though his hands were callused from years of stone work the touch was very gentle.

Wren looked to be about fourteen or fifteen years old. The top of his head reached to their shoulders and Storm thought that it would not be long before he stood before Anfang in the Testing.

"Hi Wren, my name is Storm." He motioned for the boy to sit on a nearby cot and the two of them sat down. This could be a traumatic thing for the boy. The fate of his family and friends were in jeopardy.

"We are trying to understand what happened in Speyer so we can make it better. Could you tell us what happened?"

The boy didn't have any trouble talking about what happened. He eagerly launched into the circumstances of the evening before.

"It started not long after supper last night. My parents had finished eating and my father was smoking his pipe. He did this almost every evening after supper. I heard him call my mother. He told her the smoke from the pipe was forming little figures and they were dancing in the air. I peeked out of my room and the two of them were watching as he blew smoke from his pipe into the air. He inhaled deeply from the pipe then gently blew the smoke into the air. It looked very normal to me but they were amazed. My mother would gasp and point. They did this for a long time. I just watched from the doorway of my room." He paused and looked at each man carefully. He was trying to judge whether they believed him or not. Storm encouraged him. "Go ahead, continue."

Up to this point the story was peculiar but not unusually so. Wren took a deep breath and launched into the rest of his story.

"My mother started complaining that the smoke shapes were bad things and they were laughing at her. Then she got really scared and tried to shoo them away. Noises started filling the air outside too. The village was coming alive but in a bad way. My mother started screaming and tearing at her clothes as if to fight off invisible smoke creatures that had attached themselves to her. My father ran into his bedroom and emerged moments later with his sword. He then ran out of the house screaming bad words. I tried to help my mother but she just kept screaming. When she looked at me she didn't look like the same person. Her eyes were different." He paused again, looking for sympathy from the men.

"I ran out after my father and there were many people running through the streets. Old Mr. Minson's House was on fire and Mr. Minson was lying in the street. It looked like he was dead. Everyone in the town was running through the streets, fighting, and screaming. Mr. Jenks came running after me waving a sword and screaming that I was a demon so I ran straight here to the brothers."

Storm gave this some thought.

"You said that your parents were having supper and you were in your room. You don't eat supper with them?" Wren's face turned red at the question. "I uh, my father had sent me to my room without supper. Mr. Minson complained about me tramping through his garden." His face turned red. "I wasn't taking his water gourds. I was just chasing after my cat." He set his jaw into a stubborn pose defying any of the men to accuse him of stealing water gourds.

Storm spoke to Benedict. "The fact that the boy didn't eat a meal is very suspicious; and everything started to happen shortly after supper time. Maybe there was something in the food they ate." Benedict grunted at this.

"How can something in food cause a person to have evil visions? It is food.

"What is food like when it goes bad? It gets rotten right."

"Yes, but I doubt very much that the whole town would have eaten rotten food. And food that has gone bad will make you sick not make you crazy."

"Sometimes food goes bad in a way that makes it hard to see or smell. Sometimes it goes bad in a way that you like." This train of thought gave him an idea. "Do you drink wine?"

Benedict and Uhr both stared at him. They were thinking that maybe the sickness of the village had spread to him somehow. Uhr was more alert to Storm's strange train of thought so he answered the question. "I have been known to have wine on occasion."

Storm nodded his head at Uhr in thanks. "Did you ever wonder how the wine got to be that way? It has an effect on your mind doesn't it? It is just grapes but over time it changes right?" He shot a look at the doubtful Benedict. Something happens to the juice of the grape that changes it to wine."

Again Benedict grunted but this time it was a grunt that gave a little ground to his skepticism. "Okay I can understand that it is possible that something you eat can somehow change in a way that could affect a persons mind. I could give you this if it were one or two households but the whole town?" How could that be possible? If someone had a bottle of wine that went bad or some food that went sour only they would have eaten it not the whole town."

"Let me ask you some questions now." Storm pointed at Benedict who, just like the boy, jutted his jaw in defiance, but not as severely. He had been going along grudgingly and it looked like he would have to play this game all the way out so he resigned himself to it. "Go ahead."

"Good. Do you here in the temple eat the same food as the people down in the town? We need to find out what you and they have in common and we can rule that out."

Benedict gave this a moment of thought. "We all grow food in the same fields. All the vegetables and fruits are a common element between us. And the meat is the same. Even though we are on the top of this hill we are a central part of the community."

This stumped Storm and he threw out some more ideas. "What about water? Is there only one well in the town?"

"Yes, there is only one well in the town."

Storm stood up off the cot. Maybe this was a lead.

"But we draw from that well also. There is clearly no well up here."

"How often do you draw from it? If you only get the water once a week maybe something happened to the well since the last time you drew from it."

"No we get water every day. Only as much as we need. We drew water from that well today and you had some with your meal." Benedict smiled. It felt to him like he had trumped Storm. The unasked question was: "If it's the water then how come you aren't insane like the folk of Speyer?" He didn't need to ask it though. Storm already figured that out.

"There has got to be something." Storm was speaking his thoughts out loud. It helped him to follow the logic. But this was turning into a dead end so he sat back down on the cot and spoke to the boy. "Is there anything that you did different than the other folk in Speyer? Let's pretend that this is an illness and almost everybody got sick. But you didn't because you did something different or because you ate something different. Can you think of anything like this?"

The three men stared at the boy and he spoke in a low voice. "I had water gourds." He glanced slowly up out of his embarrassment hoping to see that this wasn't some elaborate plot to catch him in a lie and to catch him for stealing Mr. Minson's water gourds. He was worried now that somehow his stealing and eating the fruit from his neighbor had somehow caused the whole town to go crazy.

Storm put his hand on the boy's shoulder. "Thank you for your help Wren. Your family is going to be okay. This is something that will pass."

He stood up and aimed another question at Benedict. "I need to speak to some more people. There has got to be something we are not seeing." His resolve was starting to slip. You could hear it in his voice. This was a strange world and it was possible that things didn't happen here the way they did back home. This thought made him laugh. Nothing happened here the way it did back home. Most of the rules of life appeared to be similar but there was no telling where things differed.

Benedict broke into his train of thought. "Wren is the only youngster that came to us but there are several adults from Speyer that have come to us seemingly unaffected by the possession. We could talk to them."

Benedict was skeptical about Storm's theory but it couldn't hurt to keep exploring the possibilities. He was faced with a town that had gone mad and his only alternatives were to send Brothers down there to bind them all and if it persisted for very much longer they would probably kill each other or die of starvation. That is if they haven't all run off into the fields or drowned themselves in the river by now.

"Rann and his wife live down in Speyer. They were there when it all started and they came to us for shelter and help. They are in the kitchen." He pointed back at the corridor they had come in.

They left the room through the corridor and went back up the curving staircase into the Temple and Storm knew they were getting close to the kitchen when he caught the scent of what appeared to be bread baking. He tugged at the back of Benedict's sleeve to get him to stop. "You bake your own bread here in the Temple?" Benedict looked at him. The wrinkles over his nose creased deeply then his eyebrows went up.

"Yes we do. We bake it fresh every day. And it is only for us here to eat. Down in the town they have their own baker —and there is only one. His name is Roald and he and his three sons bake all the bread for the town."

Benedict turned and the three of them rushed off toward the kitchen and the smell of baking bread.

Benedict went straight to a man that was chopping a large pile of vegetables. He didn't need Storm to ask any questions he knew what they were looking for so he asked Rann directly. Storm and Uhr just watched on.

"Rann, yesterday when everything went bad down in Speyer had you and the Mrs. eaten supper?"

Rann looked up from his vegetable cutting. He was shocked by the question. It came out of nowhere.

A woman who was stirring a large pot at one of the stoves behind him wiped her hands on her apron and still carrying a wooden spoon she stood along side Rann. This must be his wife Storm thought. They were in their fifties and looked comfortable together. He was very thin and she was very plump but they had a glow of satisfaction about them. It showed to Storm that life in Speyer was probably a good life. True the town was a farm town but if the fields were rich, the crops plentiful, and the winters mild it could be a very healthy and happy life.

Rann glanced at his wife as if he were asking permission to speak then answered the question. His demeanor was almost one of subservience. Down in Speyer they had a lot of respect for the Brothers up here on the hill.

"Aye, we had just finished our sup. The Mrs. made a wonderful stew." He glanced at her – looking for her approval. Judging by her figure she really liked to cook and judging by his figure he really wasn't that much for eating or maybe her cooking really wasn't all that good.

"Did you have any bread with your meal?"

Quick as lightning Rann's wife rapped him on the elbow with the wooden spoon she was holding. She didn't even consider the fact that he was cutting vegetables with a rather large knife. "He was supposed to come in from the fields early and pick up some bread at the bakers but the lout forgot. He stopped in at the pub first."

Rann broke out in a sheepish grin. "No sir, we didn't have any bread with out delicious stew." Storm picked up on the sarcasm this time. "But I had only stopped at the pub for one taste of Mead. That was all. I came round the bakery early enough but I swear that Roald closed up shop early." His wife guffawed at this and turned back to stirring her pot with the big wooden spoon.

"Bread would have ruined the delicate flavor of that delicious stew!" He reached around and pinched his wife on the bottom. She squealed then rapped him several times with the wet spoon.

Benedict took a small step away from Storm then asked him a small question that changed everything. The whole dynamics of the situation was now totally different. The small step that Benedict took was one of respect. He distanced himself just a bit so as not to intrude into Storms space or thoughts.

"What should we do?"

It was four simple words but they held a tremendous amount of meaning. An acceptance had occurred. Benedict had lost whatever remnants of doubt that he had been carrying. He stared at Storm, with his head just slightly tilted down, in wait for an answer. And as expected, Storm composed an answer that was succinct and effective. A chain of command had been established and it seemed like Benedict had waited six thousand years for it. It almost looked like he breathed a sigh of relief. The only thing that broke the spell was his constant glancing at Storm's left hand. It was as if he expected the hand to do something on its own.

Storm broke the spell by speaking. He took the role naturally without giving it a thought.

"Have you ever been sick where your body picks up a fever, you get aches, maybe you get vomiting?" The question was pointed at Benedict but both he and Uhr nodded.

"How long did it stay with you?"

At this question of duration of time Uhr couldn't control himself and he blurted an answer before Benedict could respond. "Two to Four days depending on the depth of the illness."

Storm nodded his head at this.

"This is a similar illness; the symptoms here are not nausea and temperature although they could be. The biggest symptom is wild imaginings of the mind and false visions. This illness should too run its course in a total of three or four days. But the serious symptoms we are seeing now should only last a day – maybe two. Some of the people may already be coming through it. The important thing we need to do is to keep them safe. Not allow them to hurt themselves, or each other."

He closed the distance between him and Benedict and put his right hand, fatherly on Benedict's shoulder, drawing him in closer.

"Send as many monks as you can down to the city. Their goal is to insure the people don't hurt themselves -or each other. Tell them to tie people up if need be and give them water if possible. Another day and the worst will have passed. Explain to the monks about the illness and the cause of it. And tell them to round up all the bread in the city – all of it. And make sure they don't eat any of it." Benedict nodded his head in a gesture of respect and obedience then turned and hurried off.

Storm pointed a finger at the skinny cook who was preoccupied in a lively yet friendly argument with his portly wife and redirected his attention at Uhr. "The gentleman mentioned that he had stopped in for some mead and that was the reason why he was late. Do you know who the mead maker in town is?"
"Yes, his name is Erich, but judging by the situation, if you have questions of him you may want to wait a couple of days. But the monastery has its own mead maker here. You could ask him."
"Excellent, yes. Our mead maker may be of some help. Let's first return for something to eat, the monks can handle the situation now that they know what is going on. We should eat then retire to bed. In the morning I would like to talk to the mead maker."

10. The Mead Maker's Lesson

Quote:"Beer is Proof Positive that God Loves us" - Benjamin Franklin

***

Storm just sat in the cafe and wondered about the potential change in his life. He sipped coffee and watched as people walked by. Toward midnight the intensity and number of the people seemed to grow. It was as if they had all been napping and were now coming out of their reverie and enjoying the evening. It felt like a dramatic change from his typical American life.

The pace just seemed so different. For him it was a mark of courage to be up early and start his day with a flourish. By evening it was time to hit the sack and recharge the batteries for the next day. Everything revolved around work and being "productive."

He debated whether he should just stay right there all night just in case she came back. But the excitement of the day was too much for him so he walked back to his hotel and retired with thoughts of her.

 He woke early, showered quick, and after making a call to his business partner to explain he would be unavailable that day he head directly back to the cafe with the hope of Arabella's return.

The day ground slowly in the heat and he drudged his way through it by trying various cold drinks and ordering small meals every couple of hours. The wait staff didn't seem to think anything abnormal about a man spending the day in a cafe. In America he would have been looked at as being odd.

By nightfall he had resolved to stay until the place closed -if it even closed. Maybe he had met her on an off schedule of hers. Maybe she, like most of the others, seemed to hibernate for a few hours in the early evening heat then came out late at night. As the darkness grew so did his anxiety. Maybe he would never see her again? How large was this city? He guessed it to be somewhere around two hundred thousand people. Could he find her? He spend the next several days following a very strict schedule where he would sleep three or four hours at the hotel, shower then return to the cafe.

After the first day he started roaming the area near the cafe always staying within eye-shot or returning back to it within no more than ten or fifteen minutes. His plan was to start walking ever growing circles and hitting all the likely spots she might be. And he would even start talking to people and asking about her. In the pit of his stomach he felt that maybe something was wrong. He sensed the signals she was giving and her turning and waving to him was unmistakable. She wanted to see him again. He could just tell. Well, he would find her no matter what or how long it would take. He couldn't know if anything would come of it but there are times in your life where you have to take an unexpected path just to be sure. Maybe it was just an infatuation with an exotic and pretty Spanish woman. Or maybe it was something more. There was only one way to find out and that was to see her again.

***

Uhr knocked on his door and entered without an invitation. "Come come now! The watch says it is time to start our day."

After shaking the sleep out of his eyes he played along with Uhr "And what time is it?" He could picture Uhr looking with glee on the watch he had given him.

"It is twelve minutes past the seven hour!" With that Uhr cackled in glee and Storm asked him to enter.
        "Good Morning."
Uhr was obviously in a good mood.
"I have already talked to the mead maker and he is expecting you. His room is near the kitchen so maybe we can spare a few minutes for breakfast?"
Storm nodded his head and quickly dressed.

Uhr lead him through a series of corridors and rooms and in a few minutes they entered the kitchen which was busy but quiet. The tables were filled with monks slowly eating breakfast in relative quiet. Off to the left Storm could hear kitchen noises coming from a pair of doors. Uhr lead him over and through the doors.

Inside was a food line. They grabbed some plates and made their way through the serving line.

When they entered back into the dining hall Storm could feel a difference in the quiet. There was no readily perceptible change in the sounds –he just felt like they were all aware of his presence. And though none of the monks looked his way he could tell they were all aware of him. He resisted the urge to hide his left hand under his tray.

They ate their breakfast quickly and all during the meal Storm fought the urge to switch his fork over to his right hand. The two of them finished their breakfast in the palpable quiet then returned their trays to the kitchen and walked out of the dining hall. The tension in the air released as they left. And Storm could hear a flurry of hurried whispers.

Uhr lead him to a short corridor and into a large room where the smell of fermenting beverages assaulted them.
"Erich my friend, here is the man we talked about."

With Uhr's introduction Storm extended his hand and Erich took it with a brief shake then waved an arm in a short motion as if to present his mead making operation.
Storm took the cue and looked around. It was a large room, rectangular in shape -about twenty feet long and ten feet across. Along the left wall were a row of covered wooden barrels and along the right wall a row of open barrels. In the middle of the room was a large wooden table with a variety of tools, implements, and containers. The smell of honey in the air was cloying.
He walked over to one of the open barrels along the right wall and peered into it. It was filled to within a few inches with a brown fluid and a thick layer of froth and impurities floating on the top. He grunted and turned his attention to Erich.

"Can I ask how you make the mead?"

Erich nodded his head and nervously walked over to one of the open barrels. He placed a hand on the side of it about three quarters up from the bottom.

"I fill it to here with water."

He shifted his hand to within a few inches of the top.

"Then I fill it to here with honey and stir it."

There was a long pause as Storm waited for Erich to continue but that appeared to be all and Erich just shrugged his shoulders.

"No yeast?"

The mans brow wrinkled in puzzlement.

"You mean like the baker uses?"

Storm nodded his head.

Erich responded in the negative and Storm paused for a moment.

"So you leave it open to the air for how long?"

"Until it starts to taste like mead, or about a month. Then I move it over to the other side and place a cover on it and let it set for a few more months. I have to wait a month. If I cover them too soon they rupture and spill all over the floor. The honey makes quite the sticky mess."

He seemed proud of knowing that. It seemed to Storm that it was something that the mead maker had figured out.

Storm Grunted at this but continued without commenting on the process.

"Do you have the materials to make another batch?"

When Erich nodded his head Storm continued. "Do you have any new barrels that have never been used?"

Erich shook his head. "No, but I can have one made for you. It will take a half a day.

"Good, do that. And once it is completed boil it in water for at least an hour." Erich's eyebrows raised. "Boil the whole barrel?" At that Storm nodded his head and explained.

"Did you ever think about how the honey actually transforms into mead?" Erich just looked down at his feet and Storm continued. "What happens when you plant seeds in the ground?" Erich looked up quickly as if proud to know an answer. "They grow into plants!"

"That's right and the same thing happens with mead. Except instead of using soil you are using honey and water. And many things can grow in this much like algae and seaweed grows in water. The seed that needs to be planted in the honey in order to make mead is yeast. And you don't add any yeast but your workroom here is very close to the kitchen so there is plenty of yeast in the air."

He paused for a moment to let the idea sink in.

"You probably have some success with your mead making but I would guess that a good half of the batches are undrinkable." Erich nodded his head and again looked back down toward his feet.

"Let me help you to improve that. For now on whenever you start a new batch of mead you should thoroughly boil the barrel first. This will clean it out. Then once you have added the water and honey you should also add a cup of baker's yeast. It will grow and transform the honey into mead." Erich seemed to grasp the concept. "For the first month of a new batch keep it covered but slightly cracked so it can breathe. Then you can seal it up for a few more months. You should get much better mead this way. And you will get a much higher success rate."

At the prospect of making a better mead Erich seemed to brighten and rubbed his jaw in thought. Some wheels were set in motion and it was clear that he was going to do some experimenting with his batches now that he had a grasp of what was really happening.

"But there is something I need you to do for me. The new barrel you are making for me. I want you to make me a batch of special mead. This is something that you must not allow anyone to drink." He looked Erich carefully in the eyes to make sure that point was understood. Erich nodded his head gravely so Storm continued.

"You are going to make this special batch of mead in the same way you do the others, according to the new way I have shown you but there will be one change." Erich leaned forward in anticipation of a new revelation. "I want you to go down to the city and get some bread from the tables of people we know have been affected by the madness. Only take from the tables they were eating at." He stressed this last point with an explanation. "The people who are sick have been affected by tainted bread and we want some of that bread. It does us no good to get the regular bread. What I want you to do is gather up some of that tainted bread, grind it into powder then use it rather than baker's yeast in this one special batch." Erich scratched his head so Storm explained further.

I want to make a batch of mead that has the same poisons in it that was in the bread. It may prove useful to us in the future." At that Erich nodded in understanding. "Just make sure you nor anyone else taste it. And do not handle the bread with your hands. Carry them in a cloth, grind them in a cloth and after putting it in the mead barrel wash your hands thoroughly so you don't get sick."
Again Erich nodded as if he understood everything so Storm continued on. "They are in town right now starting a cleanup. You should go down there now so you can get some of the tainted bread before they get rid of it all." He paused for a moment then asked a question. "Do you understand everything? Is there anything not clear"? Erich didn't hesitate to answer proudly. "No, I understand everything. We are making a batch of poison that is disguised as mead. It is dangerous and I should never handle any of it with bare hands, nor drink any of it." Storm grunted in the satisfaction that Erich seemed to gain his balance and catch on quickly.

He turned to Uhr. "Things are done here. I need to continue on with my journey to Vorgard."
Uhr nodded.
"We should find Benedict. He has made plans for an escort."

They made their way back through the kitchen then wound their way through the many corridors eventually coming to a large room that felt to Storm like a war room. Lots of monks were bustling around the room and huddling over various tables. Uhr and Storm spotted Benedict poring over a large map rolled onto a table. He was talking with several others.

As if sensing their presence Benedict looked up and waved them over to his table. He shrugged off all greetings. "There has been considerable trouble brewing. Scouts have brought word of large groups of Grim roaming the forests. And we also have word of GegenHounds."

The room got noticeably quieter at the mention of the creatures. "There is something going on and it seems that forces are at work. I fear something is rallying these dark creatures." He paused and looked at Storm. It felt to Storm like he was consciously trying not to look at his left hand. "I think that your quest is central to the coming trouble so I have made arrangements to aid you in your journey to Vorgard. The land between here and there has become dangerous. I would like to give you an escort of men." It wasn't an order, it was more of a question and Storm noticed how Benedict went from being the leader of everyone in the room to second in command behind Storm.

"I would like to leave as soon as possible."
Tension around the table was broken and Benedict visibly relaxed. "Good. Preparations have been made and an escort of ten trained men is awaiting your word." He grabbed a rolled parchment off the table and handed it to Storm. "This is for the lady Petra." Storm glanced down at it. It was a durable parchment roll that was sealed with a red wax crest.
Benedict turned to Uhr.
"Could you escort him to the staging area?" Uhr nodded his head and Benedict put a hand on Storm's shoulder. "Good luck on your quest and should you have the need we are here."

With that the conversation was over and Benedict returned to the discussion with his men at the table.

Uhr and Storm wound their way to the outside of the stone structure.

"I want to accompany you." Uhr blurted out. "But I am no more than a hermit who is getting on in years. I will be returning to the solitude of my cabin once my strength has returned."

He paused as if giving Storm a chance to speak. Neither of them realized it but the import of the conversation had brought them to a stop. When Storm said nothing Uhr continued. "Nevertheless I am deeply grateful for the gifts you have given me. I have much to do now, and a new direction to follow with many new things to make."

Storm clapped him on the back and gave him a quick hug. Then the two of them turned and continued their walk. In another few minutes they broke out into the morning sunlight.

They quietly crossed the stone surface to a stone building and entered. Storm's escort of soldiers were milling about inside. He assessed them. They weren't just monks. They were monks turned soldiers and they appeared just as comfortable in military gear as they were in monks robes.

One man separated himself from the group and approached.

"I am Stein, your second in command." He waved a hand at the group of soldier/monks. "Ten men, ready to go. We are packed for fast travel and armed for forest skirmishes. We have food enough for five days quick travel although we shouldn't need it all. We should be able to make stops and resupply along the way but we are prepared for any eventuality. We can go all the way to Vorgard without stopping anywhere if need be."

He pointed at one of the tables.

"There is equipment and supplies laid out for you. And the men are ready for your inspection if you so desire." Storm glanced at the men who all visibly straightened under his eye. He was surprised because there wasn't a sword among them. They all carried percussion weapons -maces and hammer. Most carried one at his belt. A few had big two handed hammers slung over their backs.

"No need for an inspection."

He walked over to the table and looked things over.

It was a complete and comprehensive setup for one man including light but durable clothing and a comfortable yet strong pair of boots. There was a variety of weapons including a mace and a hammer. It seemed that among the weapons he could choose which he wanted. He changed into the clothes and boots then hefted both the mace and the hammer. These were serious weapons but he had no training with them. So he focused on the swords and pleased with one of them he strapped it to his waist. He finished his transformation by selecting a dagger which he hung at his other hip. Finally, he lifted the rucksack onto his back and after adjusting the straps he turned to Stein. "Let's go."

11. The March to Vorgard

"All warfare is based on deception. Hence, when we are able to attack, we must seem unable; when using our forces, we must appear inactive; when we are near, we must make the enemy believe we are far away; when far away, we must make him believe we are near."
- Sun Tzu, The Art of War

There were no more formalities. The monk soldiers spent most of their lives either working the stone, practicing their arms, or meditating in silence. All of which were arts of silence. They didn't need to talk much and characteristic of every other group Storm has run into they seemed to be in sync with each other. Storm imagined their hearts were beating in the same rhythm and he wondered if his own heart had fallen into the rhythm.

Stein ordered them into a single file with Storm right in the middle – five in front of him and five behind. Stein himself was the man right in front of Storm.

The road to Vorgard passed right through the center of New Speyer so they made their way quickly down the stone finger then straight for town.

The town was reasonably quiet and monks were scurrying about. Things had calmed down quite a bit. Everything was starting to fall back into order. The next few days would be very interesting as the people came back to their senses and realization set in. Storm wondered what they would do to the bread maker and his sons once they found out what caused all of this.

They passed quickly through the small town and just before leaving Storm spotted Erich going from one building to another. He was carrying a satchel of what could only assumed was tainted bread. And in his hands was a piece of cloth. Storm considered this as the sounds of the city dimmed. The wheels were turning and he wondered just how much control he had over all of this – if any.

The band of eleven walked a solid military pace for the remainder of daylight stopping occasionally to survey the surrounding areas. The terrain east of Speyer, for the most part, was pasture and farmland and as the sun was getting closer to setting Storm spotted a small town nestled in between the hills up ahead. It was a solid days walk from Speyer to this town and it made sense. He imagined the whole of the route was very similar. This route was heavily traveled and it was advantageous to build a town, however small at every evenings stay. You could probably stay at a cozy little Inn every night across much of the land.

It was a tiny village with a dozen small buildings all huddled around one large building which looked to be an Inn. The soldiers spread out a little bit as they entered the town but Stein and another soldier stood close by Storm. Two soldiers head for the small open market directly across from the Inn. The other soldiers walked around the various buildings. Storm, Stein, and the third soldier stood in the center of town and waited. This little town had a nice market and there were vendors and people haggling over vegetables and other goods. The surrounding miles of land was probably full of farms and this was where they brought their goods. Everything looked normal and the residents didn't seem alarmed by their presence. They probably didn't know what had happened in Speyer. And maybe it wasn't strange to them that nobody had come from Speyer in the past few days.

Once all the soldiers returned with reports of "all safe" the group entered the Inn.

It was large and comfortable and pleasant smells of cooking food filled the air. It seemed like the place was well kept and well stocked. Along the left wall was a large bar and standing behind it what looked to be the Innkeeper. This was a trade route Inn and it showed. Scanning the room Storm saw a half dozen men scattered and eating meals at various tables.

The group filled two of the larger tables and once they had their rucksacks removed and were seated Stein went over and spoke to the Innkeeper then returned to his seat beside Storm.
He looked over the group carefully and said "No ale or mead for anyone. I want you all sharp. I have gotten us two rooms for the night." He looked directly at one of the other soldiers. An older one who seemed to have some battle experience. "Assess the situation upstairs, then choose rooms and bedding and set up a shift of guards. Always two guards on all night, I want one outside and one inside and they should overlap by checking on each other." The old soldier nodded his head and Storm knew it was done.

"In the morning we take breakfast here then are off." The end of his speech was punctuated by a serving woman who came out of the kitchen with a large tray of food. She placed it on one of the tables and started distributing the plates. While they started the meal the man Stein had nodded to called out names and defined the night watch.

Other than some talk about the specifics of the journey there was no conversation. Storm found it a bit unsettling. They were a stoic group.

As they finished their meals and their water they retired in pairs to their rooms upstairs.

While the monks settled into their rooms a lanky, awkward, and dark figure made its way slowly through the farmlands north of the little village. Wildlife quieted and no sounds were emitted from anything. It was as if a cold chill were blowing toward the little town. The figure was hooded and caped and in its hand was a sack. It made its way on awkward legs that moved with an uneven rhythm as if one were longer than the other or one stronger than the other.

It had been set that there would be two guards throughout the night in two hour shifts and on a peaceful night, with no hint or expectation of trouble, this would have been sufficient. This relaxation of caution was the first mistake. And often times one mistake is not insurmountable. But in this case there were two mistakes. The second of which was for the guards to separate. They positioned themselves so one was outside the Inn and one was inside the Inn. They walked their respective circuits diligently, one inside and one outside; and at certain intervals they would check on each other but the time between checks was too large and it was an opportunity that would be capitalized on.

The cloaked figure made its way slowly toward the Inn of the town. The night was very dark and very quiet and the hood over its face obscured things even more. The dark under the hood was so complete that it looked like it was simply one solid chunk of coal that absorbed any light that passed into it.

It walked itself on awkward legs to a dark corner of the market directly across from the Inn and it watched as the Monk-Soldier walked circuits around the building. It watched as the guard walked by the front of the Inn then disappeared around the right corner. In a few minutes it watched as the guard came back around the left side of the building to the front again.

It plucked at a string on the bag it carried, carefully opened it and reached inside. It pulled out its bony hand and lifted something out and up to its coal face. Something squirmed in his hand and the coal face purred at it. The squirming slowed and the cloaked figure bent over and placed it gently on the ground whispering word-like sounds to it. The thing, no larger than a man's fist, scampered on multiple legs over toward the Inn. It found a very dark spot near a stone that was against the wall of the Inn and settled in beside it.

The footfalls of the guard were very quiet as he made his circuit around the Inn. But on the unusually quiet night they could be heard as he again rounded the left side of the building and came to the front again. He didn't notice the thing huddled against a stone. If he would have looked at it it would have appeared to him like two stones side by side; One being a little darker than the other. As he passed and his back was to the thing it scampered out on awkward legs, hopped up onto the leg of his pants and climbed up his clothing to the exposed skin at the back of his neck. And before the guard could react it punctured him with a poison filled bite. The guard instantly crumpled to the ground.

Within a minute the guard raised his head then awkwardly climbed to his feet in a parody of how the spider-like creature had moved. He flexed his arms and legs then looked over at the figure hidden in a dark corner of the marketplace. The cloaked figure purred unhealthily then moved quietly out of the market and back to the way it had come into the town.

The guard continued his walking circuit around the Inn, at first on shaky and uncoordinated legs but after a few laps he had got the feel for how the body moves and he was walking in a good mimic of what he had been earlier doing. One of his laps was interrupted as he approached the door in the front of the Inn. It opened and a voice spoke through the darkness of the sill.

"Our replacements are here. We can retire to bed."

He stopped in his path and just stared at the man now leaning out the door.

"Come, come. Our shift has ended." He spoke a little louder this time and beckoned with a wave of his arms. Understanding slowly sunk in and the dazed guard walked to the door where the two of them retired upstairs to their beds as their replacements took over.

***

Storm had been getting anxious. It was three full days and about thirty cups of coffee later when he finally decided it was fruitless to just sit at the coffee shop. He started taking small walks around town each walk a little bit further than the previous. He really couldn't think of anything else to do but ever widen his circles as if he were casting a net, each cast being a bit further out than the previous. He was a good hour since returning to the cafe and he feared that his routes were starting to get random. But he heard something that he recognized. He stopped and turned slowly to his left.

Down a little side street he could hear the buzzing of a vibrant market place. There were a lot of things going on and it was all background except for one thing that rose above it in a staccato. It was the sharp remarks of a woman's voice and it was carrying itself above all the other sounds in the market. He couldn't really tell what was being said but he recognized the voice. His heart kicked into another gear along with his legs and he head down the side street.

It had to be Matilda. He could simply tell. She must be cussing at somebody. No doubt somebody had raised her ire and she was giving him a good tongue lashing.

He rounded a corner and there she was, somehow making herself appear to be the only thing, even though she was in a crowd. She was grasping a pair of sunglasses and jabbing them at a vendor while she no doubt gave him her opinion on them. It seemed to Storm that she really didn't care about the glasses, the quality, the price, or anything else. She simply enjoyed the whole process of quarreling.

He looked around, carefully surveying the market, in the hope that Arabella was here with her. Not finding her he relaxed and focused back on Matilda. There was no way he was going to lose her so he waited patiently while her tirade wound down. She and the shopkeeper had come to some sort of an agreement that she was totally right and he was totally wrong and that seemed to appease her but she decided she didn't want the glasses after all so she put them down on his cart an unceremoniously turned and walked away. She didn't make it three hurried steps when she bumped right into the unmovable shape of Storm. She looked up at him and opened her mouth. She was about to blast him for being foolish enough to stand in her way but recognition came to her and she paused and stepped back.

"Ahh, the American."

She stared right into him as if an apology were in order. All he could muster was a "Hi."

This seemed to be not what she expected so she paused and little wrinkles appeared on her forehead as she considered something. This gave him time to compose some kind of sentence that was longer than one syllable.

"Is Arabella here with you?"

She shook her head and something softened but the softening didn't make the wrinkles at her forehead disappear.

"She is home…. Sleeping…"

With that she stepped closer to him and looked even harder at him as if expecting a reaction.

It was as if she were carefully gauging how he would respond and he felt the weight of this as if it were a pivotal moment and he should choose his words carefully. But nothing would come.

For three days now he had gone over and over what he would say if he found Arabella. But his mind was a total blank because he never expected to literally run into Matilda. The silence continued and she just continued to stare until she came to a decision and broke the tension.

"Come, we go to her home."

A rush of anticipation hit Storm and he couldn't be sure but he felt that those few moments of absolute silence were really a pivotal moment in his life and if he had said something wrong his life would go down a very different path. He grinned at this and thought "Better to say nothing and be thought a fool, than to say something foolish and be known a fool." He chuckled and the two of them walked out of the market toward Arabella's home.

***

In the morning there was a big production; the final set of guards woke everyone up as the sun rose. They all quickly dressed, grabbed their weapons and made their way downstairs. Stein chose two men and gave them orders to walk around the town and make sure everything was safe for their departure. The rest of the group sat down at tables in anticipation of a quick breakfast. Noises from the kitchen indicated that breakfast was well underway.

They finished their meal in quiet and donning their packs they head out of town toward the east not realizing that something dark followed a full league behind.

They walked and the day passed quickly and without incident. They marched in single file as they had on previous days and only stopped for short rests to drink and eat. At the end of the day they made camp in a small clearing while something watched patiently from a short distance off.

Later that evening, in the middle of the night, while two guards roamed the perimeter of their little camp, one of the guards watched blankly as a figure slowly walked on awkward legs toward the sleeping encampment. The guard made no sound as the walking figure paused by a large tree and reached into its bag. It retrieved something and placed it on the ground. The guard continued his blank stare as he watched the creature scamper off in search of the other guard.

The group of travelers followed the same routine for the following two days and each night the bag opening, scurrying, and neck biting continued.

As the days passed an uneasy feeling grew in Storm. He didn't recognize it at first. It was something in the background. An off-balance kind of feeling because something was not right but the realization hadn't surfaced in him yet. On the fourth day out of the little town with the Inn things started to come together for him and he noticed the little things.

When had the group stopped walking in their disciplined single file? Why now did they walk in an almost hap-hazard manner? Why is it that nobody talked at all? True they were monks and they didn't talk much to begin with but this was totally wrong. They didn't talk at all. It was as if they were all having a conversation that he couldn't hear. It unnerved him and he started observing the individuals in the group as if hoping for a clue as to what was going on.

Early on the fourth day, when they had all stopped to eat and break their fast he approached Stein who was sitting on a rock. He broke the deafening silence not so much to get an answer but just to hear somebody say something. Things were starting to unnerve him and he thought it would be good to hear a voice in the thick woods.

"So, tomorrow is our fifth day from the little town. Are we on schedule? Will we be arriving in Vorgard tomorrow?"

Stein looked at him blankly and paused around some of his breakfast then spoke. It sounded to Storm like he had too much food in his mouth and it was distorting what Stein said.

"Yes, tomorrow Vorgard. But today we enter the labyrinth." He then turned his head back down to his food to indicate the conversation was over.

The awkward speech just heightened Storm's sense of alarm. "The labyrinth? Why hadn't they mentioned anything about a labyrinth before? This was just getting very strange." He found himself wishing the trip could be over and they could be in Vorgard. He dropped the attempt at further conversation and walked away wondering about the labyrinth.

12. The Unmaker

Sometimes paranoia's just having all the facts.
-William S. Burroughs

By mid-afternoon everything had turned dark and ominous for Storm. The group did not stop at all for any reason. They continued on with their march at what felt to Storm like a faster and faster pace. It was as if he, and they, were being impelled toward something. And this "something" was very unsettling. All through the day the monks would cast glances at him as if to check that he hadn't gone astray.

The feeling of comfort was totally gone and now he felt like a prisoner – he just couldn't see the walls. But he had the feeling that if he strayed off the path they were cutting that he would face some kind of a wrath.

In the early hours of the day he had just brushed the feeling off as some kind of paranoia. But now, as the day had unfolded he was sure that something was going on -something that he was very much fearful of. He thought about what he could do. Could he somehow separate from this group and make his own way to Vorgard? That was very doubtful. He had no idea where he was. And he was no longer sure that they were even headed in the right direction. If he tried to escape from the group would that do him any good? There were ten of them and they were all in fighting shape.

If they wanted to kill him they would have no doubt done it already. So they had other things in mind. There was another goal. And how could he have misjudged the monks this much. Early on in this trek he felt good about them and about what they were doing. What happened to change all of that? How did this turn of circumstances come about?

The questions remained unanswered. They were, at the moment, unanswerable. Maybe he would get answers when they arrived at their destination, which was something called the labyrinth. If he could trust that at all.

They never stopped to rest during the remainder of the afternoon. He could feel a sense of anticipation in them. Their pace, if anything, had accelerated as the hours pushed on until they abruptly stopped in a dense patch of forest.

Before them, on the ground, were a pair of thick granite slabs about six feet apart. And between the slabs was a dark corridor leading into the ground. The slabs and corridor looked very much like the one that Storm had gone down into to witness the testing of Ardan. Maybe there were a whole series of these tunnels all over the land. It could be an enormous series of tunnels and underground caves. And they could all be interconnected. Or maybe this was the same exact one they had entered. For all he knew they had walked all the way back to where he first came into this world.

One of the monks unrolled a bundle of torches, lit them all up, then distributed them among the group. He didn't give one to Storm who didn't even bother to ask for one. He was already in the dark mentally, might as well make the metaphor real.
They stepped right down into the stairs between the granite slabs and continued their walk – five of them ahead of Storm and five of them behind.

Stein had said they would enter a labyrinth but this didn't seem like much of a labyrinth. As far as he could tell it was one very straight and very long corridor. The only perceptible change in anything about it was the slow slope downward.

They marched for an undetermined length of time. It might have been several hours and the only thing that changed was their torches as they burned out and lit new ones. Something didn't feel right about this corridor but Storm just couldn't perceive anything except the redundancy of the walls and the slow pitch downward.

A change came into the air as they cycled through another couple of hours and another series of torches. The torches started a slight flickering and there was a perceptible motion in the air as if something changed up ahead. Maybe the corridor was ending and they were coming back out into the forest.

The light from the torches only lit up a small area around them and this was particularly constrained in the corridor so he couldn't see far ahead and it was a surprise to him when the group of them walked right out of it and into a dark open space. The walls of the corridor stopped but the stone floor continued out into the darkness as if some kind of six foot wide bridge extending on forward. He looked over the edge and saw nothing but darkness and looking up he saw the same thing. They could be in an enormous cavern so large that the torchlight couldn't reach the sides of it. The distance down could be enormous too and it felt like if he fell off the side he would fall into the darkness forever.

They continued their marching and Storm continued his pace. He feared that if he slowed down the monk behind him would push him right off the edge. He looked forward and it seemed as if he could see a vague metallic glimmer of something. He locked his eyes on this to keep his mind off the blackness below him and as they got closer something took shape.

It was a giant sword embedded right into the stone bridge they walked on. It was as if a giant had plunged his sword, blade first, right into the stone. And plunged it in deep. Only the last six feet or so of the blade was above the surface of the stone and shock registered with Storm as he realized what the sword was. It was Varheit, the sword that talked. The very sword that he saw being used by Anfang at his Testing. It was exactly the same, with the open mouth and rectangular hole at the base of the blade. The only difference with this sword being its enormous size. And it stood right in their path. The bottom part of the hole in the blade was exactly even with the surface of the stone bridge they walked on and it formed a sort of passage that they would have to walk through if they were to proceed.

They grouped up near the mouth of the sword and it seemed to Storm that they were hesitant to walk through. There was a hint of a nervous energy about them. He couldn't decipher what exactly it was that was giving them pause and he looked down to the closed eyes of Varheit but found no clue there.

Just as things seemed to be working to some sort of quiet conflict Stein turned to him and spoke through a mouth full of marbles "We take the path to the left."

Looking through the mouth of the sword he could see that the path branched off in a fork one path going left and the other going right. And each path was half the width of their original path. And with that they each took a step and passed through the mouth of the sword. Their nervousness had an effect on the marching order and he was almost left behind but one last monk motioned for him to pass through first and with that he was through.

The splitting and narrowing of the path made the walk more intense and it seemed like he could easily just barrel himself forward with a scream and waving of his arms and force the whole bunch of the stoic monks right off the edge and into the darkness. Maybe this is why they were hesitant to pass through.

They walked the path leading down to the left. And at the end of it, some fifty yards ahead, he could see in the dim torch light a door. He looked over to the other path; the path they had not taken and could see that it too ended at a door.

One of the monks opened the door and they all entered, single file, into a brightly lit gothic cathedral. That was the best way Storm could describe it. It was the biggest cathedral ever built, by far, and it had all the traditional features of a gothic cathedral. They extinguished their torches and replaced them into their packs.

They had entered through a small door that was placed exactly where there should be two large double doors to allow congregants to enter for Sunday service. A broad expanse of marble flooring lead down the length of the cathedral to a raised area on the other end and on the left and right each was a row of large marble columns that lead from where they were to the raised area on the other end. Directly adjacent and parallel to the rows of columns were rows of wooden pews filled with kneeling figures. This whole structure was built to impress and bring the person, and the eye, to the raised platform at the far end. And on that raised platform was a seated man. The seat was more of a throne. It was very large and richly adorned. Made of thickly hewn wood, polished with fine oil and sculpted by a master craftsman.

The group of them didn't move down the length of the corridor. Nor did they have to move. The impact of the place was a bit overwhelming.

The figure that was seated at the far end of the cathedral let out a bellow of a yell, jumped out of his chair and raced in long strides toward them; all the while he was shouting profanities and incoherencies. Storm saw that the figures feet were not human. They looked like the split hooves of an ox. And as the figure raced toward them the hooves made an uncomfortable clicking noise on the marble floor of the cathedral.

Storm watched in mesmerized awe as the figure quickly approached them. He was an extraordinarily handsome man with a long mane of golden hair and he was very tall and muscular. Storm estimated him to be about six feet eight inches and every inch of it was handsome muscle. But the filth that poured from his mouth betrayed the beauty of his body.

"YOU HAVE MADE ME WAIT TOO LONG."

It was such a loud remark that it was a scream and Storm could see the anger in the man's body. It was so palpable that he could almost feel a heat emanating from the man.
Not a single one of them spoke. The anger was as impenetrable as steel armor. The man, as he approached them, taking his last running steps and slowing to a walk continued with his tirade, his hooves clicking on the marble.

"THERE WAS NO NEED FOR SLEEP... OR FOR FOOD."
THESE THINGS DELAYED YOU."

He waved his long and muscular arms in the air and continued on with his rant.

"I SHALL NOT BE MADE TO WAIT."

The veins on his neck and face bulged and he trembled with his anger.
He paused for a moment, took a deep breath and then with a lightning like swipe of his hands he grabbed the nearest monk by the head, pulled the man in close and spoke in a normal voice:
"I shall not be made to wait."

He slowly twisted the man's head until it faced backward, then continued to twist until the man's neck snapped, and continued on until it faced forward again. The man's body went limp but the stone hewn arms of the raving man held it upright and continued to twist. He brought the head around for another full revolution before the muscles, skin and bone could take no more and with a tearing the head separated itself from the body and the body fell to the marble floor. Blood poured from it onto the floor in a beating rhythm. The heart was still pumping and it was flushing the blood from the body and onto the cold marble.

The Raver knelt down in the pool of blood and lifted the head over his own head then with a quick and brutal motion he brought it down and smashed it onto the marble floor. The skull cracked and distorted. And something changed in the Raver. He bowed his head, still holding the crushed skull against the marble floor, and he breathed deep. The scene was one of pure horror and Storm shut off a part of himself so he could continue to look. The kneeling man, raving with madness, just breathing, while kneeling in a slowly expanding pool of blood that pulsed in little ripples as the heart let out its last beats.

The group of remaining men stood quietly as the Raver composed himself and stood up. And as he came to his full height he brought his eyes to bear on Storm. It was a horrible few moments for Storm. He saw madness, hatred, anger, and so much more in those eyes. They burned with very bad things.
A large-toothed smile came to the face and he spoke directly to Storm.

"It takes a few moments but it happens."
Storm had no idea what he was talking about.

The smiling and the talking continued. "It takes a few moments for the spirit to gather itself."
He pointed at the bloodless and headless corpse lying in its own blood on the beautiful floor.
"And there he goes." The Raver slowly moved his arm in an arcing circle beginning at the corpse and ending at the ceiling of the cathedral."

"Did you know that if you kill a man his spirit must do your bidding? It becomes yours. And will remain so until you release it. And I never release. I am the one who doesn't release. I have unmade this man and he is now mine."

The large tooth smile broadened and the words and the smile made the hairs on Storms arms raise up in fear.

Storm looked at the headless body and the shock continued as the man's back twitched under his tunic. It was as if the muscles were still trying to flex. But it wasn't that. Something under the man's shirt was moving. He continued to watch in horror as a black spider-like creature crawled out from the collar of the shirt and scampered past the big toothed killer and down the length of marble flooring toward the raised dais on the other end.
Why hadn't he noticed that? What was that thing? Some kind of parasite?
With the large mouth smile still staring at him he looked at the monk nearest him and he could see a visible lump on the mans back. Why had he never noticed that during all their journey? He had spent a lot of time walking right behind one or another of them yet he never noticed the unusual hump that he now assumed all of them had.
This explained a lot. The thing was some kind of parasite. This explained why they had changed. They were, for lack of a better word, possessed. His whole mindset about the betrayal of the monks changed. They didn't betray him.
He wondered if the monk that was decapitated had felt any pain.

His attention turned back to the raving man and he felt as if the man were reading his thoughts. It was as if the man paused to allow him to think. The toothed smile widened and uttered a word.

"Umfolg"

The raving man turned and walked down the red of the marble floor toward the place he had been seated. The Group followed.

"Umfolg" Storm thought to himself. That was another word from his and Arabella's secret language. It meant "Follow me." And it felt very strange to Storm because he started "following" without even thinking about it. It was as if the word compelled him to follow; as if the word could not be denied. He stepped right through the blood and could feel the sick warmth of it. And he followed the crimson footprints that the monks left as they walked through and beyond it.

As they approached "the throne" members of the kneeling congregation hissed as they passed. and looking toward the raised dais Storm could see a dread figure standing at it's side. It was the awkward-walking and mysterious figure that had tried to penetrate his head while battling in the Gether. It still carried the creepy wiggling bag and he still couldn't see inside the darkness of it's cowl but he had the distinct impression that whatever was in there was sickly smiling.

The angry man set himself gently down into his throne and said "Halden" which meant "Stop." And on cue they all stopped walking. The loss of control of his own muscles was a deeply disturbing thing for Storm and once he had regained control he flexed his fists both in a gesture of rebellion and to verify he once again had control.

They all stood on the marble floor just before the raised dais so they were a good foot lower than the seated figure. It was no doubt a tactical gesture meant to keep them in an inferior position even though it wasn't needed. The verbal commands and the sheer height of the Raver were sufficient. But it needed more.

The Raver pierced Storm directly with a glare and spoke:
"I know why you are here."

This caught Storm off guard and he had very much hoped the man hadn't noticed him at all but now that he addressed Storm directly there was no way of hiding. So he replied in a cracked voice:
"Good to hear that somebody knows why I am here. It would be great if you could enlighten me because I haven't a clue."

This enraged the Raver and he jumped off his throne and launched himself at the nearest monk. He grabbed the monks head and paused. He was contemplating whether or not to screw this man's head off like he had done with the other. He opted this time not to. Instead he took a deep breath which seemed to calm the veins on his face and neck, turned and sat back down on his throne.
"You will not patronize me."
Storm nodded his head in agreement. The inference here was that heads would literally roll if he patronized the Raver.

"Why are you here?"

"That was a quick switch" Storm thought to himself. The first question must have been a bluff. Or was it?

"I don't know why I am here. I don't exactly know how I got here, or even where "here" is. This is all strange to me."

"I will not allow him the free reign to do what he pleases." The Raver lifted an arm and pointed off to his left. Storm looked over to where the point lead but he only saw the wall of the cathedral past a pew of kneeling figures.

Then the man did something so totally unexpected it shocked Storm almost as much as the decapitation. The man leaned his head down onto the arm of the throne and started chewing on it. It was a gesture of uncontrollable anger and seeing that Storm could see that all along the thick wood of the chair, the back, the arms, and even the legs there were chew marks. This Raver was like a child -A six foot eight, strongly muscled child. He was constantly on the verge of losing control. A child that, on a whim, could tear a man's head off with just the strength of his hands and forearms.

Once he had satisfied himself he turned to the hooded figure. "Look into him and tell me what you see."
The hooded figure took a slow step backward and spoke. It was an unhealthy grinding sound as if the mouth was rotted.
"He is closed to me. I can see nothing."

The rage hit the Raver in another wave and he picked up his throne, which being hewn from solid wood must have easily weighed two hundred pounds, and he hurled it at the wall where he had previously pointed.

It sailed across the width of the cathedral, over the heads of the parishioners and crashed against the stone of the wall then fell to the floor unbroken.

The Raver pointed at the point of impact on the wall. "I will not be bested." There is always a way and I will find it." He turned to the thin hooded creature. "Release the Urchne on him."

The hooded figure chattered what Storm imagined to be skeletal teeth, and reached into its bag.

He pulled his hand out slowly and revealed a black spider. It looked to be the same one that had disconnected itself from the decapitated monk.

The hooded figure cooed and placed it on the floor. And it scampered toward Storm and the group of monks. He simply stood in frozen horror as its little clicking appendages moved it toward him.

It didn't make a beeline toward him though. It zig-zagged back and forth as if it were searching for him. It circled the group and then circled again. It then hurried back across the floor to the hooded creature who picked it up and with a coo placed it back in the bag. The hood turned to the man on the throne "It cannot see him. He is not here."

This enraged the Raver.

"I WILL NOT BE DENIED. I WILL KNOW. YOU WILL NOT BEST ME."

Again the Raver pointed at a spot on the cathedral wall then turned to Storm. I will know your plot or I will watch your spirit float up to the ceiling." The venom in the statement was sickening.

Things were quickly escalating. As if they couldn't get worse? He thought to himself.

First the lunatic bluffed him, second he asked a question. Then came the request to look into him by the thin being, which was denied. Then came the attempt at possession by the spider. Each step was a deeper penetration. Lastly came the threat. Storm wondered what would be next? Would the Raver chew on him as if he were nothing more than a piece of furniture?

The raised dais seemed different now that there was no throne on it. It was just the Raver and the thin hooded creature. The Raver stared at him and smiled as if something occurred to him. Storm braced himself for the escalation. This could not be good.
"You will not leave this room alive." I will watch your spirit float and you will do my bidding." The Raver paused and stated deeper. "This may not be enough to get from you the plot that you and he have put against me. But… If you do not reveal it, your death will stop it."

Again the Raver paused and smiled.

"It is a foolish thing to keep sealed from me what I wish. And the threat of your own harm might not be enough to get you to tell me what I need to know. But maybe you will do it for another?"

This was not going to a good place. It was as if everything were racing toward a very bad conclusion.

The Raver placed his hands on his face and turned his back to Storm and the possessed monks.

He waved his arms and the air in the center of the dais shimmered. Smoke materialized and the air slowly solidified. Storm watched on as the smoke formed the shape of a bed. It was a large and simple bed made out of wood and covered with quilts. Laying in the bed was a figure.

As the smoke solidified the image solidified and became almost real and he strained to see who it was that was in the bed. Horror spiked at his chest and his heart kicked into a furious race as he recognized Arabella. There she was lying in the bed.

The Raver chuckled. "She sleeps."

Storm grit his teeth. The escalation was turning out to be a very difficult thing. This is what the Raver meant by not doing something for himself but doing it for somebody else."

"Yes, I know exactly where she is. She will be easily found." The Raver's grin broadened in anticipated victory.

A wave of emotions hit Storm. There she was, so beautiful, sleeping, and unaware of what was going on. And there was nothing he could do. It was the incident in the sinking car all over again. He wanted to cry, he wanted to scream. He wanted to grab the Raver by the throat and throttle him until he was dead. But most of all he wanted to be reunited with Arabella, or at least to know that she was okay.

"I don't know why I am here."

He pointed at the spot on the wall where the Raver kept pointing to and where he had hurled the throne. "I don't know this 'he' you keep talking about. I don't know anything." It was a confession of helplessness. He felt that if he did know something, anything at all, he would gladly tell it to the lunatic in order to protect Arabella. This was of course what the Raver desired and he would have gladly provided it. But he didn't know anything and his heart sunk at the thought of what would come next.

The Raver clenched his fists and turned his face up to the ceiling of the cathedral and bellowed in anger. Storm could feel the congregation cower in fear.

Then you shall die and you shall do my bidding." He pointed nonchalantly at Arabella. "And the same will come to her." Then he shouted loud enough for the whole of the congregation to hear: "KILL HIM."

As fast as lightning, with the reflexes of trained soldiers the monks all turned on him and the closest two grabbed him and forced him to the ground. And the congregation, composed of humans, non humans, and creatures of all kinds rushed toward him. And in a moment the group was a mass of flesh pressing down upon him. Several monks held him down while Stein lifted his hammer to deal the finishing blow. It all happened so fast that Storm didn't even have time to unsheathe his sword. He couldn't move and could only watch the arm that would bring a hammer down on his skull.

And as Stein's arm raised high to deal the killing blow a woman's voice penetrated the scene. It was Arabella. She sat up in her bed, and even though she wasn't physically there she still was there enough to speak and have it be heard. She pronounced in a loud voice a few words from their language:

"Sei frie Ihr Kettchen."

It meant "Be free of your chains." And it was directly for the monks who were being controlled by the spider-like Urchne on their backs. And with the same lightning reflexes as they had attacked and subdued Storm they now turned to his defense. They were free of the control of the Urchne. Stein shouted commands quickly and the group of monks pulled Storm up and formed a circle around him. They hacked and hammered with military precision and rock hardened muscles at the throng of worshippers that swept at them in waves. Their release from their bondage formed a pandemonium that caught the congregation by surprise and a layer of them fell dead before any of them could react.

In their tightly packed formation they slowly made their way toward the door they had entered through. Storm looked over the melee toward the dais and watched as the image of Arabella sitting up in the bed slowly shimmered. He could see a look in her eye. She was beckoning him. She needed him to come to her. The Raver stood there on the dais with it's arms outstretched; a look of surprise across its face.

It was fairly easy going as far as combat was concerned they were well armed, and well trained men, facing a mass of weaponless foes. The force of them pressing against them in a suicidal attempt to break the defense was challenging but nothing their iron couldn't handle. It was less than a minute later that the throng of foes had thinned and Storm and the monks were standing at the door they had entered. As one of the monks reached for the handle Storm shouted out. "NO." He turned and pointed at the dais where Arabella still sat in her bed and where the Raver still stood, shaking in uncontrolled anger. Storm wanted to get to her. He didn't want to leave.
The monks understood with just his one word and his point. They all turned and made their way quickly toward the dais at the other end of the cathedral.

The going was easy and they sprinted. Storm flushed and couldn't take his eyes off her. She sat there watching. He shouted to her "Gubra Da Lee." She visibly swallowed and tried to raise her arms to him. There was a yearning in her half-real and half-shimmering presence.

The Raver came out his reverie. The words that Storm shouted had stunned him. Fear came over his face and he looked over to the broken remains of his throne. It was as if he were looking for something to gnaw on. But it gained some control and lifted his arms out to his sides then clapped them together in a thunderous clap that shook the cathedral and sprung Storm and the monks off their feet. It was as if someone ignited a bomb in the chamber.
The last thing Storm heard before the darkness came was the clicking of the ravers feet. It sounded like the Raver took two running steps in a click-click sound then disappeared.

At a time later Storm awoke. He was lying on the floor and looking up at the beams of the cathedral ceiling. He rolled his head to the side and saw the other monks were coming awake too. It was as if a percussion grenade had gone off and it knocked them all unconscious. He moved his body and twisted to look over at the dais. The shimmering apparition of the bed and Arabella was gone. But so was the Raver. It set off a clap then made its escape.

The quiet was a strange counterpoint to the earlier mayhem inside the cathedral. There was no more pandemonium but the stench of death was in the air and a thin layer of fog covered the floor of the cathedral.

Storm looked around. He and the monk warriors had been unconscious for an indeterminate amount of time. Why hadn't the remaining throng, and the Raver, simply killed them -slit all their throats while they were out? It was an uncomfortable and riddling thought. Instead the Raver decided to leave. And it took the throng of worshippers with it.

As the monks revived themselves they removed their tunics and started pulling the dead creatures off each others backs. Storm walked around the cathedral, making his way to the now empty dais. There really was nothing to be done. And there was no door in that end of the large room. Within a few minutes they had all gathered near the only door– the entrance they had come in.

Storm collected his breath and his thoughts. He didn't do anything but everything went his way. It was as if everything the Raver did worked against itself. And it was the Raver that summoned the apparition of Arabella. And that was a mistake on its part because it was her apparition that saved them all.

This gave him pause to think about his own actions. He would have to be more careful about the things that he did. He did not want to make decisions that would be his own undoing.

That all raced through his mind then he settled on one very important point. Arabella was alive and she was here somewhere. There was some hope. He had been floating through this world almost directionless. He was just going where forces took him. But now he had a very distinct goal. He had to find her. She needed him. And he had to find her before the Raver got to her; if it hadn't already done so.

***

Storm and Matilda didn't walk very far when they stopped in front of a blue door in a beautiful white painted building. The whole street was either large buildings plastered together or placed very close together. The only thing that distinguished one residence from the other was the placement of doors. At least that's what he figured. He also figured it was rather ironic that he had walked either up or down this very street a few times as he made his circles in search of Arabella. He looked up at the windows on the second floor. They too were trimmed in blue just like the door. He wondered if one of those windows was her bedroom.

Matilda knocked and they waited.

A beautiful woman in her late forties opened the door and smiled at Matilda. The resemblance to Arabella was striking and this was no doubt her mother. Matilda rattled off a series of sentences in Spanish and the woman listened carefully, nodded her head a few times then looked closely at Storm as if examining him. He wondered what stance Matilda conveyed. This first introduction was important and it could go very badly for him if Matilda painted him as a crazy American.

The woman opened the door wider and with an arm gesture waved for them to enter.

The inside of the home was warm and comfortable. He loved the stucco walls that all these Spanish homes were made of. It was so much more comfortable than the sheet-rock of American homes.

Just to the right was a staircase that lead up to the second floor and Storm glanced that way hoping Arabella would come walking down.

Arabella's mother said something to Storm in Spanish and smiled – Matilda translated. "We should go out to the garden. She will make us some tea."

Matilda started forward and Storm followed. They crossed through a couple of rooms and out a back door into a small garden with a table and chairs. They sat and waited. Matilda was quiet and this seemed to Storm to be a bit out of character for her.

When Arabella's mother joined them she had a tray with tea and bread. She placed it on the table and sat down.

Matilda made a formal introduction introducing the woman as Camilla. The three of them had a conversation that lasted well over an hour and throughout the whole conversation they never spoke of Arabella until the very end. Storm figured it was an interview of sorts. They spoke about him, about his job and about various aspects of his life and his family. He learned that Camilla was not Spanish, even though with the dark hair she definitely looked Spanish. She was German. She had come to Spain in her early twenties to teach German to the locals, met her husband here, who was Spanish, settled down and had Arabella.

He was polite and cautious. He was hoping to make a good first impression, assuming he would even get the chance for a second impression. Eventually he broached the subject of Arabella.
"Is Arabella Home?"
Camilla shot a quick look at Matilda and Matilda answered for her.

"Yes, she is here."

It seemed a bit odd to Storm that she was here but hadn't made an appearance.
He raised his eyebrows in hopes of a little bit more information.

"She is upstairs sleeping."

"Oh, okay." was all he could say. It seemed a bit odd that she was sleeping in the late afternoon but who knew. It could be for any number of reasons. Maybe she worked a night shift job.

Matilda looked to Camilla. It was as if she were searching for something, permission or something more from the woman. Camilla nodded her head and Matilda turned back to Storm.

"She is not well. She sleeps very much."

This brought a lump to his throat. She was sick. That explained why she was sleeping in the late afternoon. The poor thing. In a small way it raised his spirit. At least she wasn't avoiding him.

"I am sorry to hear that she is sick. Is there anything that I can do?

I don't want to bother her or burden her mother but if there is anything I can do to help just name it. I would be glad to help." How ill is she? The flu? Does she have a fever? Has she seen a doctor?"

Matilda quickly responded to all the questions: "No, no." It is not that. I don't know the words in English. She is sick. She sleeps very much."

Hmm... he thought to himself. The language barrier could be baffling.

From there the conversation became awkward. He wanted to talk more about Arabella. If he couldn't see her, and he clearly couldn't, he at least wanted to know more about her. It was almost as if a panic was setting in. He would hate for the language barrier to be something that brought everything crumbling down. He didn't want to say goodbye and thanks for the tea with the expectation that he should never come back again. It made him a bit edgy.

They were finishing up their tea and it seemed like the "interview" was coming to a close so he started to blurt.
"Could I come back and see her maybe in a day or two? When she is feeling better?

Matilda looked at Camilla who shook her head. He knew what that meant but Matilda voiced it anyway.
"No, that is not a good idea."
He was crest-fallen. His mouth turned down and his shoulders slumped just a little bit. But the ladies picked up on his body language and Camilla spoke to Matilda then motioned with her hands for them to get up from the table.
They stood up and started walking back through the house and to the front door. Just as she grasped the door handle Matilda spoke:
"You not understand well. It is not that you cannot come back to see Arabella. We don't know when she will be better. It is best that you wait."

Something had definitely changed in Matilda. It seemed that she was coming around to his side. She could see that he was earnest in his intentions and that he was truly hurt at the possibility of not seeing Arabella again.

"When she is better. I will call you. You have telephone number at hotel?

This lifted his spirits significantly. He grabbed his wallet and rifled through it for the hotel's business card. He handed it to her and she nodded in recognition of the hotel. "I am in room 304." She nodded her head and repeated the room number.

Things seemed to at least end reasonably well and he thanked Camilla for the tea and for her hospitality and then he and Matilda exited the door.

After the door closed behind them Matilda reiterated the situation for him "When Arabella is awake I will call you. Room 304." She held out the business card and looked at it then smiled.

At that they parted and she rushed off but he just stood there a moment and looked back up at the blue framed windows hoping to get a glance of Arabella.

13. Arabella's Dream

"The City sleeps and the country sleeps, the living sleep for their time, the dead sleep for their time, the old husband sleeps by his wife and the young husband sleeps by his wife; and these tend inward to me, and I tend outward to them, and such as it is to be of these more or less I am, and of these one and all I weave the song of myself."
–Walt Whitman

This last trip to the other world was different for Arabella. She didn't fall asleep and cross over in the way she usually did. She didn't really know how she crossed over. The last thing she remembered was the horrible accident where the car was plunged into the river. She was counting the seconds between breaths that Storm breathed into her and everything went black. She woke up in her bed in the convent as if she had simply fallen asleep and crossed over like all the other times she had done it.

But the circumstances of this trip were much different. And it had now been more than a month that she was still in this world and she wondered if she had died in that world and would never return to it and to Storm.

Every evening she retired to bed hoping to wake up in her bedroom with Storm sleeping beside her. Even a small part of her wished it would even be okay if she woke up in the submerged car. At least she would be with him.

It all began for Arabella around the age of five. Her mother tucked her into bed one night and shortly thereafter she woke up under a tree in a patch of sweet smelling grass. She was in the courtyard of a convent in the city of Vorgard. She didn't know this at first but as time went on she would come to learn these things and many other things.

The women of the convent took her in and cared for her. And they gave her a new name. They named her Petra which in the old language means one who could see clearly. As she grew into womanhood she became known as the Lady Petra -the oracle who never took a man. It was rumored that if she took a man she would lose the powers of the oracle. She let the rumors say what they would but she knew it to be not true for she did have a man. Just not in this world.

She never was sure which world was real and which was not and she never spoke of that other world to her family. But in that other world she often spoke of her other life -her life in Spain.

She traveled back and forth between these two worlds when she slept. In one world when she fell asleep she would often, although not always, wake up in the other world. And sometimes she would simply sleep. And although her family and friends considered her to be afflicted with something because she slept so much she didn't consider it so. She may have appeared to be asleep in one world but she was often awake in another. So she split her time between two worlds and she was happy. Her life was rich with many different experiences. And as she grew up in one world she also grew up in the other. And in each world she had people who loved her and who cared for her while she slept.

It was an unpredictable gift. For some stretches of time she would be asleep in Spain for twenty or more hours a day which allowed her to spend much time with the people she loved in that other world. And this could last for months.

And sometimes she would sleep a scant six or seven hours a night which meant she didn't see that other world for months at a time.

She didn't lament any of this; she simply accepted it, enjoyed it, and traveled back and forth as it happened. Until things started going dark in the other world and evil powers began exerting their force on it. It was in these recent times she fretted over the world and the people she loved and each time she went to bed she hoped she could return to that world to help.

In that other world, in the city of Vorgard, she began as just a lost child but she soon became something more. Her gift for sleep and dream allowed her to walk between two different worlds but it also gave her the ability to do something more. It allowed her to open up the Gether and this ability elevated her from just another person to an oracle. By opening up the Gether to the people she changed their world.

She spent her days in that world roaming the convent, enjoying the world, the gardens, the food, the people, but she rarely left the grounds and she never took a man– never even considered entertaining a man. She loved Storm and always missed him while she was there.

It was this missing that brought her thoughts to him as trouble cast a shadow over the world. She often considered talking to him about that other world and she wondered at the gift of his left hand and if it meant anything. But she never did. Instead her thoughts began to turn to the possibility that she could bring him into this world much as she had brought this world into the Gether.

This last time she had come to the world –seemingly to stay, the convent was in quite an uproar and they were all very glad to see her return. Tales of wild and evil creatures lurking the countryside were spreading and the Gether had become a place that was unsafe. People were going into it and being killed or returning with tales of twisted happenings and vile creatures attacking.
The balance of everything was upset and nobody knew what to do. They all looked to her, as the oracle, to guide them. But she really didn't know what to do.

On the first evening of her return, after the accident in the water, she organized a trip into the Gether which upset many of the other women. It was no longer safe to travel into it. People were dying. But she insisted that she had to look if she were to find out what was going wrong.

Barmen grunted at the news and organized a group of one hundred soldiers to act as her escort. The hundred soldiers, Arabella, and her circle of nine others gathered in the meeting hall and lay down upon mats.

She awoke, in the Gether, in a dense fog. She raised her hand and could make out it's outline vaguely through the milky white of the fog. She waved her arms and whispered some words and the fog slowly retreated away from her. In a few moments it had retreated far enough to reveal the worried faces of the nine and the soldiers. Barmen was visibly relieved; having thought he might have lost her. He moved closer to her in a conscious effort to make his body a shield of hers.

Nobody spoke; the nine watched her while the soldiers spread out in a uniform circle around them as the fog continued to retreat in an ever broadening circle. They were standing on a gently rolling grassy hill as was often the case with a trip into the Gether. But the grass was not its normal vibrant green. A pall had settled on it and its vibrancy was lost. It was still green but it didn't have that vibrant green dream-like vividness. It was almost like normal real-world grass.

She looked them all over and smiled at the rhythm all one hundred and ten hearts made.

"The best way to see what is happening, or not happening in this land, is to see the land." She raised her arms slowly and the grass beneath her and the nine changed. It elevated several inches in a shape of the land. It was a detailed re-creation of the land –a map about twenty yards in size.

It appeared to be a perfect reproduction of the land. It included rivers, mountains, grasslands, and everything else. It was a beautiful little diorama of sorts and it had a palpable aliveness to it. They all tread very carefully on it so as not to hurt or damage anything.

It was a living thing and they could see and feel the flow of the rivers and the pulse of life in the various little cities. But it wasn't all as it should be. There were spots of trouble, particularly to the north where the color of the land was tainted. Unhealthiness was slowly creeping into things. They could feel it.

Arabella took a deep breath and opened herself up to the living map. She scanned it slowly and they all watched her.

A feeling was coming to her. There was a presence here that she recognized. She caught her breath and focused in on that feeling. She walked toward the west and waved her arms in a slow motion. As she did this the diorama grew and they zoomed slowly into a wooden landscape along the bank of a river.

As they zoomed in closer Arabella could feel him. It grew strong very quickly and she caught her breath in shock as her group came to a stop near a group of four men huddled around a campfire. They listened in on the conversation the four were having.

"What is he cooking for his Testing?" The tallest in the group asked. He was strangely dressed.

Another man responded:

"He is a fine cook and he has chosen something most challenging – The Mother's Blanket"

The answer had no effect on the tall man so the speaker continued.

"The Mother's Blanket is a meal that must be carefully prepared and very slowly roasted over the fire on a spit. He must clean a quail and stuff an egg into it. Then he must stuff the quail into a cleaned hare."

Arabella's heart raced as the man spoke. Not for the words he was saying but for the presence of Storm. He was here! He had come into her other world -this world. She looked at him while the man continued to speak about the Mother's Blanket.

He looked good, he was healthy. His hand was bandaged but he seemed to be in good health -if not a bit shell shocked.

She waved her arms and her group moved in even further. Now they were all standing around the campfire with Storm and the three men that were with him. She resisted the urge to reach out and touch him. He wasn't really there. Or more correctly, they weren't really there. It was as if they were just watching a movie. They could see what was going on but they couldn't be seen.

She turned to Barmen.

"Do you know where this place is?"

"It is far to the west, somewhere along the Rhyme. It seems the young man is undergoing his testing so they mustn't be far from a testing stone." And as if reading her mind he added: "We could find it. But it would be a two week journey. By the time we arrived the young-ling would have finished his testing and the group will have returned to their town or village. No telling from which one they had come."

She moved closer to Storm. She wanted to touch him, to talk to him but couldn't. She just stared and let the yearning wash over her. She embraced it. It made her feel more alive. And she took heart at the fact that he was here, alive, and in good condition.

Barmen, noticing her focus on the tall man, broke her reverie.

"Who is he?"

The whole group of a hundred soldiers and nine woman gasped in unison when she replied.

"He is my husband."

And that was the last coherent thing that happened. Everything quickly turned into a tempest of sounds and actions as the howling of a GegenHound pierced the air around them.

Storm and his group didn't hear it. It wasn't happening to them. It was happening to Arabella and her group.

She waved her arms and her group retreated out away from the scene by the river. Again they were standing in the fog of the Gether with the miniature map of the world under them. And the pulling out was just in time for the onslaught of the Hounds to hit them.

Barmen's voice rose about the clamor of iron and snarls.

"My lady, we must move back to our starting point."

And as if on cue the group of soldiers moved as a single unit toward where they had first entered. Along the way they fought off the assaults of Hounds, Grim, and Vile.

When they arrived at the place where they entered she uttered the chant of return and everything went black as the group- the ones still alive – left the Gether and returned to their lives. All except for Arabella who returned to the darkness of sleep. This happened often and they would protect her and carry her until she returned to them.

14. The Labyrinth

"The greatest trick the Devil ever pulled was convincing the world he didn't exist" – Charles Baudelaire

Storm, and the remaining monks stood outside the closed door of the cathedral and regained their composure. The Raver and the throng of worshipers had to also leave through these doors. So they must be out here somewhere. Maybe they were waiting in ambush. But then again, this world seemed to bend rules in strange ways. Maybe they just appeared inside the cathedral when summoned and were subsequently summoned out.

For all he knew, when they passed through that door they entered another world and the cathedral was no longer behind it.

Storm was reeling in a sea of confusion. Arabella was here in this world, and she seemed to be okay. He couldn't think straight and didn't know what to do. Stein however took control of the situation. It was good that he was back to himself.

Stein was assessing the party, talking to each of the soldier monks in turn. They had lost one to the Raver and another during the melee of escape. Their number now was eight monks and Storm. The nine of them were all in good shape though. None had sustained any serious injury.

Once Stein had everything under control Storm assessed their environment. They were not in the same place they had initially come through. That place had a long and slender stone bridge inside a cavern and it had lead to the sword they walked through. There was no stone bridge here and no cavern. They were now inside a corridor, a wide corridor that stretched off beyond their torchlight.

They had two choices now. They could go back into the cathedral, that was if it would even still be the cathedral. Or they could move out into the corridor and see where it leads them. He had a feeling that now they were in the labyrinth that Stein had spoken of during his possession. And it seemed to Storm to not bode well. The worst kind of labyrinth was the one you didn't realize you were in. How could you find your way out if you didn't even know you were lost?

Making your way into a labyrinth could be of help when it came time to make your way back out. But, if you didn't know you were in a labyrinth that would be no help. Might as well just have been plucked out of the Gether and plopped right down into the middle of it.

Stein didn't waste any time. With military precision they reviewed and checked their supplies and gear and moved forward into the dim light of the corridor.

They walked for what definitely was a long time and the corridor twisted, turned, branched off, and revealed plenty of doors to them. When they came to a door they always opened it and at least looked in. It was very difficult going and several times Storm considered that they should return back to the doors that might lead into the cathedral. But he was not very sure if they could find their way back.

They had quickly taken a very conservative stance and were burning only one torch which cut their visibility; but it would be worse if they would end up deep in this labyrinth with no torches. If that were to happen they probably could sign themselves off as good as dead.

One of the monks was assigned the task of keeping a map and they all looked for little clues that might be of help – things like a slight broadening of a branched corridor which could mean it was a main corridor or a slight feel of air moving which could point them toward the outside. They were also very sensitive to any sloping that they found and always moved in what appeared to be an upward direction.

They used every tool they could think of to help them puzzle their way through the labyrinth. They even used their blades to scratch marks on the wall at every intersection. This way they could know if they were moving into a corridor they had previously come out of. But in all their walking they never came across a single scratch they had made.

After what seemed like a very long time of walking Stein ordered a halt and they all sat down to have a very small meal with a small portion of water. The rule of conserving was in full force. Then without a word they formed a small camp in the corridor and Stein assigned guards so they could get a little sleep.

He broke up the monks into groups of four. Each group would take a shift of two hours. This time no guard would be left alone – they would always be in pairs. One pair on one side of the corridor, and the other pair on the other side. This time there would be no surprises from the Urchne.

Storm rest his head on his pack and fell right to sleep hoping to have a dream of Arabella.

In what Storm guessed to be morning he awoke to Stein shaking his shoulder. Nothing was wrong, Stein just nodded and Storm sat up. Some of the monks were sitting in a circle and brainstorming what they should do. He joined the conversation and Stein brought him up to speed.
"There is no telling how big this maze is. And we don't seem to have crossed our own path. It could very well be the end of us. Our water supply is low."
It wasn't pretty but it was realistic. And that pretty much summed up Stein's view of everything. The hard facts are all he dealt in.

He listened as they discussed their options and possible strategies, which weren't a lot. And half the discussion was spent on making sure they rationed what food and water they had so they could continue on for as long as possible.

The talk of surviving for as long as possible brought up a thought and Storm added his opinion.

"Do any of you remember anything while you were under the possession of those things?" Stein nodded his head.
"Yes, we talked about that and we remember all of it, even though we were powerless to do anything.
Storm grunted and continued.
"We keep talking about this being a maze but at one point the creature that had possession of Stein referred to it as a labyrinth."

They all looked at him waiting for more.

"It might not matter and it could just be a preference in words but a maze is very different than a labyrinth – technically. A maze can have dead ends and lots of different paths. But a labyrinth actually only has one path through the whole thing."
Stein spoke up.
"So if this truly is a labyrinth then we will eventually find our way out?"
Storm nodded his head in answer and Stein added: "Assuming we can stay alive long enough. No telling how big it is."

Storm asked their map maker for a paper and something to write with then drew out the rough shape of a labyrinth.

"A traditional labyrinth will look something like this. It is a spiral that continuously wraps around itself in a series of layers. Each layer will be larger than the previous and eventually you come to the end of it."

"There could be side paths that break off the main path then re-join it further on. This could be why we haven't run into any dead ends. There aren't any. What we might want to do is try to make sure we stay on what we believe to be the main path and mark off the distances. If this is a labyrinth and it does fold around itself we should be taking turns at either longer or shorter distances – depending on whether we are moving to the outside or the inside."
He looked around at the group and they all seemed to understand.

"My guess is that the cathedral was at the center and we are, hopefully, moving our way to the outside. The only real question is whether or not the labyrinth turns to the left or the right.

They spent another day walking and then another night sleeping. By this time their rations were very thin.

The going was slow and arduous. It was getting very serious. To die of simple starvation after everything would be a real tragedy. Dying in this world at the hands of some evil creature was a terrible thing but it would be better than dying this inconsequential end. A slow and painful death by dehydration and lack of food. It would be an irony fitting of a universe run by a trickster.

They marched for indeterminate periods of time and slept for even more indeterminate periods. All the while they got weaker. They scratched marks on the walls and made diagrams in their maps. It was an exercise in extreme determination and they were getting weaker by the hour. The group of them were all exhibiting symptoms of dehydration and short periods of cloudy thinking. He found himself thinking over and over that it wouldn't be much longer.

They broke for a rest from their walking and some of the monks went through their now nearly empty backpacks. Stein wrestled something out of his pack and walked over to Storm holding it out in his hand. Storm reached out his hand and took it. It was a water gourd. It was a bit shriveled but it probably still had a lot of water in it. "Thanks." Was all he could muster the strength for. He stabbed his front teeth into it and squeezed. Water trickled into his mouth for a long draft. He looked at the other monks that he could see in the dim light of the single torch. None of them were eating or drinking. He tried to think clearly and it seemed to him that he hadn't seen any of them eat or drink for quite a while now. At least since before the last sleep period.

"I have been the only one eating or drinking?" He croaked through a dry throat. Stein nodded.

"How long has it been since any of you have had water?" "Maybe three days."

It hit Storm like a hammer on the head. These men had given everything they had and then gave more. It made sense to start rationing out the food and water to just him because things were not going well. Eventually more ground could be covered by one all alone after the rest had died or simply could walk no more.

The discipline they had, and the love, welled a lump in his throat. And a feeling washed over him. It was something he hadn't felt in a long time –inadequacy. He stared into Steins grim face and thought about how much these people loved their life and their land. And he thought about how willing they were to sacrifice for it. This brought him to thoughts of what happened to Bherin and then what happened to Ty. The inadequacy overwhelmed him. How could he possibly measure up to this life or death commitment that seemed to come easy to them.

Stein broke his concentration "Get some sleep. I fear tomorrow will be the last day we can accompany you."

Storm curled up against the wall clutching the crumpled water gourd. And as he fell asleep all he could think of was that there had to be some way to get them out of this. There had to be a way. There always was a way. He smiled because those words were very similar to what the Raver had said. He wondered if he was being his own worst enemy just as the Raver had been.

The dying don't sleep well. And they rarely dream. Dreaming takes energy and the dying don't have a lot of that to spare. But Storm was dreaming. It was pleasant. He was back in the fields outside of a village. He and Ty …. Well Arden now… were looking for water gourds. It was a little bit different this time because he could hear a rhythmic click-clacking of wood and water somewhere off in the distance. It was as if Uhr's shack were somewhere nearby. He thought about the beautiful water running through the wooden sluices and it made his dry lips hurt. That would be so good. Maybe he would just look around for that shack and the water.

But first he would pluck this one water gourd. That would be almost as good as a clear stream. Just a little effort and he could drink. He bent down and reached for the gourd and it screamed then scampered off. A gourd rat! There goes his water. He heard Ty laughing off in the distance "Sometimes things are not what they appear." was all that Ty said and the words hit Storm like a lightning bolt. He woke up.

They were in a forest somewhere. The monks were all asleep in various positions lying on the forest floor or leaning up against trees. They were out of the labyrinth. He mustered up some strength, stood up and walked over to Stein.

"Wake up." He muttered, but Stein didn't rouse. He got down and shook the man by the shoulders and Stein roused groggily.

"We are out of the labyrinth." With those words the man summoned up some energy and sat up slowly to look around.

What happened? How did we get out?"

That the man had the energy to actually ask two questions was a good sign. This was a man who rarely said anything and never asked even a solo question.

"Well, we weren't in a labyrinth. It was another place. Something like the Gether. We were actually walking around the forest for all these days. We just thought we were in a labyrinth. It was an illusion." He paused to let that sink in.

"I think it happened when that Raver clapped his hands. Remember how we were all knocked out?" Stein nodded his head. It seemed to make sense.

"I had a dream, and in it I realized the labyrinth was an illusion. And just like that, with the realization of it, the spell was broken. So here we are, out of a labyrinth we never were in to start with. He grinned at his own cleverness. And Stein grinned in a sympathetic reaction.

"Ok, we need water, grab some skins and go look for water.' He pointed in a direction. "Go downhill, that will be your best chance to quickly find water. I will rouse the others." This made sense to Storm so he rummaged through their supplies and found a couple of empty water skins then shuffled off while Stein checked on the others one by one.

It didn't take him long to find a nice little stream. He drank greedily then filled the water skins and made his way back. All the while he had a certain sense of satisfaction. After everything they had been doing for him he finally could actually do something for them. It was a good feeling. The inadequacy faded away with that thought.

When he found his way back to them he saw they were all gathered around a little fire that somebody had started. The warmth was probably doing them some psychological good. And the fact that the ordeal was over probably gave them some strength.

They passed the skins around in silence and started out slowly. Just a few sips each and then a half hour later they drank a little more.

It appeared that they had come out of the labyrinth at some point in the early afternoon. And over the course of the next few hours Storm made runs for water and they continued to drink and gain their strength. He monitored them quietly and as each one made a trip behind a tree to relieve his bladder Storm checked him off a mental list. Looks like nobody suffered from kidney shut-down. They would probably all be ok.

As the day closed Stein suggested he grab a large pan and an axe and go look for a rotted log. They found one and he spent some time digging out grubs and insects. They added water and cooked that up into a strange insect stew. It didn't taste too good but it was really good for all of them. They all had a fair portion of it then fell off into a healing sleep.

Over the course of the next two full days they continued to rest and build their strength. Storm continued to help them gain their strength and by the third morning of the third day they were all strong enough to continue on with their journey. It didn't take them too long to get oriented and realize they had previously walked quite a ways to the north-west which took them off their path to Vorgard but it could have been worse. At least they hadn't walked south.

15. Vorgard

Of stone and water the one with no shape is the stronger.
- The Book of Varheit

Storm and the group of warrior monks marched toward Vorgard for several days. Each day they ate, rested, and regained their strength. On their fifth afternoon they broke through a line of trees onto the top of a rocky ledge. Across a small forest, then a long open field, was a beautiful city built from light colored stone. Stein pointed and said "Vorgard."

It was the consummate medieval city -walled all the way around with a large castle keep near the center. And as the day progressed and they got closer he could make out more details.

A main wall circled all the way around the city and from their vantage point they could see two roads leading to that wall with a large gatehouse at each point.

In the center of the city was another wall that circled around the main keep or "castle."

The whole thing was set up in two concentric circles creating a good defense. The first wall going all the way around the whole city was the first line of defense. It encircled several square miles of territory.

The second interior wall covered an area that was probably just a few hundred square yards. It had what seemed to be some kind of outer courtyard with buildings then it had the keep.

That keep was a big stone structure and it was the last line of defense.

The design of the whole city was quite remarkable. But one thing stood above everything else. The city was nestled against the river Mid. One long section of the wall went right up to the river. And the water lapped at it's base. And from their vantage point on the hill They could see that there was an extensive series of canals and water ways running through the city and through the castle. It was a water city with a water castle. The overall effect of the light colored stone contrasted against the blue of so much water running through it was quite remarkable. Those various canals and water ways also made for excellent defense against attackers. There were no doubt lots of bridges that could be lifted, removed, or even burned if needed. And that would hinder the movement of any attacking force.

They quickly found their way down the ridge and crossed the valley in a couple of hours finding themselves at the open main gates of the city.   And they simply walked in.

This seemed like a good sign to Storm. They didn't have the city closed down. The main gates were open for all to come and go as they needed. There were guards but they seemed relaxed and unconcerned.

Stein lead them through the city and it was not how Storm pictured a medieval city. He thought it would be dirty and mucky with sewage in the streets and rats everywhere. And it wasn't. It was clean, vibrant, alive and very well kept. The residents were active, busy and seemed happy. Their economy no doubt was doing well.

And the water was everywhere. There were small six foot wide canals and large twenty foot canals. There were waterfalls and small pools. And it seemed like there was a fountain in the center of every open space. All that clean running water no doubt had a positive effect on the residents. Water was life and health.

Maybe his preconception about a medieval city was just a little too much tainted by tales of the black plague.

On their trek through the city they passed over a half dozen bridges and passed under several more. And as they got closer to the castle they passed through a market with lots of people going about their daily business. It was fun. Storm, while anxious for his goal, tried to enjoy the feeling as they passed through the life of it all.

It took them about fifteen minutes of purposeful walking and they came to the second inner wall. This one had a gate that was closed.

"Who goes there." A voice shouted from atop the wall.

"We are a contingent of monks from Speyer and we come to see the Lady Petra."

There was a flurry of talking on the wall and then a pause.

"The lady awaits you, the gate will be opened."

And with that the gate opened and a group of guards greeted them.

"Come, I have sent a guard to notify the lady of your arrival. She has foreseen you. Follow me."

Storm choked back a rush of emotion. She's alive. And she is here.

Passing through this second set of gates changed the feeling of things. There was a wide open space. It was a stone courtyard, and there were small buildings along the wall both left and right. And across the courtyard stood a staircase leading up to another door and into the keep.

They passed by several more sets of guards and into the castle. It was beautiful, well built, and decorated tastefully without being ostentatious.

Finally their guard escort brought them to a large marbled room. A carpet ran down the length and all the way to three large chairs. They were clearly thrones of some type. This felt like a room where the king would sit and hear from the commoners of the kingdom.

They crossed this room quickly and at the back they entered another room. It was a smaller chamber, lushly decorated and very comfortable. It was a hearing room where people would discuss the issues of the kingdom.

The guard gestured for them to sit at a large table but none of them moved to the table. The anticipation made them all nervous. It was better to stand.

They mulled around the room for several nervous moments and nobody spoke. Then a small door opened at the far end of the room and a familiar face came out. It was Barmen, the personal guard of the Lady. Storm remembered him from their meeting in the Gether.

And behind his large frame were several other men and women. And then there was another person. Storm stood frozen. All he could do was crane his neck. And it happened.

Arabella stepped through the door. His eyes met hers and they both paused in shock. Storm stumbled across the room on shaky legs. And in the next moment he embraced her. He felt the warmth and the shape of her and he listened as she choked back tears.

Both groups of people waited silently. Storm's group of monks felt satisfaction over their worry, having achieved their goal of getting him to a meeting with the lady. The group of men and woman that entered with her felt a mixture of emotions including shock at seeing their oracle with a man. It really was true. She did have a husband. And this appeared to be him.

This fact was something that seemed to complicate the whole problem that the world was facing.

"I brought you here. I wanted you here. I didn't know what else to do. These people, me, we all need you. She paused and looked in his eyes. "But I didn't know how to get you here. I never brought anything over with me."

It caught Storm by surprise. This was the woman who rarely put two sentences together. Yet, it all came out of her quickly in a long paragraph of need.

It further confused everything. And even though he found her. It made things even more complicated. The riddle seemed to expand further out.

They simply embraced for a very long moment feeling the nearness of each other was a comfort. The last time they were together was in the cold water of a river. And this erased all of that.

She took his hand firmly and lead him toward the door she had earlier come out of. Both groups of people saw the cue and followed along.

The door opened into another room, large but not as large as the previous. This room was more functional. It was a war room of sorts, less on decorum and more on function. There were more men in here and they were busy with various tasks including poring over maps on walls and tables.

Arabella lead him to the center of the room. There was nothing there. It was a big empty square about ten feet on a side. And marked off by a rectangle drawn on the stone floor.

"We will talk more, this evening. But as of right now let me help you understand better."

She lifted her arms and the square in the center of the room started to take a shape.

It became a miniature landscape – a beautiful three dimensional map complete with rivers, mountains, grasslands and everything a world would have except all in miniature.
People, soldiers, monks, women -everybody in the room gathered around the edges of the rectangle on the stone floor. Their eyes going back and forth between him and the map. Their curiosity was pointed in two different directions. They wanted to see what the lady would explain and they also were curious about this new man.

Arabella tucked a hand under Storms upper arm and pointed with the other hand. A small glowing light, a firefly of sorts, rose over the map near where they stood.

"This is Vorgard, where we now stand."

She waved her free hand as if to encompass the room they were standing in.

Her pointing hand returned to the diorama map. And the firefly over Vorgard moved as she moved her hand.
And there, to the North, a blight has invaded. It's a sickness and it is being wielded by something or someone.

He watched as the firefly floated to the North of the map. And grew uneasy as the lush greens of that part of the map turned brown and gray. It was a time lapse of a rot. What happened to an orange if you just let it sit on a table. A small spot turned to mold and the mold quickly spread.

Barmen, standing to Arabella's right, spoke.

"The rot spreads. GegenHounds, Vile, and many other types of tainted creatures have been making their way south. And as you have seen, the rot has also spread into the Gether."
He paused and nobody else spoke so he continued. He was a leader. It was in him.

"We have been gathering forces and strength to protect what we know. And we have made many exploratory excursions. It all comes to the same. The rot is here and it spreads. We can't stop it. We don't know how to. We don't know what has started it nor why."

Arabella continued his thought. And looked into Storm's face.

"And that is why you are here. To find the source and stop it.

Storm added his thought.
"Chop off the head of the snake and the whole snake dies."
A murmur went around the room.

"Okay, so who or what is the head of the snake?"

He looked around but nobody answered.

Barmen broke the silence.

"We don't know. He or it is hidden to us. There is a feeling but nothing that we can see distinctly. It is closed even to the lady Petra."

Storm came out of a deep thought to the realization that the room was quiet. Two dozen people and not a peep. Everyone just stood quietly staring at him.

If someone throws something for him to catch he swore right there to catch it with his right hand.
He didn't say anything more. He just grit his teeth. Of all the things that could happen this was a good outcome. He found Arabella, or she found him. Either way they were back together. And that was really the best thing. He would have to take all this other stuff one step at a time.
The group in the room, typical of these people, all came to a unanimous decision without so much of a word. They all felt that the introduction and summary was over.
They started to split up. People returned to tables and maps. They resumed the work they had been planning when he had entered the room. The meeting was over.

Storm walked around the room with Arabella on one side and Stein on his other. He asked various questions and people gave him different briefings of a sort. Telling him about the situation in various parts of the world and about various patrolling parties that had been sent out to defend towns or gather information.

It was all quite a lot. But he welcomed the fact that something was being done. It was all just a stop-gap. Something to slow the rot until he found the actual root of the problem and fixed it. That's what they were all thinking.

They spent hours working with the people going over plans and reports. Coming up with ideas on what they should do. Meals started coming into the room and people were taking breaks to have their supper. Arabella spoke to him. "Let's have our supper in my quarters. There is much for us to discuss."

She brought him down various corridors and through several doors until they came to her chambers. Storm looked around. It was quite a beautiful room but not overly done. Opposite the door they came in was a doorway that lead out onto a balcony. He could see a blue sky through that doorway. And on the wall to the left was Arabella's bed. Opposite the wall with the bed was a small table with a pair of chairs. They sat there and Storm pulled his chair close to hers so they could speak more tenderly.

For the next half hour Arabella told Storm her whole story. Of how for her whole life, since she was five, she was traveling between this world and the world the two of them shared. And how her long bouts with sleeping were somehow tied to the gift of the travel.

Her talk was interrupted by the sound of a goblet hitting the floor. They looked up from their table to see a young woman, a serving girl, carrying a serving tray of food. She stood in the doorway with her mouth open.

"It's a man. In… in your room." She blurted.

"Arabella smiled gently "Yes, this is my husband."

The serving girl took a few more moments to regain her composure. She finally closed her mouth and walked over and placed the serving tray on the little table. Then rushed to the doorway where she had let the goblet fall.

"My lady, I will return with more drink."
She curtsied and left.

The conversation continued on for several more hours and each filled in the other on what had happened since they had bee so abruptly parted. Through the door in the balcony darkness started to set in as the sun grew tired and retired in a red glow.

So they retired themselves to the bed and the last thing Arabella said to him before laying down was "I fear that if we sleep side by side tonight we will awaken to our life in the river."
Her brow wrinkled and she stared into his eyes.

He paused and looked at her. And he could feel her heart. He could feel the beating of it. And he could feel his own heart beating in his own chest. And he knew that the two hearts with beating in a beautiful synchronization."
"No, that won't be. On the tomorrow we will have many things to face. But that won't be one of them."

16. The Blacksmith's Task

The Hotter the fire the purer the gold. - The book of Varheit

In the morning, while they were getting ready the serving girl returned with another tray of food. This time she knocked before entering. She didn't say anything but was flustered and nervous. She couldn't stop glancing at Storm. After placing the food she quickly left with a curtsy and without a word.

They had their breakfast then went to the meeting room. As with the day before there was a lot of activity. Barmen spotted him and waved him over to a table.

"There have been more skirmishes here, mostly coming out of the north. The progression continues. He waved a hand over a table with a map on it.

He looked at Storm and paused. Waiting to see if there was a question. Storm didn't say anything so he continued.

"Scouts have reported a large force of Vile and Grim to the north." He pointed out a spot on the table map. "It is clearly an army, well supplied and moving this way."
Now Storm spoke up.

"How long have we got?"

"Three weeks, maybe four. They are a large force and gaining in their strength as they travel. A large force like that, even rabid, must move slowly or risk falling into chaos."

"I can venture a guess here. If Vorgard falls then everything else soon follows."
"That's right." responded Barmen.
"It feels like a poor metaphor but cut the head off the snake and the rest of the snake dies."

The group at the table visibly tightened at the reference to them being the snake. That was reserved for the darker half. Not the good half.

Storm looked over the map on the table. It was a diorama. A miniature three dimensional landscape – and beautiful. This one wasn't conjured. It was hand-made. Another rendition of the land. Itself also being very beautiful. And there was a healthiness about it, a lush green growing of it, and the people were the same way.

He looked around the room and they were all looking at him. That was the very moment everything changed in his head.

He was no longer the confused man stumbling through a strange world. Everything had fallen into place for him. They needed him, the left-hander, and somehow Arabella summoned him to this world, her other world, in order for him to help.

He didn't fully understand the why of it all. But when did anybody? Whether it be in this world or the other? It felt good to have a real goal. A goal that was pure and clear to see. These people needed help against a rotting that was spreading through their land.

He and Arabella spent the morning moving from group to group, reviewing plans, helping where they could.

At midday most of the people had found their way to the kitchen. Storm, Arabella, Barmen and a few other high ranking soldiers from Vorgard had spent the entire morning together formulating plans and deepening their bond. Eventually they made their way to one of the dining halls And they ate quietly until Storm spoke.

"I have been thinking about your weapons."

With that everybody at the table stopped eating. It was as if they knew what was coming.

Everything here is iron. And iron is great. But as far as I can tell nothing is steel. You have no steel. Except for that sword that talks. What was the name of it?"

Barmen answered the question.

"Varheit."

Storm nodded his head. "Yes, seemed to be steel to me. I think I can teach you how to make it. Then we can have some much improved weapons – swords, knives, spears. They can all be of steel rather than iron. That would make quite a difference in a battle."

He looked around the table. They all were in shock. One of the soldiers broke the silence. "It is as the book of Varheit foretold. You would teach us to make steel."

He didn't know how to handle that one so he just continued.

"The castle has a blacksmith?" Nobody answered but he continued. "And a potter?"

"I would like to meet with them as soon as possible. The process takes quite a bit of time. And time is something we don't have a lot of." One of the Vorgard officers rose from the table. "I will have them summoned immediately."

They all finished their meal quickly and as they rose Arabella spoke. "I will go to my chambers."

Storm almost tripped on his chair.
"Are you okay? Do you feel sleepy?" The though of her falling off to sleep brought a vision of losing her back to the other world, possibly even the accident in the water.
"No." She grasped his hand. "You have much to do. As do I. The people of the castle and the city are near panic at the coming trouble. I and the women with me have much work to tend to. We will be back together this evening." At that she kissed him then turned to leave. He hadn't noticed before but two young women were standing behind her. He wasn't absolutely sure but he thought that maybe they had been following them the whole morning. One of them was the serving girl from the night before and from their breakfast. He was sure of that.

They returned to the big meeting room and weren't there long when someone approached. "The blacksmith and the Potter are both here." He pointed at a door. Storm went immediately over. And he beckoned for Barmen to come with him. It became a bit of an entourage. There were six of them walking through the door one at a time. He thought for sure this was more of a personal body guard – for him.

They entered into the room, it was a comfortable meeting room of sorts with a table and lots of chairs around it. But the two men awaiting were standing. Probably due to nervous energy.

One of the men was big and burly with thick arms and broad shoulders. The other man was thin with quick darting eyes and large hands that seemed to be very dexterous.

Easy enough Storm thought. He walked over to the big burly man and put out his hand in a gesture of a handshake. "You must be the blacksmith."

The man looked at him in a long pause. "No, I am the potter. He is the blacksmith." He pointed a thumb at the slender man standing beside him.

Storm choked on that a little bit, er. Ahh....uhhh...." He tried to choke out an apology with his outstretched hand just grasping at air.

The awkward moment extended a few more seconds then the whole room burst out in a laugh.

The big burly man, while laughing, grasped Storm's hand in a firm shake then clapped him on the back with his other hand.

Once the laughter died down the man released Storm's hand. He had a twinkle in his eye.

"Yes, I am the blacksmith. My name is Eisen. And this" He pointed his thumb again at the other man "Is Carullae the Potter."

At that Storm laughed. It was a relief in pressure. It felt good to laugh and the room had a good feeling. Some people just had that gift to change the mood of a room or of a group no matter the circumstances. And Eisen had that gift.

He extended his hand to Carullae and the introductions were complete. "Let's go out to the courtyard. We can talk as we go."

As they walked Storm explained to the two craftsmen that his plan was to teach the Smith how to make steel. And with that statement the disposition of the Smith changed. He got much more serious about things.

They came to a stop in the inner courtyard of the castle. There was a fair amount of room. But he thought they might need more. "This will have to do for now." He can get them started on it. They can plan the logistics of it as they understand the process.

Storm's entourage of body guards spread out a bit in the courtyard which kept him safer but also gave them room to walk about.

He stopped at a spot near the wall and asked for somebody to get him a stick.

Once the stick arrived he drew a circle on the ground about two feet in diameter. Then he drew another circle around it, about eight inches larger.

He turned first to the potter.

"You have a clay that is fired in an oven? Something that dries and turns very hard but can resist very high temperatures?"

"Yes, it is found by rivers. We keep some on hand."

"Good, build a structure here out of that clay. The inner circle is empty. The wall of the structure goes from the inner circle to the outer circle. And make the structure about as tall as a man's waist." The potter seemed to understand so he continued.

"And put a hole in the bottom at the ground, about the size of a man's fist. Then put a second hole opposite that one and about two hands up from the ground.

This is the first of many." He pointed along the wall. We will need to make a lot of them."

"These are called stack furnaces. With these we will turn iron ore into steel."

"Do you have the resources?"

The potter paused for a moment. "Yes, I have apprentices, guild workers. We have some of the clay on hand and can gather more from the river. And we can get some in the city from various sellers."

Storm nodded his head.

"Great. If you need anything the full resources of the castle are at your dispose. If you need men, coin, materials, carts, anything at all. Just send for it."

The potter sensed that his mission was assigned and he was dismissed so he bowed his head and hurried off.

Storm then turned to Barmen.

"You are familiar with smelting?"

The smith nodded his head.

"That's good. You smelt iron ore into iron. We are going to go another step and turn that iron ore into steel. It is much much better than iron. But in order to do that we need charcoal. It has a high carbon content."

The smith raised his eyebrows at the comment about carbon content.

Storm went on. "It's the black stuff left over when you burn wood. It is that carbon content that makes all the difference. If we get the fire hot enough and for long enough the carbon from the charcoal will bond with the iron and create steel. That's pretty much the whole story."

The smith nodded his head in agreement. But Storm could see he didn't really grasp the concept. Or maybe he was just skeptical.

"No matter. You are a smith. Once we get going you will get a feel for it. And I am sure you will make improvements to the process. A little trial and error will do us good."

It is two steps. First we make charcoal with a very high carbon content. Then we burn that with air flow and the iron ore to make steel. And the airflow means bellows. Each clay furnace is going to need two bellows, and they need to be pumped throughout the entire process."

The smith seemed to grasp this.

"We are going to need a lot of cut wood. Small pieces about the size of your forearm. And lots of them. And they have to be a hardwood, no softwood. Hardwood is best. And fairly dry. Nothing too green. It will be to make our charcoal."

"How much will we need?"

"We will need a lot of it. And I think we are going to need someone who can oversee this whole project. There is a bit of complexity to it and the logistics will be a bit tricky."

Barmen put a hand to his chin.

"The quartermaster will have someone that can manage this smoothly."

Storm turned to the smith and with his stick drew some more on the dirt of the courtyard.
"Ok, so it is a two step process. First we make the charcoal in barrels then we use that charcoal in the clay foundries, along with iron ore to make the steel.

For the next several hours Storm, the Smith, and the quartermasters appointed man in charge went over the plans and how they would make steel from iron ore.

And Storm was pleased by the fact that they seemed to be an organized and disciplined group because over the course of their discussion people had been bringing in barrels for the charcoal and another group of people, he assumed to be potters, were already hauling in clay for the furnaces.

It was with a bit of satisfaction that he and Barmen broke off the training session and went in search of their supper. The smith remained at the work site and was very pleased with what was going on. He probably wouldn't retire for the night just from excitement at what he was undertaking.

After their supper the remainder of the day was spent meeting with more people and making more plans. Everyone wanted Storm's opinion on pretty much everything. He wasn't exactly sure why but he accepted it. Did their group-think just take over and they all accepted him as their lead? Was this something that came of their hearts all beating together? Did they all decide things together also?

The last thing he did before retiring to Arabella's room was discuss with Barmen about setting up some kind of a council of people that could run things for him, make decisions, and get things done. If he was going to be the lead in all this he was going to need a small team of people to help him.

He returned to Arabella's quarters and as he walked in the door he saw her lying in the bed, maybe asleep. He froze in the doorway. The door still open.

When she was actually sleeping he never knew for how long she would be asleep. He just accepted it and let her quietly be just as her family had done for most of her life. And in all that time nobody knew that she wasn't actually there but somewhere totally different - in a different world, other than the sleeping world.

He shuffled over and sat in one of the chairs. And as he slid off a boot he heard her gently say to him "Gubra Da Lee."

He looked up and there she was, lying in the bed, on her side, with her eyes open and looking at him and smiling a gentle smile.

"Gubra Da Lee sparrow."

In the morning Storm spent some time just embracing Arabella while they lay in bed. When he got up to dress he told her he would meet her at breakfast but first he would make some rounds and check on the progress of things.

He rushed off to the inner courtyard to see how things were developing.

He walked out into the morning chill of the courtyard and was shocked by what he saw. The area was totally different. Many people had been working all night. He would imagine it was scores of people, maybe more. There were scores of barrels burning wood, many of them were sealed and leaking smoke out of their tap holes. That was to keep the pressure on the wood and the fire. It would impregnate the wood very well with carbon.

And there were already half a dozen clay furnaces built and more partially built. Everyone was busy. Wheel barrows full of material were moving around and people were scampering about. It all was a good sign.

The blacksmith spotted him, put down some papers on a barrel and waved him over.

They wished each other a good morning and the smith launched excitedly into questions.

"Overall I have a pretty good sense for what we are doing. And we are going to experiment with the furnaces, vary the ore, the amount of charcoal and the burn times. We should be able to get a good sense for what works well. Once of course we can get to hammering on the err…. Steel."

He said it as if it were a holy word.

"One important question I have is how much? How much steel will we get from these furnaces? Knowing this will also give us a feeling for how much ore to put in."

Storm put out his fists.

"Hmm…. Each furnace should yield somewhere around three or four fists."
The blacksmith seemed disappointed.

"That's about it from these furnaces." He walked the smith over to a furnace and pointed at the top. You get a good fire going then you add the ore at the top, and the ore slowly makes its way to the bottom where it will form a bloom. The time it takes to travel to the bottom is important. Too much iron and it doesn't go, or it doesn't pick up enough carbon."

The smith still seemed disappointed.

"It's okay, this is how you will learn. In the future, you will be able to make larger furnaces to yield larger blooms of steel."

The smith finally spoke his disappointment.

"Well, it just looks like we aren't going to be making a whole lot of swords. We don't have the time to yield all the steel we need"

Finally Storm understood the disappointment. It was all about the impending battle.

"I think maybe our wisest course of action is arrow tips and spear tips." With them made out of steel our foes armor will be of no use. Steel arrow tips, spears, and maybe pikes, will easily penetrate where iron ones would not."

The smith lifted his shoulders and his disposition changed a bit.

"Yes, that is true! Arrows are quick and easy to make. Spear tips too. We can get a lot of them made in plenty of time. I have already sent out word. Every man with the ability to work metal will be coming in to help with steel. That's everyone from the city and the surrounding towns and villages. We should have quite a workforce. The sound of hammering will ring through the castle."

      The next two weeks passed quickly. The smiths were busy at work making steel and forging arrows and spear tips. Everyone had a sense of purpose and a sense of hope.

Storm spent time every morning with the smiths. But after a week it was evident that they didn't need his help anymore. They had a handle on what they were doing and how to go about making steel. The furnaces were cranking out blooms of steel on a daily basis and it was getting better in quality. And the master smith had already started the making of a larger kiln so they could churn out much larger blooms of steel.

The whole city was industrious. Food was being stored, weapons and armor being made, plans being made, and each day marched their enemy a little closer to them.

Storm and Arabella spent as much time as they could together in the following weeks and one night while sitting out on her balcony Storm spotted Orion slowly coming up over the horizon. And he thought to himself "Has it already been a year that we have been here?"

17. Precursor to Battle

"Only the unknown frightens men. But once a man has faced the unknown, that terror becomes the known."
- Antoine de Saint-Exupéry

It was three weeks into the preparations, Storm and Arabella lay sleeping in their bed. No moon cast a light from the balcony and the room was very dark. And Storm awoke with a start. Arabella lay quietly sleeping by his side and the room was filled almost to waist height with a fog. It was much like being in the Gether.

In the corner of the room, off to the right was a darkness. It was a figure, a presence, and Storm knew it. He had met it before. Even though he couldn't really see it he knew it was the same thing that had visited him many years ago in that little apartment near the library.

He tried to move but couldn't. Maybe it was terror that bound him or maybe it was that presence. He couldn't tell which but it didn't matter. The effect was the same. He couldn't move anything but his eyes and he just stared at the darkened area in the corner of the room. And he watched as the waist high fog slowly swirled into the room and poured itself out the door to the balcony.

How long he lay there he didn't know. His sense of time was changed. It was as if he really were in the Gether. Or maybe in some place that was both this place and that place.
But this time the terror didn't last until dawn and the proclamation of a cuckoo clock didn't interrupt the trance. It was the sound of a ringing bell that made the interruption.

Someone was ringing the church bell in the keep. Storm shifted his focus from seeing to hearing and the sounds of the keep, the castle, and the grounds came into his awareness.
There was fighting and screaming going on. At first it started with screaming but after a minute or two the clashing of iron could be heard from various directions.

Arabella screamed, and the spell was broken.
The darkness in the corner of the room was gone and Storm was freed of restraint. He jumped out of the bed, grabbed his sword and rushed to the balcony.

The courtyard was filled to the waist with a slowly swirling fog and people were running in various directions and fighting dark shadowy figures.

The church bell got louder and the castle seemed to come awake. Lights began springing up in various doors and windows and the sounds of fighting got louder.

The bell was a warning and it was working. Some kind of malevolence was attacking the residents of the castle and they were coming awake in defense against it.

He rushed back to the bed and grabbed Arabella who was sitting up and appeared to be in shock. She didn't say anything. She was just staring at the space in the corner where the dark presence had been.

"We have to stay safe."

As he said this the door burst open and three armed men rushed in. They stopped and assessed the situation then one hurried out to the balcony and posted himself in the doorway, as a guard.

Storm quickly took charge of the situation.

"What do we have?"

One of the guards spoke up as the third one posted himself in the doorway leading back from where they came.

"There is some kind of attack going on. It came from somewhere within the castle. We don't know where, or how. But it is a small force of creatures. And they wrought havoc in the beginning. The guards of the castle, and some from the city have responded quickly. Once the alarm sounded things turned pretty quickly."

He paused.

"There is some strange magic here. The fog is pouring all through the castle and it doesn't appear to be coming from anywhere. It is just here."

Arabella broke the line of thought.

"The world and the Gether have been blended in some unnatural way. The two places were touched together somewhere. And this is how the fog.... and the creatures passed over from there to here."

"Stay here and protect the lady from harm. I am going to see what can be done."

Barefooted, wearing his bed clothes, and armed only with his sheathed sword he rushed out of the room, through the outer room, and into the outer corridor. He looked both ways and to his left, just as he turned his head that way he caught a glimpse of a dark figure darting around a corner.

He chased after it and turned the corner just as it disappeared into a room -opening and closing the door behind itself without even touching it.

He ran down the hall, grabbed the handle and burst into the room. It was very dark. He couldn't make out anything but small differences in light. The torch on the wall in the hallway was too far away. It didn't reach light into the room. He stood still and quiet not three feet into the room. This was Aria's room he thought. She was one of Arabella's maidens. He had never been in the room so he was unsure as to the layout. But it was probably a single room, maybe with a window – maybe not. And there was no telling where the bed was. He squinted in an attempt to see anything and craned his neck in an attempt to hear anything at all.

It was unnerving to wonder whether he would just be struck down in the dark. A blade to the heart? A talon to the eye? He waited in the dark, just a sliver of orange light behind him -listening and trying to look.

And it happened. He heard three short but sharp clicks on the stone floor. They came in rapid succession and each one was closer to him than the previous. And instead of turning or moving he drew his sword out of its scabbard and swung it in a sweeping arc from his right, out of the scabbard, and to his left, at waist height. And he connected with was most likely flesh and bone. As the slash and crack sounded Aria screamed from about five feet to his left. He guessed she was in her bed.

A body hit the stone floor and moment's later, alerted by Aria's scream footfalls moved down the hallway.

"In here."

A guard carrying a torch entered the room and Storm could now see the situation. Aria was sitting up in her bed. Her face pale, her eyes wide open. But she appeared unharmed.
At Storm's feet was a dark twitching body. Blood pooled around it and around his bare feet.

They dragged it into the hall.

"Never seen anything like it sir. And it isn't the only one. There are more of them crawling around the castle."

It was thin and pale with very large eyes, humanoid in shape but it's feet were odd, almost hoofed. It's the talons on those feet that brought about it's death, and saved Storm's life.

He looked back into the room. Aria was climbing out of her bed. She was shaking but appeared to be physically okay.

He turned to the guard. "Come, let's search for more."

They made their way slowly through the building, checking rooms as they went. As they progressed they ran into various guards and soldiers all doing the same. And as they got to the courtyard the sky was beginning to lighten and the fog at their feet was disappearing.

He walked around the courtyard in his bedclothes and with bloodied feet assessing the situation – his ears alert.

The castle had quieted. There were no more sounds of fighting and no screaming. It seemed that the attack, if it could be called an attack, had come to an end.

He grabbed up soldiers and guards as they passed and organized them into groups sending them out to make sweeps of the castle and grounds. They were to gather up bodies of both the creatures and humans. And they were to help any wounded.

It seemed like a small skirmish. And it seemed like some kind of suicide mission.

"Why this attack? It didn't seem to make any sense. Maybe it was some kind of scouting mission."

He looked over at the various furnaces. They all seemed okay. Everything was still burning as it should. Some smith's were still working them. Almost oblivious to the events of the night.

They recovered from the attack quickly and by morning light everything had returned to normal castle life. Although there was tension in the air. Few things are as unnerving as a surprise attack upon a sleeping castle.

Storm's council of advisers were effective. Everything was flowing smoothly. Bodies of the dead were being handled well and the bodies of the attackers were piled up in the courtyard.

They gathered in the meeting room and a lively discussion ensued. But everything was just speculation. They couldn't come up with anything solid or substantial.

As the morning progressed and the discussion continued information flowed into the meeting. Eleven dead, fourteen more injured. Thirty four dead creatures and an undetermined number escaped. General opinion from guard was that none of them escaped. It didn't seem to him like they had any intention of escaping.

So what was their goal? Was it simply to kill as many as they could? Was it to terrorize and demoralize the occupants of the castle?

As the questions turned from what they were doing to how they got in Arabella walked into the meeting room and answered them.

"There has been a tear in the Gether. That place and this place sometimes touch in a different way. The creatures came through that touching. It is a tainting and it is unhealthy."

A long silence overtook the room. None of them could really grasp what it meant. But they all knew it didn't bode well. One man broke the silence.

"Can they do it again?"

Arabella paused and looked around the room. "I don't know. But, if it was done once I would venture the guess that it can be done again. It must take a lot of effort and energy though. I can't see it being a nightly event."

They didn't have much to go on but this all seemed reasonable so they set a new schedule for a larger contingent of guards to be patrolling the castle each night. This would at least give them more warning if there was another surprise attack from within. The Captain of the Guard would insure that they would be ready if it happened again.

By afternoon everything had returned seemingly to normal and Storm set out on his usual rounds to check on the progress of various groups including the smiths. His mind was heavy with worries though. Scouts report the attacking army about a week away now so they were running out of time. And the "why" of the nights attack was something he couldn't shake. There had to be a reason other than harassment.

In the courtyard he walked over to one of the smiths. The man was laboring over a furnace, pouring more iron ore into it. Storm watched him, not wanting to interrupt. Once the man had loaded the furnace fully with a batch of ore there was a pause in his work and Storm spoke.

"How goes the work? Are we on schedule? Is anything needed?"

The smith didn't respond. He just stared at the red glow.

Storm placed a friendly hand on the man's shoulder and the man slowly turned his head and looked at Storm with vacant eyes.

Storm recoiled -and took a single step back. He had seen that empty look before. It was the same look the group of guards had as they escorted him to see the Raver. And this time he recognized exactly what it meant.

This man was possessed by an Urchne! Storm just stared with his mouth open. The man continued to look over his shoulder directly at Storm, one eye focused blankly on him. And something on his back squirmed. It was a lump and it moved ever so slightly.

But it saw that he recognized something and the second that Storm spent in shock was enough time for it to act. And it was a single step back that saved him or at least saved his eyesight.

He couldn't comprehend fast enough what happened next and the shock is what froze him for almost too long. The smith/Urchne reached a hand into the top of the kiln and grabbed a hand full of burning coals. And then turned and swiped at Storm's face.
Storm's reaction was autonomic. He didn't do it intentionally. It happened too fast. He just instinctively jerked back his head to avoid the blow. And the step back he had taken was just enough to put his eyes out of reach of the coals.

He smelled the burning flesh of the man's hand as it passed by him and he could feel the heat of the coal. And the really disturbing thing about it was that the face of the attacker was blank. There was no feeling in it at all – no feeling of hate and no feeling of pain. Any normal person grasping a handful of hot coals would be writhing in pain, their face a tortured mask.
But that little bit of reaction and the small amount of time gave him enough time to react with his thoughts rather than just instinct.

The hand passed by his face and continued in an arc as if the man had just thrown a heavy object and it would take time for his body to recover from the motion.

Storm sprung at the arm and grasped it with one hand. Then with his other hand he lashed out at the face of the attacker. Several fast and heavy blows with his fist knocked the smith out and his body crumpled.

Storm assessed himself quickly, looking over his own body to make sure he wasn't burned and to insure the Urchne hadn't somehow detached from the blacksmith and scampered over to him. While people rushed over to his aid he gave thought to the situation. "At least now he knew why they did this unexpected attack in the night. They wanted to know the secret of how to make steel. All of the fighting and the dying was just a distraction to get control of a smith.

He just looked on as guards stripped the shirt off the smith and looked at the parasite. One of the guards ran off and returned a few minutes later with a bucket of pitch. They coated the thing with a thick layer of pitch and watched as it convulsed then detached itself from the blacksmith. As it tried to make it's escape they made quick work of it with knives.

18. The Battle for Vorgard

The War room was full of soldiers. They were in final preparation for the upcoming battle and all of the various team leaders were going over their final plans. Storm and his advisers were poring over a large map on a table and the scouting commander was making his final briefing. But his job was coming to an end - tracking the enemy force was no longer necessary. It's advance parties had arrived and made encampments north of Vorgard and the brunt of the force would arrive over the next day or two.

For the past few days they had been sending out war parties to scatter and harass the advance teams but the enemy numbers grew too large and more just kept coming. So the Vorgard soldiers and scouts had retreated to within the walls around the city. That was the line of demarcation. And it is where the true battle would begin.
Scouts estimated their numbers to be at twenty thousand and a mix of Vile, Grim, GegenHounds, humanoids and more. There were many strange beasts and creatures in the mass. Many of which have long been forgotten in the memories of people.

The steel furnaces had done a remarkable job. The smiths and all their assistants had found a good recipe and process for making steel, and the blooms were turned out daily and quickly hammered into spear and arrow tips. They even had used steel for other purposes including replacing banding on the major gates to the city and the major gate to the castle. Every little bit would help.
Everything that could be done had been done. Men of all ages had been coming in from all over the countryside, and they were quickly armed with something or other and given rudimentary training on their weapons and assigned to groups of seasoned troops. And many families from the North-lands have been coming into the city in search of refuge. The hoardings were full of grain and dried foods in expectation of a siege or a long drawn out battle. The one thing they didn't have to worry about was water. Being a water castle meant that running water, and reservoirs of clean water were everywhere. But Storm had a feeling that it would not get to the point of a siege. One way or another this battle would not last very long.
Nothing more could be done but wait so Storm returned to Arabella's quarters.

She was sitting at the little table near the bed, worry lines on her forehead.

"I have to sleep."

The words froze him half way to sitting. She didn't mean the normal sleep that they had both been experiencing for the last month. She meant one of those sleeps. The sleeps where she slept for an undetermined period of time. He sat down slowly. It was a subject they had been avoiding. What would happen? Would she return to the river?
"Are you sure? You can feel it?"
She nodded her head.
The two of them sat in silence for a very long time. A breeze blew into the room from the balcony door.
Everything was coming to a crux -to some kind of conclusion and apparently from every direction. A large force of evil was gathering outside the walls of the city and even if they managed to get through that there still was the possibility that Arabella might fall into her sleep here and wake up in the river-sunk car. He couldn't voice any words. His mouth was dry and his throat was constricted.

"Do you think you will return to the….. the car and the river?"

The words were hollow. He felt as if he were not in his body, he was just listening to someone else say them.
Maybe she knew. She had been doing this all her life. Maybe something else would happen.
"I don't know. I never know. But I do feel the sleep coming on to me. It's always the same feeling."
He came back to his body, pulled by a sick feeling in his stomach and a dizziness in his head. How do you fight something like this? You can't take a sword to it. And you can't run and hide from it. The loss of control in the situation was unnerving him.
She continued with her thoughts.
"I feel that I will return to our other life. And that probably is the river. But how much time has passed is unknown to me. Time here and time there passes very differently. I think that once I have fallen into the sleep here we will have time."

He detached himself from the nausea in his stomach and looked up at her.

He watched in horror as she stood up and walked over to the bed. She turned and sat on the edge.

"I love these people. I love this life. These things are only rivaled by my love for you. Will you save them? Can you do this for me?"

He wanted to shake his head in a no. While this world was quite beautiful in it's way, and while he did feel love for the people it wasn't the same for him. She had been coming here and experiencing all of this for most of her life. For him it had only been a year.

But he couldn't say any of that. All he could do was nod his head and say "Gubra da lee."

At that she smiled and raised her arms in request of a hug. He rushed to her and hugged her until she relaxed, letting her head fall on her pillow.

He remained sitting on the edge of the bed for an hour, carefully watching her. Dreading what might happen. But nothing happened. She slept quietly as she always did whether is was a normal sleep or one of those long sleeps like she just now slipped into.

He left the room and walked down the hall then knocked on Aria's door. She immediately opened it as if she were waiting just on the other side. They paused just staring at each other and he managed to get out around a dry throat "She is sleeping."

Aria gasped, paused, and regained control. She knew that he meant it was one of those mysterious sleeps where she could be gone for days. She passed quickly through the doorway, squeezed by him, and rushed down the hall to Arabella's room.

He continued down the hall and stopped two guards making their rounds patrolling the halls and corridors. He pointed at one. "The lady has fallen into the sleep. Post yourself outside her door as guard." Then he pointed at the other guard. "Go inform the captain of the guard of the situation with the lady. He will want to know so he can make arrangements for her."

The two guards nodded their heads and without a word each rushed off to do his appointed task. Storm returned to the War room.

It was busier, and much more crowded, than it had been over the past few days. The extra bodies were monks, dressed in armor. He made his way to the command table where a knot of men stood and Stein greeted him.

"The monks of Speyer have come." Stein waited for a response from Storm but didn't get one so he continued. "They are armed and ready for battle -and quite formidable."

"How many are they?"

"All of them, five hundred, but of more value than that."

He ushered Storm closer to the table where a map lay.

"Scouts report a lot of activity within the enemies camps. It looks as though they may attack tonight." He paused again then continued. "The monks of Speyer arrived several hours ago and went right to business. Leadership has been poring over maps of the city, the keep, and the surrounding grounds."

And no matter how we look at it the whole situation doesn't look good."

And with no warning, no fanfare, and no desire from anyone for it a bell starting ringing somewhere in the city.

The command room went silent.

The pause, and quiet, in the room, lasted five seconds then broke as they all started briskly moving. Armor clanged and weapons make scraping sounds as they were withdrawn from scabbards. And without a single word from the whole group they all briskly moved to the various exits around the large room.

Storm exited the room to the sounds of more bells. Other than that he heard people rustling about. And coming from the north end of the city he heard a low rumbling of noises. It was too far away to be distinct. It was a muffled mix of battle sounds.

Everyone in the castle and everyone in Vorgard had an assignment. They all had things to be done once the battle started. This had been carefully planned and Storm was the only person who had no assignment. He had not been tasked with anything.

So he turned and started in a trot across the courtyard.

He exited the main gates of the castle courtyard into the city and turned to the north; He had gotten a hundred feet when he realized there were several monks following tightly behind him. Their hammers were drawn and they were ready for battle. It looks like a bodyguard had been assigned to him. It was Stein and the same group of monks that had traveled with him all the way to Vorgard. With two new monks to replace the two that had died. All the monks instilled a sense of confidence in him. But he knew these monks very well. They had been through a lot together.

He would head for tower three. While he moved he reviewed the overall battle plan.

They would heavily man the walls and gates encircling the city. Archers could bring a heavy toll to enemies from their vantage point on the wall. This gave them a good advantage for a period of time. Once the onslaught got too big and the gates could no longer be held they would all retreat to points within the city. Archers could climb to upper levels of buildings and melee combatants could hold various choke points along streets and waterways. This again, along with the fact that they all knew the city, and the enemy didn't would give them yet again another advantage. The various waterways were again another advantage; not just in the health of the residents of the city but in how they formed a network of barriers that were difficult to cross. And small bridges were re-worked so that they could be brought down quickly by one man and a sledgehammer.

All of this would be watched over from several towers in the city. Command groups would use colored flags to help soldiers on the ground know where they were needed and where the enemy was moving.

After all of this was exhausted and the encroaching enemy was still moving they would move all remaining forces to the fortress complex. It was the stronghold and their last line of defense. The woman and children of the city were already making their way to it. The first line of defense at the outer walls and gates would hold long enough for every non-combatant to get to the safety of that inner fortress.

His thoughts finished as he started up the stairs in tower three.

The command group in tower three had a good vantage point to watch over the whole of the city. They could see much of the wall surrounding it. They watched and unfurled colored flags to let the combatants know where help was needed along various points and various gates. The first few hours went reasonably well. The walls and the gates were held.

But they all knew their enemy was just testing them. Feeling things out. Finding out where the weak points were. It would get worse.

And as the sun set the battle subsided. Within the course of half an hour all sound of conflict was gone and the walls went quiet. And that was it for day one.

The enemy, while in a rush, was in no hurry. It clearly was a sign of intelligence. A plan was being formed. They tested the city and learned what they needed. The next attack would be focused.

He returned back to Arabella.

He passed the guards at her door and slowly opened it as if not wanting to wake her. It seemed silly because he so very desperately wanted to wake her.

The room was quiet and a little bit of moon shone through the balcony window. And he wasn't surprised that Aria had climbed into bed with Arabella. The two of them slept quietly, Aria with one arm around Arabella.

She evoked that feeling in people. There was a purity to her and a tenderness that brought out gentle feelings in people. He knew that feeling. She brought it out in him.

He sat down in one of the chairs by the small table and fell asleep.

19. The Gatehouse

He woke to the ringing of bells.

Day two of the battle for Vorgard had begun. This time he would head to tower one. That was the tower nearest to the main western gate. That gate is at the road to Speyer. It is the largest entrance to the city and the attacking forces had paid a lot of attention to it on the previous day. He had a hunch that it would be the place where they would attempt their breach.

He kissed Arabella gently on the cheek and made his way out of the castle; Stein and the contingency of monk bodyguards a few steps behind him.

Before they could arrive at the door to tower one they were detoured. The sounds of a pitched battle was coming from the west – the direction of the main gate. He broke into a trot and the monks kept pace.

They turned a corner to face a wide walking bridge over a waterway that lead into the courtyard for the main gate. The whole area was blanketed in a thick layer of fog that was almost knee deep. They had managed to do again what they had done the other night. They got a contingent of forces into the city without breaching the gate or going over the wall. It had something to do with the mysterious fog.

And the goal of the contingent was clear – to open the main gate and let the enemy forces in the easy way. The battle was fierce and covered most of the courtyard with the serious action happening at the gatehouse where the mechanism for opening and closing the gate was.

It wouldn't be easy for Storm and the monks to get to it. There was a number of Grim with hounds standing on the bridge between them and it. They weren't attacking anything. Their goal clearly was to hold off reinforcements while the gatehouse was taken and the gate was opened. It was smart and it looked like it wouldn't be long before it happened. It did surprise him that the Grim were showing restraint. It went against their nature.

Once that main gate opened it would be the beginning of the end. The attacking force would pour in unimpeded. They would be forced to already move onto the second stage of their plan – retreating to the inner sections of the city.

Storm looked the bridge over. It was made of stone and wide enough for five men to walk across side by side. The parapets, or stone railings, on each edge of it were about waist high. The fog didn't cover them completely. The walkway surface of the bridge was cobblestone and it bowed slightly up at the center. It made for an excellent place to make a stand to hold off enemies. In this case Storm and his group of monks were the "enemies".

He head straight for the bridge. And the Monks, having assessed the situation just as he had, were right beside him. The group went up the slight incline toward the Grim at the mid-point of the bridge and the hounds attacked first.

The GegenHounds quickly closed the distance and in just a few seconds Storm was in the middle of a maelstrom and slashing with his sword. The sound of the monks hammers cracking skulls rang in his ears.

The hounds were just a sacrificial opening round -something to just soften them up. Before the last of them was dispatched the Grim had closed the distance on the bridge and joined in the melee. With normal city residents or poorly trained soldiers it would have been an easy one-two punch. But the monks were well trained, and well conditioned. The hounds posed very little challenge. And with the same efficiency they turned their hammers to the Grim.

They cleared the bridge within three or four minutes then paused and all looked across the courtyard to assess their next move. The battle continued in parts of the courtyard with the most activity happening near the gatehouse. The fighting had decreased. The soldiers were possibly holding. Storm thought that maybe he and the monks would be enough to turn the tide of the battle. Sometimes just a small number of men, in the right place, at the right time, could make a significant difference.

If they could dispatch the enemy here the gate would remain closed. And just as they started their sprint toward the gatehouse the gate started to lift. It went up just a foot then stopped. Clearly there was a desperate battle for control of the mechanism that controlled the gate.

They were forced to slow their rush to the gatehouse as they discovered that the knee deep fog hid bodies. Dead soldiers, Grim, and Vile were laying all over the courtyard and it was difficult to see them through the fog. One of the monks tripped on something and fell to the cobblestone.

The fog made Storm think of The Gether. Maybe this mysterious fog was somehow linked to The Gether.

Some Vile and Grim, along with hounds, came out of the gatehouse to meet them. Storm kept his eye on them as they approached and behind them he saw the main gate close back down. Maybe Storm and the monks have already turned the tide of the battle by taking some of the enemy away from the fight for control of the gate.

Things looked promising. They have the enemy in a pinch - trapped between Storm and his group crossing the courtyard and whatever forces were defending the gatehouse. Things could turn quickly in their favor.

Twenty yards from the gatehouse Storm came to a stop and he stared.

A very tall figure came confidently walking out. Storm rubbed his eyes. Maybe he had some blood blurring his vision. He looked again. He didn't want to believe what his eyes were seeing. But as he and the group of monks got closer he became sure of it. It was the Raver. The muscled psychotic they had encountered in the cathedral. The one who chewed on furniture and tore the heads off of people. The monks recognized him too. Storm thought he could hear some of them gritting their teeth.

The Raver looked right at Storm, pointed a finger at him and screamed! Vile and Grim came pouring out of the gatehouse. It seems they no longer cared about the gate. The Raver screamed and again pointed at Storm.

"LEAVE THE GATE BE! THAT ONE, THE ONE WITH THE SWORD IN HIS LEFT HAND. HE IS THE ONE WE SEEK. KILL HIM."

The horde moved quickly across the courtyard, some of them stumbling and tripping, and the Raver followed behind in a casual walk. And in a few moments the whole flow of their approach changed. The monks started backing up, back to the bridge. It would be a good choke point. A place they could hold and defend while they waited for reinforcements. It was just a very few minutes ago they were attacking defenders of the bridge. Now they were the defenders of the bridge. And they might be able to win the battle from that vantage point even though they were significantly outnumbered.

Storm wondered if the Raver, in his anger, had once again made a mistake. The better choice would have been to get that gate open to allow reinforcements to join the fight. It seemed the Raver was determined, in one way or another, to destroy himself.

The horde reached the bridge just as Storm and the monks turned to defend. They were right in the middle of the span -the center section where it is a little bit higher than the ends of the bridge. It was yet another advantage, albeit a small one. Hammers started swinging, swords and hammers clashed, men and Vile alike shrieked and screamed in fury. The monks, who were always in control of their emotions, were driven beyond their norm. Maybe it was that the presence of the Raver reminded them of how helpless they had been with the Urchne attached to their backs.

Across the courtyard Storm got a glimpse of the gatehouse. Some soldiers were coming out and making their way quickly across the courtyard. They would join in the fray. And that would be the end of the Vile, the Grim, and the Raver. That squad of filth would be trapped from both sides, on a bridge, with nowhere to go but over the edge and into water below.

The Vile and Grim felt the squeeze, and increased the tempo and fury of their attacks but it was of no use; the battle was turning quickly against them and with the main gate firmly closed there were no reinforcements coming to help them.

In just a few minutes the swinging hammers of the monks had brought down most of the snarling foes. It came down to just the Raver and a few of his larger underlings furiously fighting Storm and a few of the monks.

The Raver stopped and dropped his sword. It's strong presence affected everything on that bridge and the pitched close-combat battle decreased in pitch. The the Raver extended both his arms out to the sides as if he were on a crucifix. And everyone on the bridge knew what that meant. The Raver was going to clap. And the last time he clapped, in the cathedral, it knocked them all unconscious sending them into the labyrinth.

Storm panicked. And everything slowed down.

In times of high stress things passed quicker. Everything happened and was done before you knew it. But in times of extreme life-or-death stress things passed slower. Every motion, every color, lingered. And as Storm panicked he felt that feeling of time slowing down. He made a quick two step launching run. The first step was on the back of either a Vile or monk that was dead. The second step was onto the waist high parapet of the bridge. He had enough momentum and force to launch over a Grim and right at the Raver as it's hands were coming together. He held his sword out in front of him as it were a lance, and he were a jousting knight. His sword was directly aimed at the Raver's heart. If it even had one.

One of the monks, recognizing the coming clap, had thrown his hammer at the Raver. But the monk didn't anticipate Storm's jump. The hammer didn't make it to it's intended target. It hit Storm right on the hand that grasped his sword. It broke both the guard of his sword and his thumb. And it changed the trajectory of the sword. It veered off its intended course and penetrated deep into the pectoral muscle of the Raver, going all the way through it's body. Storm thought maybe he got a lung.

With his thumb once again broken he couldn't hold onto the sword tightly and as his body hit the Raver's he lost his grip on it. But he didn't fall to the ground. The Raver, having it's clap interrupted followed through with the motion of it's hands coming in and clapped them on either side of Storm's head. Then started to twist. The strength of the Raver's hands and arms was overwhelming and Storm kicked and contorted his body, bringing his hands up trying to grasp at the Raver's wrists. This would take the weight of his body off his own neck. The twisting started him on the path to a blackout. He could feel the blood supply to his head decreasing as the Raver brought him in close and spoke:

"When you die you will be mine. You will do my bidding. And I will never release you. I never release."

And as the Raver finished those words a monk's hammer slammed into the back of it's head and several teeth popped out of it's mouth and into Storm's face. The force of the hammer blow sent the Raver and Storm over the parapet of the bridge, twenty feet down through the fog and into water.

And as the darkness crept into Storm and everything turned to a muted black his last sensation was hearing a familiar "click click". He imagined it was the Raver choking, and chewing on, it's own broken teeth.

Appendix: Excerpts from the book of Varheit

Passage Root
How an escapement works
How to Make Mead
How to make Steel from Iron Ore

PASSAGE ROOT

THE BOOK OF VARHEIT

+ FOUND UNDER CANOPY OF TREES
+ AVERSE TO SUNLIGHT
+ SINGLE BLACK BLOSSOM
+ LEAVES TINTED PURPLE
+ ROOT BULB EVOKES
         TEMPORARY RESURRECTION

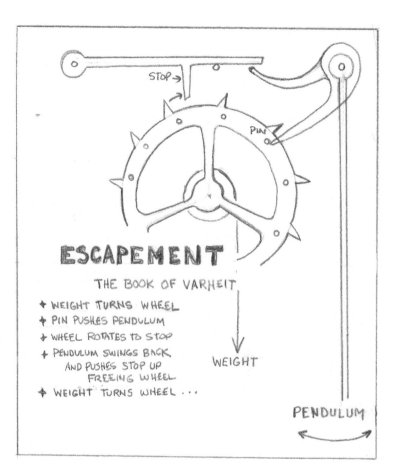

ESCAPEMENT

THE BOOK OF VARHEIT

STOP →

PIN

- WEIGHT TURNS WHEEL
- PIN PUSHES PENDULUM
- WHEEL ROTATES TO STOP
- PENDULUM SWINGS BACK
  AND PUSHES STOP UP
    FREEING WHEEL
- WEIGHT TURNS WHEEL ...

WEIGHT

PENDULUM

WATER

HONEY

YEAST

COVER LOOSELY
ONE MONTH

SIPHON MEAD

MAKE MEAD

THE BOOK OF VARHEIT

+ THREE PARTS WATER
+ ONE PART HONEY
+ ADD TEASPOON YEAST
+ COVER LOOSELY WITH CLOTH
+ ONE MONTH - SIPHON OFF MEAD
+ DISPOSE OF SEDIMENT
+ BOTTLE

DISPOSE
OF
SEDIMENT

THICK WALLED
CLAY FURNACE

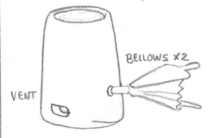

VENT

BELLOWS x2

ALTERNATE
LAYERS

CHARCOAL

IRON ORE

CHARCOAL

IRON ORE

MAKE STEEL

THE BOOK OF VARHEIT

* BUILD FURNACE OF FIRE CLAY
* ALTERNATE LAYERS CHARCOAL/IRON ORE
* BURN — CONTINUE ADDING LAYERS
* CONTINUE FOR FULL DAY
* BREAK OPEN — REMOVE STEEL BLOOM

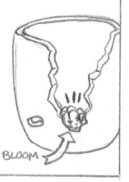

BLOOM

Printed in Great Britain
by Amazon

12122102R00139